Forever My Love

The McKinleys
Book 2

Kimberly Rae Jordan

THREE**STRAND**
P R E S S

A CORD OF THREE STRANDS IS NOT EASILY BROKEN.

A man, a woman & their God.

Three Strand Press publishes Christian Romance stories

that intertwine love, faith and family.

Always clean. Always heartwarming. Always uplifting.

Copyright ©2015
By Kimberly Rae Jordan

CHAPTER ONE

BROOKE McKinley glanced over at her son, watching as he very precisely measured the batter into the paper-lined muffin tins. A lock of his hair, a few shades darker than hers, slipped down across his brow.

Setting the dirty measuring cups into the warm water in the sink, Brooke said, "When these are done, we'll take some across to Mrs. Davis. Do you think she'll like them?"

"Yep. She loves blueberry muffins."

"I think she'll be particularly pleased when you tell her that you made them." Brooke rinsed the measuring cups and set them in the dish drainer to dry. She wiped down the counter with a wet rag, glancing up when the doorbell rang. Using the edge of her apron, she wiped the sweat from her forehead then lifted the strap over her head. "Finish filling the tins but don't put them in the oven until I get back."

She dropped the apron on the counter and headed for the front door. Moving away from the kitchen did nothing to cool her off. They'd picked one hot day to do their baking. She hoped it wasn't anyone too important at the door because she was answering it in her shorts and tank top. If they didn't like it, too bad. It was just too hot to be wearing anything else.

Whoever had pushed the doorbell wasn't standing directly in front of the screen door. She'd left the inner door open earlier in hopes of getting a good cross breeze through the house. Hadn't really worked, she thought as she reached out to unlock the screen door and push it open.

When her gaze landed on the man standing on her porch, Brooke wondered momentarily if by opening the door she'd opened a rift to another universe. Perhaps the heat was messing with her. Or maybe it was just that it had been ten years since she'd last seen him. All Brooke knew for certain was that the man in front of her was the last person she'd expected to be standing on her porch any day, let alone a boiling hot Saturday afternoon.

The guy looked like Lincoln Hamilton and yet... didn't. The Lincoln Hamilton she'd known would never have been caught dead in pressed slacks, a cotton button-up shirt and loafers. And that haircut. Way too conservative and precise for Lincoln Hamilton. Clearly ten years had changed him in ways she could never have imagined.

Whatever the reason he had for standing on her front porch, she wasn't going to give him the pleasure of thinking she recognized him after all this time, especially since he really didn't look the same. "Can I help you?"

The man pushed his sunglasses to the top of his head. Familiar blue eyes set in a face of sharp angles and planes regarded her seriously. "Brooke McKinley?"

Okay, so they were both going to play the *I don't recognize you* game. "Yes, that's me."

"My name is Lucas Hamilton." The man held out his hand. "I'm wondering if I could talk to you for a few minutes."

Lucas Hamilton? Brooke automatically shook his hand, her mind scrambling for an explanation. Lincoln had never mentioned having a brother. Especially not one that looked so much like him. She stepped out onto the porch, letting the screen door close behind her.

"I'm here about my brother, Lincoln."

Brooke crossed her arms, resisting the urge to glance over her shoulder into the house. "He's not here."

The man—Lucas—nodded. "Yes, I know." He cleared his throat. "I am here because you and your son were mentioned in my brother's will."

Brooke's eyes widened. Lincoln actually knew about Danny? And this visit was regarding his *will*? "What's happened to Lincoln?"

Lucas glanced away from her, but not before she saw grief in his eyes. "The plane he was in went down. No survivors."

The air whooshed from Brooke's lungs. It had been years since she'd seen the man. In that time, she'd gone from affection—she would never say she had loved Lincoln Hamilton—to hate to anger and then simply...nothing. But it still wasn't easy to hear that her son's father was gone. She had always hoped for his sake that Lincoln would come around and at least try to be a father to their son. Now that would never happen.

"I'm sorry for your loss," Brooke said. Though she had no feeling of grief for Lincoln's death, she knew it had to be difficult to lose a sibling.

Lucas looked back at her, his gaze now devoid of emotion. He reached into his hip pocket and pulled out a folded paper. "Lincoln had this with his will."

When he held it out, Brooke just stared at the envelope. She recognized it. Ten years later and still she recognized it. It was the letter she'd sent to Lincoln to let him know he was going to be a father. She'd sent it to the apartment where he'd been staying while they'd been dating.

She'd never received a response, so she'd just assumed he hadn't gotten the letter. Now she knew he had. He'd just chosen to not acknowledge it. Or his son.

Anger burned in her gut. What right did he have to mess up their lives now? If he wouldn't claim Danny in life, he didn't get to claim him in death either.

"I don't understand why you're here. Lincoln wasn't a father to my son."

Lucas seemed to realize she had no intention of taking the letter from him, so he shoved it back into his pocket. "I know he wasn't the father he should have been to Danny, but with his death, Lincoln has made sure that he—and you—are taken care of."

"I don't want anything from him," Brooke said, pulling her shoulders back. "Danny and I are just fine on our own." She didn't miss his glance at the house and then the neighborhood. "Money isn't everything."

Lucas lifted a brow at that remark. "I know my brother wasn't the man he should have been when it came to his son, but there's no need to reject what he's offering for him now. It could change Danny's life for the better."

As he said the words, Brooke realized it wasn't the money she was rejecting. There was just something about *this* man that had her wanting to avoid him having any say in her life. At least Lincoln had understood her. Had understood her desire to live without anyone controlling her life. Back then she had lived for the adventure and the fun. In fact, that's how he had lived his life, too. Brooke didn't think for a minute that Lincoln had died in a plane crash on his way to a business meeting. He'd probably been flying somewhere to watch a volcano erupt. Or maybe to swim with sharks. Or to catch the biggest wave ever. The man had been an adrenaline junkie. And she'd loved living that life with him for four short months. She'd asked him a couple of times why he didn't need to work and yet seemed to have an abundance of money. He'd said he did work but that his family was also financially well off.

"Mommy?"

Jerked from her journey down memory lane, Brooke turned to see Danny standing on the other side of the screen door. She glanced at Lucas and saw his gaze was pinned there, probably trying to get a clear look at his nephew. His dead brother's son. She was at a point of no return because once Lucas got a look at Danny, he'd know without a doubt— if he even had any—that the boy was Lincoln's son.

With a sigh and fervent hope she was doing the right thing, Brooke turned toward the door and opened it. Looking back at Lucas, she said, "Would you like to come in?"

Without hesitation, Lucas nodded and followed her into the entryway of her small home. Danny had moved to the side to let them in. Brooke went to him and slipped an arm around his shoulders. With a quick movement, he swiped at the errant curl that once again tumbled across his forehead.

"Sweetie, this is Lucas Hamilton."

Danny shot her a startled look. He knew the last name. It was on his birth certificate. It was part of his last name. *Daniel Lincoln McKinley-Hamilton*. A mouthful for sure, but Brooke had wanted him to have her name as well.

"Hello, Danny," Lucas said.

Brooke felt a spark of sympathy for this man who was clearly still grieving his brother's death. She had no doubt he felt as if he were looking at his brother. Danny was Lincoln's mini-me in every way but personality.

"Hello." Danny shook the hand Lucas extended to him. "Who are you? You look like my dad and have his last name."

"Your dad was my twin brother."

Twins? Well, that explained the similarity in appearance.

Always one to pick up on subtleties in a manner that went far beyond his years, Danny said, "Was? He *was* your twin brother?"

"Why don't we go sit down?" Brooke suggested. Though she'd never hidden the identity of Danny's father from him, she wondered then if she shouldn't have been a little less open about the man. But that was the decision she'd made, so now her son was going to have to grieve a father who'd never taken the time to meet him, let alone be a regular presence in his life.

Once seated on the couch, Brooke kept her arm around Danny's shoulders. She pressed a kiss to his hair, trying to figure out the best way to break the news to him. Some might say she shouldn't tell him, but she'd never held back before. She'd always encouraged him to experience the full range of emotions in his life. To appreciate the beauty. To laugh at the funny. To cry at the sad. And to grieve for a loss.

"Lucas came today to let me know that Lincoln has passed away." Brooke felt the jerk of her son's body right to the very core of her heart.

He bent his head, no doubt to keep his tears from spilling in front of this stranger. Brooke pulled him tight to her side and wrapped her other arm around him.

Resting her cheek on his hair, she said, "Go ahead and cry, sweetie."

Though he'd never met the man, Danny knew a lot about him. Every question he'd ever asked about Lincoln, Brooke had done her best to answer. Lincoln's picture was in a frame on the nightstand beside his bed. But now feeling her son's shoulders shake silently, Brooke wished she'd been less forthcoming with the information about the man. Her answers and the stories she'd told Danny about Lincoln had made him very real to the little boy. And she knew he harbored a hope that one day his father might come to meet him. Now he'd have to grieve that man in a way he might not have had he not known so much about him.

"You told him about Lincoln?"

Brooke looked up to find Lucas watching Danny. She sensed his emotions were close to the surface as he observed his nephew's grief. "Yes. I didn't think it was fair to lie to him. He deserved to know about the man who played a part in bringing him into this world. Lincoln became very real to Danny because of that."

"I didn't realize," Lucas said, his brow furrowing. "I'm afraid we knew nothing about Danny until after Lincoln's death. If we had..."

"Danny was Lincoln's responsibility, and it was his decision whether or not to be part of his life. Of course, I wish he'd made a different choice, but the fact that he didn't doesn't mean that Danny shouldn't know about him."

Lucas continued to stare at Danny, his gaze full of emotion then he said, "Would you let him meet my mother?"

"Your mother?" Brooke was taken off-guard by the question. In truth, she'd thought very little about Lincoln's family. Of course, he would have had parents, but Brooke hadn't spent much time thinking about them. If he couldn't be bothered getting to know his son, she wasn't going to waste time wondering about the grandparents or aunts and uncles Danny might have on the Hamilton side.

"Yes. She's been totally broken by Lincoln's death. Seeing Danny would go a long way to helping her heal, I think."

"Let me talk with Danny about that first, please." Brooke wasn't going to agree to anything until she and Danny had a chance to discuss a few things first.

A frustrated look crossed Lucas's face, and for a moment, Brooke thought he was going to argue with her. She sensed he was the type of man who was used to getting his way. Well, he was in for a rude awakening in dealing with her. She wasn't going to just say yes to everything he suggested. If it wasn't best for Danny, she would be saying no.

When he gave a quick nod, Brooke returned her attention to her son. She rocked her body back and forth as she held him close. Her world had been ripped apart when she'd been a little younger than Danny was now, and confusion and fear had ruled her life. She hadn't understood her family's rapid departure from their home in Africa. Hadn't understood the reason for the underlying emotional turmoil as they'd tried to adjust to a new life in the cold temperatures of Minnesota. Because of those experiences, she'd determined that if she were ever a mother, she wouldn't hide difficult things from her children. That she would help them to understand as best they could for their age. And she'd done that with Danny.

But right then she was questioning her decision. If Lincoln had remained a shadowy figure in Danny's mind, his grief would have been less intense. Less real. Instead, he mourned a man who had become very tangible to him through the memories Brooke had shared over the years.

The only consolation was that once he had grieved his loss, Danny could move forward without having the constant wondering if his father might one day show up and claim him. Of course, now she'd have to contend with another Hamilton man—one very different from the one she'd known ten years ago.

CHAPTER TWO

Lucas watched the woman and boy sitting across from him on a faded fabric couch. He hadn't been sure what to expect when he'd showed up at the house earlier. In fact, he wasn't entirely sure why he'd even come at all. The lawyers could have handled the initial contact.

But something had propelled him out of the house on a Saturday afternoon to find them. And so he sat in an easy chair that was anything but easy on his behind. At least one spring poked through the covering of the chair, and the temperature in the cracker box size house was likely only a degree or two cooler than hell.

Trying to distract himself from his discomfort, Lucas focused again on Brooke and Danny. Watching her with his nephew, he had no doubt the boy was well loved even if his home environment wasn't the best. The house was in an old neighborhood and apparently had non-functioning air conditioning. This very maternal display by Brooke seemed to be at odds with the women Linc usually spent his time with. Those women had been as eager to jump out of planes, rappel down sheer rock surfaces and race fast cars as he had.

Brooke McKinley didn't immediately strike him as that sort of woman.

Maybe it had been her looks that had drawn Lincoln in. Lucas would have had to turn in his membership card to the red-blooded man club if he didn't notice her appearance. The white shorts she wore showed off legs that seemed to go on forever. And like her arms, they were lightly tanned. The dark blue tank top left her shoulders bare, and he could see a smattering of freckles on them. Her light auburn hair was pulled back in a braid and from the looks of it was crazy long. Most the women he interacted with wore their hair styled, never just...long. Her make-up free face revealed a few more freckles across her nose and cheeks.

She glanced up then, her light blue-green gaze meeting his. Lucas didn't know why he felt a bit abashed at having been caught staring. Surely she would understand his curiosity about the woman his brother had fathered a child with.

After a moment, she looked back down at Danny. "Why don't you go to the bathroom and wash your face, sweetie? I'm going to put the muffins in the oven."

Danny nodded and without looking at him, stood up and walked toward a room near the front of the house. After the door had shut behind the boy, Brooke got to her feet as well.

"I need to finish up what we were doing when you arrived," she said with a wave toward the kitchen.

Though the open floorplan would have allowed him to still see her as she worked from where he sat, Lucas got up and followed her. He stood, hands on his hips, watching as she picked up one of the muffin trays on the counter and opened the oven to slide it inside. Once she'd put the second one in and closed the door, Brooke moved to stand behind the counter. She picked up a cloth that sat there, but instead of using it to wipe the floured surface, she twisted it in her hands.

Finally, her gaze met his. "You're not taking my son from me."

Lucas tipped his head to the side. "Why would you think I'd do that?"

There was a flash of annoyance on her face. "Don't think I've missed the way you've looked around and judged how we live." She motioned toward him. "And it's clear you have money."

Lucas looked down at himself. How exactly did his outfit tell her that? It wasn't like he'd shown up in one of his suits. "I'm not here to take your son away from you. But honestly, would it kill you to get the air fixed?"

"There's nothing wrong with it," Brooke said, dropping the cloth onto the counter and crossing her arms.

"So why don't you have it on? It's the hottest day of the year, for Pete's sake."

"Lifestyle choice." She paused. "And how do I know you're not going to take Danny from me? Take your word for it? Sorry, but I don't know you."

"I can see you love Danny and, apart from the heat and the not-so-great neighborhood, I think you're giving him a good home. Besides, I'm not worried about that right now. Like I said when I introduced myself, you and Danny were mentioned in Lincoln's will. Money will no longer be an issue for you."

Brooke was silent for a few moments, her brows drawn together. "So if Lincoln was so willing to provide for Danny after his death, why didn't he want anything to do with him while he was alive?"

Lucas moved to sit on a bar stool at the counter. "I really don't know. I knew nothing about Danny until Lincoln was officially..." He swallowed and cleared his throat. "Until Lincoln was officially declared dead. My best guess was that given the lifestyle he liked to live, he didn't want to be tied down with a family."

"Well, I wasn't wanting him to marry me," Brooke said as she leaned a hip against the counter. "I just wanted Danny to have a chance to get to know his dad."

"I'm sorry Linc didn't step up and take on that role. From what I see, it was definitely his loss."

"That's for sure." Brooke nodded vigorously. "Unfortunately, it was also Danny's loss."

"You've told him a lot about Lincoln?"

"Yes. I don't volunteer information, but if he has a question, I always answer it honestly."

Lucas glanced toward the closed door behind which Danny had disappeared before saying, "Like I said, I don't want to take him away from you, but I would like the chance to spend some time with him. He's my nephew." He hesitated. "And, I know my mother would like to meet him, too. This has been a rough time for her. Especially this last week."

This time it was Brooke's gaze that went to the closed door. "What happened exactly?"

Lucas let out a long breath as he rested his arm on the counter. "We're not sure. He'd been gone for almost five months with only sporadic contact. From what little we've been able to piece together, he'd left Miami in his plane with a flight plan set for the Bahamas. He made it there and went on to Turks and Caicos and then the Dominican Republic. His next stop was apparently supposed to be Jamaica, but he never made it."

"How did you know he was missing?"

"He'd made plans to meet up with some friends in Jamaica. When he didn't show up, they started putting out inquiries. One of them knew who he...was—a Hamilton—and contacted the company to leave a message for me." Lucas took another deep breath and let it out. "The local authorities sent out search parties to see what they could find. They were able to locate pieces of the wreckage fairly quickly. Unfortunately, they didn't find his body."

Brooke frowned. "When did this happen?"

"We first heard about the accident four months ago." Lucas stared at the floor, still finding it difficult to believe that his brother was gone. "But it was just this week that they finally contacted us and said that based on their examination of the wreckage and where the plane went down, they didn't think he could have survived the crash. The officials there declared him dead on Wednesday."

A light touch on his hand surprised him, and he looked up to see Brooke watching him as her fingers rested on his. Her gaze was sympathetic. "I'm very sorry for your loss. Lincoln was definitely one of a kind."

"He was that."

Brooke's hand slid from his, and she straightened, her gaze going past him. Lucas turned to see Danny walking toward them. As he went to stand next to his mom, Lucas got his first real good look at the boy. It was like a punch in the stomach to see a miniature version of his brother standing in front of him. He knew it was a bit ridiculous because he saw a similar image every time he looked in the mirror, but this boy looked even more like Lincoln than he did. Danny's hair fell in familiar long curls almost to his shoulders. The only thing that was markedly different was the color of his eyes. He had blue-green eyes like his mother's instead of the gray of his dad.

Danny glanced down at the counter. "Are they in the oven?"

"Yep. Can't you smell them?" Brooke said as she tousled his hair. "Feeling better?"

The boy hesitated before nodding then turned his gaze to Lucas. "You're my uncle?"

"Yes. Your dad was my brother."

Danny looked at Brooke. Some sort of communication seemed to pass between mother and son because Brooke slipped her arm around his shoulders and said, "If you have questions, go ahead and ask them. I think Lucas will answer as best he can."

Lucas hoped he wouldn't disappoint the boy. In all honesty, he hadn't been as close to Lincoln in the past ten years as he'd been when they were kids and into their teens. They may have been identical twins, but they couldn't have been more different in personality. In time, those differences had driven them apart. He hadn't approved of the steady parade of women through Lincoln's life. He hadn't understood his insatiable need to put his life in danger on a regular basis.

Lincoln had definitely been more like their father in that regard. Though his father had tended to take more risks when it came to his business, he'd still had a need for the excitement and thrill that came with living on the edge. Lucas, on the other hand, was much more like his mother with his cautious approach. Unfortunately, she'd spent a lot of years worrying first about her husband and then her son. Lucas had struggled not to be angry with both of them for what they put her through.

As he looked at Danny, he hoped—no, he prayed—that this boy had not inherited that aspect of his dad's personality. If he had, he hoped his mother wasn't around to have to spend hours worrying about the actions of her grandson the way she had with her son.

"What did he like to do when he was my age?"

Lucas wasn't sure what he'd expected Danny to ask, but at least that question was one of the easier ones to answer. "Well, he loved anything with wheels. He lived on his skateboard. Mom yelled at him a lot about using it in the house. He also had a bike that he liked to jump off ramps. When he was your age, he raced go-karts and did some dirt track racing later in his teens. Even did a little dirt bike stuff. In the summer, we spent a lot of time in the pool, too, and in the winter, my dad would take us snowboarding. What kinds of things do you like to do?"

"Riding my bike is my favorite thing. Mom and I usually take our bikes when we need to go anywhere as long as there's no snow. I do have a skateboard, but I fell last summer and banged up my elbow. Had to wear a cast for a couple of months. After that, I just kinda stuck with my bike. I do like to swim though. I take lessons at the community center." He glanced at Brooke. "I'm pretty good, right, Mom?"

"Yes, you are a superb swimmer." Brooke smiled. "He also knows how to bake, cook and garden. I'm determined to raise a well-rounded boy who appreciates all aspects of life."

"You enjoy doing those things?" Lucas asked, almost laughing at the idea of Lincoln stepping foot in a kitchen.

Danny ducked his head but then nodded. "Mom said if I like to eat, I need to learn how to cook. And she makes it fun."

A ring tone sounded, and Brooke picked up a cell phone from the counter and looked at the display. She held it out to Danny. "It's for you."

He took it and walked a little ways away before pressing it to his ear. He was back before Lucas could think of anything to say to Brooke.

"Can I go with Mike? His folks are taking him the Mall of America."

Lucas saw emotion flash across Brooke's face but couldn't identify what it was.

"I don't know, sweetie, it's a bit unexpected."

Danny took a couple of steps toward her and said softly, "He said it's their treat."

Brooke's shoulders slumped, and her head dipped. "Okay, baby. Be sure to say thank you for that."

"I will, Mom. I'm going to get changed." He said a few more words to the person on the other end of the line then returned he phone to Brooke before heading back to the room he'd disappeared into earlier.

When the timer went off, Brooke picked up a pair of hot pads. Lucas watched as she set the pans on the counter in front of him. His stomach rumbled at the delicious aroma that wafted from the golden brown muffins in the tins.

Brooke looked at him, a smile lifting one corner of her mouth. "Would you like one?"

"If they taste as good as they smell..."

"They're better," Brooke said with clear confidence. She flipped one pan over and then quickly, with her bare fingers, righted the muffins on the wire racks then repeated the process with the other pan.

She reached into the cupboard and pulled out a small plate. After setting it in front of him, she put a muffin on it. "Want some butter?"

"Sure." Lucas touched the muffin but jerked his fingers back. How had she handled them?

This time she had a full smile as she put a container of butter and a knife on the counter next to his plate. "That's not a move for beginners."

"Well, I guess I can't argue that I'm definitely a beginner when it comes to baking."

She reached over and quickly removed the paper on the muffin. When she broke the top from the bottom, steam rose up. Setting the pieces back on the plate, she said, "Best to spread the butter on them while they're warm."

"Thank you." Lucas used the knife to get some butter from the container and smeared it on the muffin.

"You're welcome." Brooke picked up the cloth and wiped the counter with quick movements. ""You never baked with your mom?"

Lucas paused with a piece of muffin halfway to his mouth and laughed. "My parents had very old-fashioned views of the gender roles. Women did the kitchen related stuff. My dad would have had a fit if he'd found us boys in the kitchen. That was left up to my mom and my sister. Although, in reality, neither of them spent any time there either."

"You have a sister?"

Lucas finished chewing the bite of heaven he'd just put in his mouth. "Did Lincoln not talk about his family at all?"

"Nope. That wasn't the sort of relationship we had."

Now that sounded like Lincoln. Danny was proof of just what kind of relationship they'd had. "Yes. My sister, Lindsay, is six years younger than Lincoln and me. It took Mom that long to convince Dad to let her try one more time for a girl."

"Spoiled much?" Brooke asked with a lift of one eyebrow.

"Just a tad." Lucas smiled as he popped another piece of muffin into his mouth. "But she's a smart cookie. Keeps us all on our toes."

She set a glass of cold water on the counter in front of him. "You mentioned that your mom would want to meet Danny. What about your dad?"

Lucas took a gulp of the water, appreciating the first coolness he'd encountered since entering the house. "My dad passed away several years ago."

Before Brooke could respond, Danny reappeared. His hair was pulled back into a ponytail, and he'd changed into a pair of long jean shorts and a black T-shirt with a DC Lantern Corps symbol on it.

Lucas gestured to the shirt. "Life?"

Danny looked down at his shirt then up at him with a heartbreakingly familiar grin. "Yep. You a DC fan?"

"A bit. Your dad was a bigger fan than me." Lucas glanced over at Brooke. "In fact, I'm pretty sure he had that same T-shirt at one time."

Brooke nodded but then said, "Danny picked that one out all on his own with his birthday money." The chirp of her phone drew her attention. "Looks like they're almost here."

Danny gave his mom a quick hug. "Thanks for letting me go."

As he watched them, Lucas reached into his back pocket for his wallet. He pulled out a few bills and held them out to Danny. "Here you go, bud. Buy yourself something to eat and maybe find something special for your mom."

"Hey—" Brooke said as her son reached out to take the money from him. "You don't need to do that."

"I know I don't. Consider it an uncle privilege." Lucas rested his hand on Danny's shoulder. "Have fun."

"Thanks." Danny beamed at him. "I will."

He was relieved to see a smile on the boy's face instead of the tears of earlier. It as probably good that he had the chance to go do something fun after receiving the news he had. Lucas much preferred to see the boy smiling. "See you around."

Danny nodded. "I'd like that."

From the look Brooke shot him as she followed Danny to the front door, Lucas didn't think his mother was as receptive to the idea. Too bad. He'd told her he wasn't going to take her son from her—and he wouldn't—but he and his family had a right to get to know the boy. Especially now that he was their only connection to Lincoln.

When Brooke came back into the kitchen, anger radiated from her in waves. Lucas stayed on his stool, not saying anything, just watching as she jerked a cabinet open and pulled out a basket. She plunked it on the counter next to the muffins then opened a drawer and snatched out a piece of fabric before slamming it shut. Lucas winced but still said nothing. He'd had his fair share of experiences with fiery women. Though his mother was fairly laid back, Lindsay was anything but.

Brooke began to pick muffins up and put them into the basket. Thankfully, she didn't inflict her anger on the innocent baked goods. She'd just flicked the corners of the fabric over the muffins when her phone rang.

If at all possible, the scowl on her face got even more fierce.

CHAPTER THREE

WHAT do you want?" Brooke barked into the phone when she pressed it to her ear. "Yeah, I know that's no way to answer a phone, but I'm not in the mood to deal with men today."

A pause. "Well, true. I'm never really in the mood to deal with you men, but that goes double for today." She shot a dark look in his direction.

Lucas almost laughed. That sounded so much like something Lindsay would say. He had a feeling these two would be a man's worst nightmare if they ever got together. Too bad for him it was just a matter of time.

"So what *did* you want?" Brooke demanded. She continued to move around the kitchen, putting away the remainder of the muffins.

When she suddenly stilled and then looked in his direction, a glint of humor in her eyes, Lucas got an uneasy feeling. Again...so much like Lindsay.

"Actually, I *will* be bringing a date to your wedding."

A smile was spreading across her face as fast as the feeling in Lucas's gut that he was going to end up having to do something he didn't really want to.

"You don't need the name. Just put *Brooke's date* on the place card." She paused. "Yes, it's a guy. And no, it's not Danny. He's already a given since he's in your wedding party. Yes, I'll have him at the rehearsal dinner on time."

When the call ended, Brooke set the phone back down on the counter and returned to what she'd been doing before the phone rang. Lucas continued to watch her, waiting for the other shoe to drop. Maybe now was a good time to make his escape—his departure.

He started to stand up, but she glared at him and pointed back at the stool. "First...eighty dollars? Really? What does a ten-year-old boy need with eighty dollars?"

Too late. Lucas sank back down. "Was that how much I gave him?"

Brooke's mouth dropped open, but she quickly snapped it shut then said, "You didn't even count it?"

"Well, no. I just wanted to give him some money to spend."

"Thanks to you, I'm gonna be getting a phone call from my mom asking what's going on."

"Why's that?"

"Because Mark's parents are friends of my family. They attend the same church as my parents. I'm sure they're going to comment to them that Danny showed up with a wad of cash."

Lucas shrugged. "So tell them."

"Oh, I will, and then I'll show them." That glint was back in her eyes.

"Show them?"

"Yep. You, Mr. Uncle, are going to be my date at my brother's wedding."

Considering the side of the conversation he'd heard, Lucas wasn't entirely surprised by this turn of events. He knew she expected him to object. "Sure. That sounds like fun."

Brooke's mouth once again dropped open. She finally said, "Fun? You think that sounds like fun?"

Lucas shrugged. "Sure. It's not my wedding. And I have no trouble getting dressed up. I do it every day. Toss in time with my nephew, a chance to get to know his family, and a beautiful date. I'd be foolish to turn it down."

She glared at him even as a flush of pink swept up her cheeks. Snatching the basket from the counter, she said, "I'll be back."

Lucas spun on his seat to watch her marching toward the front door. It squeaked as it opened and then slammed shut behind her. He hoped she hadn't grabbed a set of keys as she left or he might be finding a nice long scratch down the side of his Lexus LX parked in front of her house.

He had to admit that he was beginning to see what might have drawn Linc to this woman. There was likely never a dull moment when she was around.

"You looking for something, dear?" Mrs. Davis asked.

Brooke glanced away from the large window in Mrs. Davis's living room that looked out on their neighborhood. Or more precisely, the house right across the street which happened to be hers. "No, just keeping an eye on the house."

"Do you have company? I noticed that car parked in front of your place. As my grandson would say, it's a fine set of wheels."

Brooke had noticed it was indeed a fine set of wheels as she'd walked—stomped—passed it on her way over with the muffins. It had probably cost the guy more than the average person made in two or three years. No wonder eighty dollars was nothing to the man. She wasn't used to that kind of thinking.

"Danny not around?"

"He went to the Mall of America with his buddy. But he's the one who made the muffins. He was supposed to come with me to give them to you, but I'm afraid we both took second place to terrifying rides and too much junk food."

Mrs. Davis chuckled. "I remember those days. I seemed to come in second place to a lot of stuff at that age. Thankfully, they usually get their priorities straight."

Brooke knew that Mrs. Davis's sons took good care of her. It was one of the reasons she was still able to live on her own even though she was well into her eighties. Unfortunately, the older woman had tried to fix her up with a couple of her grandsons who weren't nearly as responsible as their fathers.

She touched the pocket of her shorts and then the other one. Rats, she'd left her phone on the counter. The man had her more rattled than she wanted to admit. Glancing at the clock on the fireplace mantle, Brooke figured she'd been there for about fifteen minutes now. Was he ever going to leave?

"Well, he's a fine specimen," Mrs. Davis commented.

Brooke's gaze shot to the window. Sure enough, Lucas Hamilton had exited her house and was now standing beside the driver's door of his luxurious wheels. He had his hands on his hips, looking around the neighborhood. She was confident he didn't know which house she was in, plus Mrs. Davis had made sure her curtains allowed her to observe without being observed.

"Do you need to go speak with him, my dear?" she asked, leaning forward in her seat. "He looks like he might be looking for you."

"I'll catch up with him later."

"You don't want to let one that looks like that get away, dearie."

Brooke sighed in relief as he got into the car and pulled away from her house. "There's more to a man than his appearance." She'd been taken in by this particular set of looks—well, a slightly different version—before, and she wasn't keen to repeat that mistake.

She stayed to visit with Mrs. Davis for another fifteen minutes before returning home. And even though she was reluctant to leave the air-conditioned coolness of the older woman's house, she was eager to get back to her own place.

Once home, she let out a long breath as she walked through the house to the kitchen. She spotted her phone sitting on top of a piece of paper on the counter. The thought of him looking through her things to find something to write on gave her a funny feeling. She slid the paper from underneath her phone.

Now was that any way to treat a guest? Running off on me? ☺ Thanks for the muffin, by the way. It was so good, I helped myself to another. I figured you owed me that much for making me wait around for nothing. Since you weren't here for me to give you my contact information, I put it in your phone under "Mr. Uncle". Call me—or text if you prefer—with the details of our date. Would love to hear from Danny as well.

Brooke snatched up her phone and tapped the screen to get to her contacts. Sure enough, not only had Lucas added his info, but he'd also taken a picture to go with it. She found herself laughing as she looked at the photo. Arched brow, wide eyes and duck lips. The ultimate selfie. Sinking down on the stool he'd been sitting on when she'd left, Brooke realized it had been quite some time since a man had made her smile—let alone laugh. He'd certainly run her emotions all over the place since he'd shown up on her porch such a short time ago.

She was going to have to be extra careful around this man. He had the potential to be a complication she didn't need or want.

Lucas hit the button on the remote and waited until the door was up to guide his car down the sloped driveway to the garage. He turned off the ignition and stepped from the coolness of the car. Though warm, the room was still cooler than Brooke's had been. After making sure the door was closed, he took the stairs two at a time to the main floor of the house. The kitchen area was empty, so he wandered into the living room.

"He was a loser, Mom. I don't care how cute you think the guy was. He was boring and all he wanted to do was talk about himself. It was like he was a personal salesman where his product was himself. So very unattractive."

Lucas grinned as he walked toward where his mom and sister sat in the living room. His mom was sitting very properly in her chair, but Lindsay, wearing shorts and a ratty old T-shirt, sat sideways on the couch, her bare feet planted on the cushion.

"Darling! Where did you disappear to?"

Lucas went to press a kiss to his mom's cheek before settling into the chair next to her.

"How are you not dying from the heat dressed like that?" Lindsay asked.

"I had a meeting." He'd debated all the way back to the house how much he should share with them.

"A meeting?" Lindsay asked. "Dressed like that?"

"Wasn't a business meeting. It was a personal one."

"Personal? That sounds more interesting. Who with?"

"What if I said it was none of your business?" Lucas tossed at her.

Lindsay grinned. "I'd say tell us anyway. You know I can get it out of you one way or another."

She'd learned young that she could get physical with her older—and bigger—brothers but that they couldn't retaliate. That had meant they'd endured everything from pinching and punching to tickling. Lincoln had gone after her a couple of times, but she knew that Lucas wouldn't. So she was right. He would tell her just to protect himself from whatever sort of torture she decided to hand him.

"I went to see Brooke McKinley." Satisfied that he'd managed to make two of the more talkative women he'd ever known go silent, Lucas leaned back in his chair, legs stretched out in front of him.

Lindsay swung her feet off the couch and turned to face him directly. "And? You're not allowed to drop a bomb like that and say nothing more. What's he like?"

If it had just been Lindsay, he probably would have dragged it out, but for his mom's sake, he knew he couldn't delay answering. "He's an interesting mix. He looks a lot like Linc although his hair is a little bit lighter. He wears it long and it curls like Linc's. He likes to ride his bike but after hurting his arm on his skateboard last year has avoided that ever since."

He pulled his phone from his pocket and tapped the screen to get to his pictures. When it had become apparent that his hostess wasn't going to return, Lucas had taken the opportunity to look around a little bit. He'd found photos of Danny on the wall in the living room and had used his phone's camera to take pictures of them. Not the best quality but at least they would give his mom an idea of what he looked like.

He handed the phone to her. "There are five there."

Lindsay scrambled off the couch and dropped to her knees beside her mom. "Oh my word! He looks just like Linc."

Lucas watched as his mom silently swiped through the pictures. He knew it would be hard to look at them at first, but he hoped that it would also be healing for her to have a link to her son.

When she finally looked up, her eyes glistened with tears. "He's beautiful. When can we meet him?"

"I'm not sure. Today went pretty good, but his mom is concerned about him. She told him all about Lincoln."

Lindsay wrinkled her nose. "So does he hate Lincoln for not being there for him?"

"Not at all. In fact, when she told him that Linc had...passed away, he started crying." Lucas sat forward, bracing his forearms on his thighs. "His mom is an interesting woman. She kinda reminds me a bit of you, Linds."

His sister gave him a skeptical look. "I'm sure that thrilled you."

"She doesn't hold back much, but she's also created a very...soothing and safe environment for Danny. When I got there, they were making blueberry muffins together. It seems she's always encouraged him to ask any questions he had about his father. And she told him to ask me about Lincoln, too."

His mother looked back down at the phone in her hand. "What did he ask you?"

"He wanted to know what Lincoln had been like when he was his age."

Lindsay sat down on the floor, drawing her knees up to wrap her arms around them. "Well, you'd be the best person to know that. So, did he want to know about us, too?"

"He and his mom had no idea about any of us. In the months Brooke and Lincoln were together, apparently he never told her anything about his family. From her comments about it, it sounds like she didn't share about hers either."

"So you don't think she'll oppose us wanting to meet him? Getting to know him?" his mom asked.

"No, I don't think she will. But she's very much a woman in charge of her own life. It will have to be on her terms. I think if we show that we're willing to let her take the lead on this, she'll not make it difficult."

"Does she not realize how difficult we could make *her* life?" Lindsay demanded.

Lucas sighed. "Linds, she owes us absolutely *nothing*. She tried to let Lincoln know about his son, and he didn't step up. She's raised that boy on her own and has done a great job of it from what I was able to see." He gave her a hard look. "You will *not* make this difficult for her. The most important person in all of this is Danny, and I think his mom is the best one to determine how this will work for him. She hasn't painted Lincoln in a bad way to Danny, which—given how he treated her—she had every right to do. On that alone, we need to give her what she wants."

Lindsay scowled at him, but when she said nothing, Lucas knew she'd gotten his point.

"She has my information, so even though I know it will be hard, we just need to wait until she contacts us. If I don't hear from her in a few days, I'll give her a call."

"And what if she's taken off with Danny by then?" Lindsay asked.

"She's not going to do that."

She tilted her head. "You seem very confident about trusting this woman you only spent such a short time with."

"I can read people. You know that. She has a made a home for herself and Danny. A sudden move like that would upset him, especially now that he's met me. It seems to me she puts Danny's needs above hers and while she might not want us in his life, I think she knows it's important to him. You'd react just like she did, Lindsay."

"Well, I doubt that since I'm never going to have kids."

"Lindsay," his mother admonished her. "Don't say that."

"Why? It's true. I've always said you wouldn't be getting grandchildren from me."

"Lincoln always said that too, but I'm very glad that things turned out differently," his mom said. "Maybe it will be the same for you."

"If someone contacts me to let me know they're pregnant with my child, we'll have a problem on our hands."

Lucas couldn't help laughing.

"You two," his mom said, her affection for them clear in her gentle smile.

He was glad to see something take the sorrow from her face, even if it was for just a few seconds. "Well, I'm going to go change into something more comfortable. Maybe go for a swim."

"I might join you," Lindsay said as she pushed herself to her feet.

Lucas climbed the stairs to the second floor and the room that had been his until he'd turned twenty-one and moved out. It had once again become his for the past four months. Ever since news had come about Lincoln, his cleaning lady had probably spent more time at his place than he had.

As he passed the closed door that led to Lincoln's room, Lucas paused. Something he'd seen at Brooke's house had triggered a memory. He gripped the doorknob and turned it. The dark, mustiness of the room told him that his mom was still not allowing the staff to clean in this room. He reached out and flicked on the light, blinking as the room was flooded with brightness.

He stood for a moment taking in the state of the room. The staff had been cleaning it regularly up until the news of his disappearance, so it wasn't messy. But what Lucas was most interested in were the paintings on the wall. He stood in front of one, staring at it. The painting—done in rich, vibrant colors—was of a waterfall. The perspective was looking down over the top of it as if the painter was getting ready to jump. He had always figured that was what appealed to Lincoln. No doubt his brother had jumped off his share of cliffs. But now Lucas wondered if it was something else.

CHAPTER FOUR

Lucas's gaze dropped to the right-hand corner of the painting as he pulled his phone out. He quickly found the picture he was looking for. Dropping to his knees, Lucas held his phone up next to the piece of art. Sure enough, the signatures matched.

BLK

Lucas straightened. He was fairly certain that Brooke hadn't given this painting to his brother. He glanced at the other two that hung on the other walls. Their styles were similar to the one he'd just checked. He walked to the side of the large bed and leaned over to look at the one over the headboard. That one had the back of a young boy with dark brown curls in the lower right corner looking from the edge of a cliff toward where another figure—a man—flew with wings out over a stormy ocean.

He'd seen the painting before and had always assumed that Lincoln had been drawn to the figure flying free. Now Lucas realized that Lincoln *was* the figure flying. And the boy watching him was Danny. Brooke had perfectly captured the relationship between her son and his father.

It was a poignant painting. Reminiscent of the story of Icarus he'd read in high school. Only this time it was the son watching the father fly...higher and higher. And just like Icarus, Lincoln had crashed into the water below.

Lucas turned from the painting and sat down on the edge of the bed. He was fairly certain if he looked more into Lincoln's possessions he'd find more paintings. He wondered how Brooke would react to the news that Lincoln had been the one buying her art. Clearly, in the only way he knew how, Lincoln had been taking care of his boy through the purchases of his mother's paintings.

"Ah, Linc. Why couldn't you have been happy with a life here?" Lucas braced his hands on the bed and bent his head as pain pierced his heart.

Though they'd had different outlooks on life and different ways of finding fulfillment, they had still been brothers. Twin brothers. Worst of all was the knowledge that he was fairly certain that Lincoln had never made things right in his spiritual life. Whenever he'd tried to talk to him about God and having a personal relationship with Him, Lincoln had brushed it aside. Now he'd have to live with the regret that he hadn't tried harder.

"Luc?"

Taking a deep shuddering breath, Lucas looked over to see Lindsay standing in the doorway. Without saying anything more, she walked over and sat down on the bed next to him. She slid her hand along his arm and linked her fingers with his. Letting out a long sigh, she leaned her head against his shoulder.

They sat in silence for several minutes. Lindsay wasn't very visible with her grief, but Lucas knew she felt Lincoln's loss as keenly as he did. Now it was just the two of them when it had always been three. Their triangle had become a straight line. He had always figured that this would be how Lincoln's life would end given the way he lived it, but it didn't make the reality any easier.

Lucas pointed at the painting above the bed. "Brooke painted that and the other two in here."

He felt Lindsay straighten beside him. "What? These paintings?"

"Yes. When I was at her house, I saw a painting on her wall that looked familiar in its style. I took a picture of the signature and compared it to the one over there and it's a match."

Lindsay moved away from him, crawling on the bed toward the one he'd been looking at. Going up on her knees, she braced her hands on the wall and stared at the painting. After a few seconds, she glanced over her shoulder at him. "Is this what I think it is?"

"Probably. If you're thinking it's her interpretation of Danny's relationship with Lincoln."

"She's good. I always wondered why Linc bought these paintings. The style is very similar so I knew they were all by the same person. I asked him about them once. He just said something about supporting a budding artist and that they were an investment."

"They were. An investment in his son." Lucas stood up and walked to the desk where Lincoln's desktop computer sat. There was a scattering of papers on its surface. "I'm just a bit concerned if Brooke has been relying on the money from those sales. My guess is he bought them fairly regularly, but now it's been at least four or five months since he last bought one. Could explain..."

Lindsay came to stand next to him. "Could explain what?"

"Why she didn't have her air conditioning on today. That house was like a furnace. She said it was a lifestyle choice when I asked her if it was broken. I'm wondering if it's actually because she can't afford to run it." Lucas dragged a hand through his hair.

"She's going to have plenty of money soon," Lindsay commented as she picked up a piece of paper from the desk then set it down again.

"Not soon enough if she needs it now. Processing the will could end up taking more time than she has." Lucas sat down at his brother's desk. "I need to figure out where Linc was buying those paintings."

"I thought we were going to go for a swim," Lindsay said as she perched on the edge of the desk.

Lucas slid open the main drawer. "I think this is slightly more important. We can swim later."

"Okay, let me help." She grabbed a handful of the papers on the desk and began to shuffle through them.

Lucas smiled as he bent to pull files from the drawer. She might talk a tough line, but in the end, she would do what she could for the nephew she hadn't even met yet.

Brooke sat on the back porch, hoping that the gentle breeze would kick into something more like a gale force wind. Worry ate at her as she stared out at the small patch of land she claimed as her back yard. Her garden was dying with the heat and lack of rain, and she couldn't justify spending the money to water it.

It had been a long time since she'd been this short of cash. Given that she'd chosen to paint as her career, she'd learned early on to budget any money that came in, to not spend anything extravagantly. But this dry spell had taxed even the reserves she'd had in place. When her mom had called to ask her to come to church—as she did each Saturday—Brooke had said no as usual, even though she wouldn't have been able to go even if she'd wanted to. She was pretty sure she would have run out of gas on the way.

Though it was an excuse, it wasn't the real reason she declined every week. They would have given her a ride if she'd expressed an interest because they came each Sunday to pick Danny up for Sunday school and church. While she wasn't thrilled with church and the faith of her childhood, when they'd offered to take Danny, she'd left it up to him if he wanted to go or not. He'd said yes and hadn't missed a Sunday since.

She knew her parents hoped that one day she'd come with him, but Brooke wasn't sure if that would ever happen. Right then she was in need of a major miracle, and so far God hadn't come through for her. After paying rent, she had barely enough money for one more week's worth of groceries and that was even buying much less than she usually did.

Lucas had said that she and Danny had been mentioned in Lincoln's will which no doubt would involve money at some point, but the problem was she needed the money now.

In the meantime, she had to connect with Lucas again about the wedding. She still wasn't sure what had prompted her to invite him. Maybe it was to shock her family. Maybe it was to put him on the spot. Either way, she had a feeling it was going to end up biting her in the butt.

She picked up her phone from beside her on the porch step. Text or call?

Text. Definitely.

Seeing his picture on his contact page made her smile again. Trying not to dwell too much on that, she brought up the screen to text him a message.

Wedding is next Saturday at 4 PM. Need to be there by 3. Semi-formal. Reception is at 6.

She kept a grip on the phone, waiting to see if he replied. As the minutes ticked by with no response, Brooke laid down on her back on the porch. She stared up at the roof, trying to find the desire to paint. She knew she needed to keep working, but it was hard to find the motivation when her other paintings weren't selling. She had three at Dorie Kennedy's gallery that had been there now for almost eight months.

Any day now she was sure Dorie was going to call her to come and pick up the paintings. And then what would she do?

Brooke pushed herself back up to a sitting position. This melancholy funk she'd been in for the past few days wasn't like her. Rarely did she let things like money get her down. She always tried to keep an optimistic outlook on their life for Danny's sake.

But since Lucas Hamilton had shown up two days ago, there had been no way to put a positive spin on Lincoln's death. She wasn't sure how to deal with all the feelings that were mixed up inside her since she'd heard the news. What they'd had hadn't been about love between them. They'd loved life. They'd loved the thrill of adventure. Yes, they'd shared a brief—very brief—physical intimacy, but it had never been a heart connection. Still, he'd been a friend and even though she'd hated him for how he'd treated Danny, he had given her the greatest thing in her life. She wouldn't do anything differently if it meant giving up Danny.

She pulled her legs in, wrapping her arms around them and bent her head down to rest on her knees. Hot tears dripped onto her thighs. She grieved for a man lost too young. She grieved for a friend with whom she had shared the most thrilling adventures. But mostly she grieved for her son who would never have the chance to get to know his father.

Danny hadn't cried again since that first day—at least around her—but she'd seen him looking through the small album of pictures she had of their time together. Pictures of them on the tops of cliffs. White water rafting. Bungee jumping. Parachuting. All the adventures they'd shared.

She couldn't bring herself to look through it yet. Not because of anything she felt for Lincoln—that had long since gone—but it was painful to think it was that zest for life that had led to his death. At least he'd died doing what he loved. Gallivanting around the world on another adventure.

"Brooke?"

She jerked her head up to see Lucas standing a few feet away from her. Looking down at her phone still clutched in her hand, she said, "You didn't text me back."

"I was driving home from church when I got your text. Thought I'd just come by."

Well, that explained why he was once again dressed in what she'd call business casual. His hair was perfectly styled, and he had the beginnings of a five o'clock shadow. The white heavy cotton shirt set off his hair and tanned skin.

Why was she even noticing these things?

"Danny's not here."

He came to where she sat and settled down next to her. "Are you okay?"

"What?" Lifting her hands to her cheeks, she swept the wetness away. "Yeah, I'm fine."

When she glanced at him, she saw that he didn't look convinced, but apparently he was a smart man because he didn't press. "So where's Danny?"

"He's with my parents. They pick him up for church each Sunday."

"You don't go with him?"

"Nope. God and I aren't on the best of terms."

"Why's that?"

"Why are people ever not on the best of terms with God?"

He paused then said, "Usually has to do with people assuming that God is responsible for all the bad things that have happened to them."

Brooke shot him a look. There was no judgment in his words and surprisingly, none in his expression either. "Something along those lines."

"But you still let Danny go to church?"

She shrugged. "When my parents offered to take him, I let him decide to go or not. His choice was to go."

When Lucas didn't respond, Brooke didn't bother to try to fill the silence. The stillness of the hot afternoon was broken only by the distant sounds of cars and children at play. Brooke loved afternoons like that. Heat aside, she loved to be outside and to hear the world alive around her.

Lucas leaned his elbows on his legs, his fingers intertwined. He wore a watch with a thick leather strap on one wrist, but no other jewelry.

"You're not easy to find information on."

He turned to look at her. "What do you mean?"

"I did a little searching after you left on Friday. There isn't much info on you and even less on Lincoln."

Lucas nodded. "That's the way it's supposed to be. My dad was more visible, but there's been no need for that for me or Lincoln. Both of us preferred to keep a low profile. Since our names are really only associated with the overall company—Hamilton Enterprises—and not the individual companies we own it's much easier to keep from being too interesting."

"When Lincoln mentioned he had family money, I just assumed it was something like an inheritance from old money. But he did actually work for his money, right?"

Lacus nodded. "He had a deal with my dad that as long as he stayed in touch, he would only have to work four months out of the year. The rest of the time, he could wander the globe as he wanted. He actually ended up working a lot more than that because he took his work with him."

"What did he do? Danny would ask me, but I had no idea."

"He designed computer games. Or rather, he designed the games that people go online to play with other gamers. He oversaw one of the largest MMORPG's on the internet. With a group of other programmers, he designed a huge virtual world and then wrote a storyline with quests and stuff like that. I never really understood it, to be honest. I'm not a gamer myself."

"Danny enjoys computer games, but I keep a close eye on what he plays."

"As you should. I'm pretty sure the game Lincoln helped develop isn't appropriate for kids Danny's age."

"Good to know. I try not to let him spend too much time on his computer or gaming systems. My brother bought him one for Christmas along with a couple of games."

"I was always surprised that Lincoln enjoyed something that actually required him to sit still for any length of time. He told me that there was a thrill in creating things like his virtual world that while not an adrenalin rush like his other adventures, was exciting and gave him a sense of satisfaction."

"Maybe you could show Danny what Lincoln did. Not that I'll let him play it, but just to give him another perspective on his dad."

"I can do that," Lucas said with a nod of his head. "In return, could I ask you to do something as well?"

Brooke was leery to commit to anything, but surely it couldn't be too bad. "What would that be?"

"Bring Danny to meet my mom."

She stared out at the back yard. It was hard to remember that Danny had had another family. Another set of grandparents and aunts and uncles. It had been just her side of the family for his whole life. She looked back at Lucas. "I will do that as long as you agree to a couple of things."

"Okay. What are they?"

"First, I will let Danny make that decision. He's dealing with a lot right now. I want to make sure he feels up to it."

"I agree with that." Lucas arched a brow. "And your other thing?"

"I want him to be treated as himself. I know he looks an awful lot like Lincoln, but he's not. He's very different from his dad personality-wise. I need people to respect that and treat him special because of who *he* is, not because of who his father was."

"That's reasonable. It's not like my mom doesn't already live with someone who looks like Lincoln."

Brooke stared at him, trying not to smile. "You live with your mother?"

CHAPTER FIVE

BROOKE'S heart skipped a beat when Lucas grinned at her question. "Well, yes, actually I do."

"That must be quite the draw for the females you come in contact with."

"It's not generally what I lead with when conversing with women," Lucas admitted. "But I do actually have my own place. I've just been living with my mom and Lindsay since we got word about Lincoln. I imagine I'll move back to my condo at some point."

"You don't have a girlfriend?" Brooke wasn't sure why she asked the question, but if she was going to spend time off and on with him, she'd rather have a heads up if there was a potentially jealous lover in the picture.

"No. I haven't had time recently to devote to a relationship. Before that, I seemed to lose most of my girlfriends to Lincoln."

"What?"

"They seemed happy enough with me until they met him. One told me it was like being with a more vibrant alive version of me."

"Well, that's a horrible thing for someone to say."

Lucas smiled. "Not really. The first time it happened it hurt because I wasn't expecting it. After that, I didn't let myself get too involved with a woman until she met Lincoln. If she was still interested in me after having Lincoln turn his charm on her, then I was willing to consider a more serious relationship."

"You make it sound like you and Lincoln would put the women to the test."

"I guess you could say that. It was bad enough that some of them were simply there for the money. Our little test was a good way to weed out the shallow gold diggers."

Sitting there beside Lucas, Brooke couldn't imagine a woman choosing Lincoln over him. But then she was looking at it from a completely different perspective. She'd already had Lincoln in her life and experienced the not-so-attractive side of his personality. The stability Lucas showed was far more appealing at this stage in her life.

Not that he was offering it to her. And not that she was wanting it. She hadn't been on a serious date in years and planned to keep it that way. She had no interest in having just a sexual relationship with a man anymore but also had no interest in marrying one either. Basically, she had no use for a man in her life. So why bother dating? The few she'd gone on had been to appease her mother and Mrs. Davis.

"You mentioned you have a brother," Lucas said. "Do you have any other siblings?"

Brooke fought the urge to roll her eyes. Of all the subjects... "Yes, I have a sister, Victoria. She's a few years younger than I am."

"Is she married?"

"No, my brother is the only one in a serious relationship. Victoria jokes that her dating pool is a little shallow so she hasn't found anyone she's interested in dating yet. She's a little person."

"A what?"

"A little person. She was born with dwarfism."

"Really? Does that run in the family?"

"If you're asking if either of my parents have it, the answer is no. But, strangely enough, my brother's daughter also has it. It isn't hereditary in that way, and it's extremely rare for two people in the same family to have it without being a direct relation. Victoria has a good chance of having a child with dwarfism, but the likelihood of my brother and his girlfriend—soon-to-be wife—having another child with it is rare."

"So it's the three of you?"

"Sort of." It had been almost six months, and Brooke still wasn't sure how she felt about Alicia.

"Sort of? That's an odd response."

She shrugged. "We have a half-sister that we just found out about a few months ago."

"It sounds like there's a story there," Lucas said.

"Yep. But not one I really like to talk about."

Before Lucas could say anything more, Brooke heard Danny's voice calling out for her.

She stood up just as the back door flew open. "Hey, sweetie."

Danny wrapped his arms around her in a quick hug. His gaze went past her as he stepped back. "Hi."

"Hey, Danny. How's it going?"

"It's going good." He looked back at Brooke. "Grandma and Grandpa are inside."

"Really?" Of all days. Usually, they would just drop him off since they always said hi when they picked him up. She'd asked Danny not to say anything about Lucas and the news of Lincoln's death. But as she looked toward the screen door leading into the house, she knew it was too late.

She walked to the door and opened it, immediately spotting her parents where they stood together in the middle of her hot kitchen.

"Hello, darling." Her mom came and gave her a hug, the scent of her perfume wrapping around Brooke like a familiar embrace. "We were at the store and picked up a few things for you."

Brooke saw the bags on the counter that looked like more than just a few things. They did that every once in a while. She had a feeling Danny had mentioned something about their rather bare refrigerator. "You didn't have to do that."

"I know," her mom said with a smile. "But we like to be able to help out."

She knew the moment the door from the porch opened and fought back a groan. It had been too much to hope that Lucas and Danny would have just stayed out on the porch. Her mom's eyes lit up, a curious expression on her face.

Brooke turned to see Lucas standing just inside the back door with his hands on Danny's shoulders. The similarity in their appearance was striking, and Brooke knew she was likely hoping in vain that her parents wouldn't notice it.

"Hello." Her mom was heading in Lucas's direction, her hand held out. "I'm Caroline, Brooke's mom. And this is my husband, Doug."

Lucas took her hand and shook it and then took the one her dad offered as well. "I'm Lucas Hamilton."

A smile still on her face, her mom turned toward Brooke as if looking for more of an explanation.

Brooke sighed. If she didn't tell them the truth, they would likely assume he was Danny's father, given the resemblance and the last name. She had just hoped for a little more time although his presence at the wedding would have raised questions as well. "Lucas is Danny's uncle."

"Uncle?" her mom said as her gaze went back to Lucas. "I do see a family likeness."

Lucas nodded. "My twin brother, Lincoln, was his father. I contacted Brooke this week to let her know that he had passed away. They were mentioned in his will."

"Oh my." Her mom's eyes rounded at the news, and her gaze shot to Brooke before going back to Lucas. "You have our condolences for your loss."

"Thank you."

"We'd better be on our way, dear," her dad said as he slipped his arm around his wife's waist.

Brooke wondered if there would ever be a day when she would be able to look at her parents together without her stomach twisting. To this day—twenty-some years later—she still didn't understand how her mom had been so forgiving of what he'd done to her.

It wasn't like he'd been, say, a dentist or bank teller who had slept with some random woman with no connection to their lives. No, he'd gotten involved with someone her mom had known. Someone who had been part of their large circle of friends and co-workers in the mission. Worst of all, the woman had been their teacher. So there hadn't just been the humiliation of having her husband cheat on her, but to know that all the people they worked with knew exactly who it was. And then he'd had to confess and apologize before being sent back to the States where speculation had run rampant about their abrupt departure from Africa and subsequently their mission. Humiliation on top of humiliation, and still she'd taken him back.

Brooke couldn't understand it. That's why even though she'd been involved with Lincoln physically, she hadn't loved him. The trust required for love hadn't been there. Her upset with him came from his treatment of Danny. Their son had deserved better. She hadn't cared that he'd skipped out on her. She had actually expected that he would eventually.

Her mom gave her a hug. "We'll see you at the rehearsal, right?"

"We'll be there," Brooke assured her. She wasn't entirely sure how, but she would make sure that Danny was there to perform the duty he'd been given. He had been thrilled when Eric and Staci had asked him so she would do what she had to make he wasn't disappointed.

She walked with them to the front door.

"Any chance you two might come for dinner one night and bring Danny's uncle?" her mom asked, trying with little success to hide her blatant curiosity. "We'd love to get to know him since he's practically family."

Knowing better than to outright refuse, Brooke would also never commit. "I'll see what he says."

"Okay, I'll give you a call." One more hug and her parents were walking across her front lawn to where their car was parked.

Brooke watched through the screen until the car pulled away from the curb. She turned to see Danny and Lucas behind her in the hallway.

"I'd love to," Lucas said.

Brooke glanced up as she walked past him to the kitchen. "Love to what?"

"I'd love to go to dinner at your parents' place."

She spun around to face him. "Uh. No. That's not going to happen."

"Why not? Like your mom said, we're practically family."

Brook looked from Lucas to Danny, who stood at his uncle's elbow. The mischievous grins they both sported were unnervingly similar. "No. She's no doubt noticed you're not wearing a ring. Dinner would be a matchmaking affair. She has two single daughters, after all."

"Two? I thought you said there were three of you."

Danny snorted in laughter. "Grandma doesn't try and match Mom up with anyone anymore."

"Yes, she knows better than to do that now," Brooke said with a grin at Danny. She liked to think the matchmaking catastrophes had been as much about the men her mother had chosen as they had been about her aversion to dating, in general.

Lucas looked down at Danny. "You're going to have to tell me about them sometime."

Danny was vigorously nodding his head as Brooke said, "No."

Again they both looked at her with those grins. This did not bode well for her future. Already Lucas had found an ally in Danny. Eric and her dad tried to make time for him, but Brooke sensed that Danny had found a connection with Lucas that had been missing with them.

"No," she said again as she marched toward the kitchen. The bags from her parents still sat on the counter awaiting her attention.

Trying to figure out how to keep things from spinning out of her control, Brooke pulled a couple cans of soup out of the first bag. Lucas and Danny joined her as she opened the cupboard to put them away. She stared at the nearly empty shelves and quickly shoved the cans in and shut the door.

"Want some help, Mom?" Danny asked.

"That's okay, sweetie. Why don't you and Lucas go and chat? You could show him your room." She looked at Lucas. "If you have the time."

His gaze went from the bags on the counter to the cupboard and then to her. "Sure, I've got lots of time."

She watched him rest his hand on Danny's shoulder as they walked toward his room. How had everything changed so fast? Just four days ago, thoughts of Danny's father had been the furthest thing from her mind. As far as she had been concerned, Lincoln Hamilton was in her past and that was where he was going to stay.

Only he hadn't. Even in death, he was back in her life. And she didn't know what to do now.

Returning her attention to the bags on the counter, she quickly put their contents away. As much as she struggled in her relationship with her parents, they never allowed that to stand in the way of offering her help. She might be more reluctant to accept the help if it wasn't for Danny. What she might be willing to endure herself was far different from what she'd make her son suffer through.

Maybe it was time to look for a *real* job. Goodness knows no one considered her art as a steady income. And though it had been in the past, that certainly hadn't been true lately.

Lucas looked around Danny's room. Though it was obviously a room that belonged to a pre-teen boy, it lacked the trappings he and Lincoln had had at that age. Their rooms had been expansive with big beds, and they'd each had a television and a game console along with a computer.

Danny had a single bed pushed into one corner of the room, neatly made with a spread featuring the DC characters he seemed to favor. He had a simple desk under the window that was completely bare. No doubt being out of school meant no books or papers that needed his attention. There was a dresser next to the desk and posters on the wall.

"I got some medals from track last year." Danny opened the bottom drawer of his dresser and pulled out a box.

"You like to run?" Lucas moved to his side as he set the box on the desk.

"Yep." He gave him a sideways glance with a grin so much like his father's that it took Lucas's breath away. "They weren't for big track meets or anything. But next year when I'm in middle school, I hope to be able to make the team."

Lucas took the medals Danny handed him, not too surprised to see that most of them were for first place. "Your dad liked running, too. But he didn't really like to be on teams. He just wanted to run."

"I like to race." Danny's eyes sparkled. "And win. Mom says doing my best is important and while I don't have to win every single time, I need to *want* to win every single time."

"Your mom is smart." Lucas handed the medals back to Danny. There was a part of him that just wanted to shower this kid with everything, but something told him Brooke wouldn't appreciate that. And honestly, it didn't appear that Danny lacked anything of true importance in his life.

The doorbell rang, and Lucas heard the murmur of voices. A moment later, Brooke appeared in the door of the bedroom, a young man at her side.

"Jeff!" Danny hurried to where they stood.

"I told Jeff you two could ride down to the park for a bit." Brooke grasped Danny's upper arm. "Remember the rules. And Jeff, you have your phone?"

The other boy nodded. "Text when we get there and when we're on our way home."

"Perfect." She gave Danny a quick hug. "Just for an hour though, okay?"

"Yep." Danny looked at him. "See ya."

Lucas smiled. It did his heart good to see his nephew had friends to spend time with. Running off to play with boys in their neighborhood hadn't been something he and Lincoln had been able to do. They hadn't gone to a public school so it wasn't like there had been classmates who lived next door. They had friends, but spending time with them had meant coordinating schedules and utilizing chauffeurs since riding bikes anywhere off their property had been out of the question. Not that they hadn't done it on occasion, but the times they'd gotten caught hadn't made it worthwhile. At least not for him.

Left alone with Brooke, Lucas decided to revisit a couple of things. "So, I'm serious. I'd like to have dinner with your family."

Brooke shook her head before turning around and walking back toward the kitchen.

Lucas followed her. "Why not?"

"It's just not a good idea."

He sat down on the stool at the counter and leaned his arms on the smooth surface. "Why is that?"

"I already explained it."

"So you're worried your mom's going to match me up with one of your sisters? Maybe one of them is my soul mate? Maybe this is supposed to be." It probably wasn't nice to jerk her chain, but it was kind of fun.

CHAPTER SIX

LUCAS tried not to grin as Brooke's mouth opened then snapped shut. She glared at him before turning to open a cupboard and pull out a couple of glasses. "Did you want something to drink?"

"Sure. Just water is fine."

Brooke took a large bottle of water from the fridge and poured it into the glasses. As she slid one across to him, she said, "For the record, I don't believe in soul mates, so I'm not too worried you'd find one at my mom's dinner table."

"You know, if you find the idea so abhorrent, you don't have to join us. I could just pick Danny up and bring him back after dinner is over." He took a sip of the water, grateful for the coolness of the liquid in the warmth of the kitchen. "It's not like I wouldn't meet them all at the wedding anyway."

"Why don't we talk about setting up something for Danny to meet your mother?"

Well, that hadn't been what he'd set out to get from her but it was a nice result of her efforts to avoid the discussion of dinner with her family. "Sure. When would be a good time for you?"

"I did say Danny needed to agree first."

"He agreed," Lucas said as he traced a finger through the condensation on his glass.

Brooke's brows drew together. "What? You asked him?"

"Not really. When you came inside, he asked me if I had parents. I assured him that I did—the same set his dad had."

"And he asked if he could meet them?"

"He said that he liked your parents and would like to meet his dad's parents, too. Of course, then I had to tell him that my father had actually passed away."

Brooke graced him with a sympathetic look before she sighed. "So, I guess we go ahead and set something up then."

"It won't be that bad. My mom is really quite nice. My sister, on the other hand..."

"Is...?"

Lucas grinned. "Kind of like you. I figure you two will either hit it off or hate each other on sight."

"Well, she's got something going for her right off the bat."

"What's that?"

"She's not a guy."

He laughed. "That she's not, but don't ever tell her she can't do something because of it. More than one person has ended up eating their words after such a statement."

Brooke let out a long breath. "Okay. Our schedule is pretty flexible with it being summer. The only days that won't work this week are Friday and Saturday because of the rehearsal and the wedding."

"How about dinner on Tuesday night? I have to work but can swing by to pick you up afterward."

She hesitated then nodded. "Can I bring anything?"

Lucas almost laughed until he realized her offer was sincere. Considering his mother probably wouldn't even lift a finger to prepare the meal, he hadn't thought about Brooke helping out in any way. "How about you and Danny whip up something like those muffins you made the other day? They were delicious."

Brook nodded. "We can do that."

He could see she was distracted by something, but didn't press her. And for now he'd leave the topic of dinner with her family on the back burner. He drained the rest of the water in the glass and stood up. "I guess I'll leave you to your day. Tell Danny goodbye for me."

Though he wasn't in any rush to leave, Lucas knew with Danny gone there was really no need for him to linger. When he'd decided to find them, he'd imagined he'd be most interested in getting to know Lincoln's son, but now he found that he was equally interested in getting to know Danny's mother.

"Thanks for stopping by." Brooke picked up his glass and set it next to the sink. "Sorry Danny keeps disappearing on you."

"It's quite alright. I'd rather get to know him on his terms, which means I don't want you to force him to hang with me when there's a better option available to him. I was a ten-year- old boy once. I would much rather have hung with my friends than an uncle."

"Thank you for understanding. I'm trying to let him fit this into his life in a way that's comfortable for him."

"Is he doing okay with it? I'm not sure how to ask him that."

"All things considered, I think he's doing pretty well. The mourning he's doing is for more of an idea than a person. He's never had a father. My dad or Eric would step in if things popped up where a father-figure was needed. Sadly, in this day and age, he isn't the only kid with an absentee father."

"Well, for the record, I don't think the decision Lincoln made regarding Danny was the right one. And while I'm not looking to fill my brother's role in Danny's life, I would like to be there for him in whatever capacity he might need."

Brooke nodded. "For now I'll leave it up to him to determine what that might be."

"Is there anything you need or that I can do for you?" Lucas asked.

"No." Her answer came without hesitation and with a shake of her head.

"Okay. If that changes, let me know. Otherwise, I'll be here Tuesday around five thirty to pick you up."

Lucas didn't prolong the visit after that. Though he wouldn't have minded spending more of the afternoon there, he knew he'd probably pushed his luck by just showing up in the first place.

As he pulled away from her house, his mind went to the week ahead. First up on Monday would be a visit to the gallery where it appeared Lincoln had bought his paintings. Though he'd never paid much attention to art before, he was about to become the proud owner of at least one Brooke McKinley original.

Brooke stared at the number on the display of her phone. It had been far too long since she'd received a call from Dorie Kennedy. She just really hoped the woman wasn't calling to ask her to pick up the paintings that hadn't sold. It had been months since the last sale. Before that, every two to three months a sale would come through. Dorie never identified the buyer, just said that they would name their price, and it was always way more than Brooke had hoped her paintings would fetch.

"Hello, darling," Dorie greeted her when she answered.

"How are you doing, Dorie?" Brook sat down at the table, bracing herself for what was to come.

"Just fine. Well, I could do with a little less heat, but other than that, certainly can't complain."

Just spit it out, Brooke wanted to tell her but she indulged in the chitchat Dorie always enjoyed.

After five minutes of updating Brooke about the latest antics of her furbabies and the cruise she was planning to go on in December, Dorie finally circled around to the point of her call. "Listen, darling, it's been a few months since you last made a sale."

Six months, two weeks, and five days to be exact. "Yes, I'm sorry about that."

"No need to apologize, darling. And I didn't call you to make you feel bad. I was actually calling because someone came in this morning and bought the three paintings I had on hand. So...you need to bring me some more."

The air whooshed from Brooke's lungs. Someone had bought *all* the paintings?

"Darling, you there?"

"Yes. Sorry. Just kind of surprised. *One* person bought them all?"

"Yep. One person."

"Is it the same person who's bought my other paintings?"

Dorie paused. "No. This is a different buyer. This one wants to remain anonymous as well though."

Brooke supposed it was too much to expect that she had two buyers who would be willing to pay the big bucks for her stuff. Even having one had been a one-in-a-million. She did some quick math in her head. If they paid what Dorie had priced them at, she'd be good for a few months at least. And this time around she would get off her duff and be proactive about her finances. She'd put all her eggs in one basket and was two weeks away from being out on the streets. No way could she let that happen again. Even with an inheritance pending, she just couldn't count on that any more than she could count on the sale of her paintings.

"I figure you might be anxious for the money, so I've sent the check over with a courier."

"Really? Oh, Dorie, thank you."

"You're welcome, darling. And when you've got some new pieces, give me a call. I have some holes to fill now."

After she hung up, Brooke sat staring at the phone. Last night she'd lain in bed, worried about what was to come if she didn't find a reliable source of income. Lucas had mentioned her and Danny being in Lincoln's will, but she didn't feel comfortable taking the money for herself. For Danny, sure, but she wasn't entitled to anything. She had provided for her son by herself for ten years now, and she would continue to do so. Whatever inheritance he was due to receive from Lincoln would be for his future. What had her most worried, however, was the present.

So last night for the first time in—well, longer than she could remember—Brooke had prayed. It hadn't actually been a prayer, more like an attempt to bring her situation to God's attention.

I could really use some help here, God.

Of course, it may not have been her pathetic attempt to reach out that had brought about the sale of her paintings. She knew her parents prayed for her on a regular basis and had clearly been aware of her tight finances since they'd brought her groceries. Perhaps they had prayed for God to provide for her. That was the more likely answer. After all, why would He give her any attention when she'd done her best to distance herself from Him?

Thank you, God, for providing. Just in case it had been her prayer, she wanted Him to know that she was grateful.

"Hey, Mom!" Danny came flying in the back door, letting it slam behind him. "Can we go to the pool?"

"Sure, but first I'm waiting for a delivery. Once that gets here, we can go."

"You don't need to take me. I can get a ride."

"Who else is going?"

"Jeff, Pete, and Jesse. Jeff's mom said she'd drive us so you don't have to."

"Okay. I need to run a couple of errands so if you get back before I do, can you just hang at Jeff's?"

"I think I can, but I'll ask before we go."

"Thanks, sweetie."

He was just heading out the front door with his swimming stuff when a courier vehicle pulled up. Brooke took the envelope he handed her with anticipation. After signing for it and saying goodbye to Danny, she went back inside.

Standing at the counter, she took a deep breath before slipping a finger under the flap to break the seal and slide the check out. Her mouth dropped open and once again she felt herself struggling to catch her breath.

This buyer put the other one to shame. What this latest buyer had paid for those three paintings would be enough to live on for at least two years. Three, if she was careful with it. She stared at the check as she sank down on the stool at the counter.

It was made out from Dorie's account so there was no way to know who the actual buyer was. The more she stared at it, the more the questions started to come. Although it wasn't as common as it had once been, it wasn't unheard of to have some sort of benefactor in the art world. Up until meeting Lincoln, she'd been waiting tables and painting when she could. He had actually encouraged her to try to find a gallery to showcase her work, had even made some suggestions.

After he'd left her, she'd decided to give it a try. She'd gone to the different galleries he'd mentioned and after seeing the type of art Dorie featured in her gallery had approached her about bringing in some of her work. Dorie had agreed they'd be a good fit and ever since then had been the conduit through which her anonymous benefactor had purchased her paintings. Those purchases had allowed her to stay home with Danny.

But as the wheels in her head started turning and the timing of things fell into place, Brooke felt a little sick. The purchases had stopped six months earlier. Lincoln had gone missing four months ago. Which would have been a month or so before another purchase would have been made. And now, just days after Lucas appeared in their lives, another purchase was made. A large one.

Had Lincoln been the one buying her paintings all these years? Had that been his way of supporting his son? Brooke closed her eyes and let out a long breath. It made sense, in a strange sort of way because it would have eased Lincoln's conscience. He would have been able to continue to live his life knowing that his son was taken care of but without having to deal with him personally.

Anger bubbled up inside Brooke. For years, she'd assumed it was someone who thought her paintings had worth buying them. Instead, she had a strong feeling that they had been purchased as a means to an end. Not by someone who valued her work but by someone who used them to assuage any guilt they may have felt about not being in his son's life.

And Lucas? He was no better than his brother. She'd known he wanted to help out. The fact that she'd resisted his help should have been enough to warn him off. But no, he had to go and take things into his own hands. And once again, her paintings had been used.

Of course, she had no real proof of her theory, but it fit so well she had a hard time believing it was all a coincidence. She didn't bother phoning Dorie to ask because, in the past, the woman had told her the condition of any future sales was that they remain anonymous.

The anger was tinged with discouragement as well. Her work had sat in Dorie's gallery for the past six months, and no one else had wanted them. Maybe she'd been chasing a pipe dream with her painting. It was quite possibly time to put aside the dream of being an artist and settle into a real career. This latest check would allow her to go back to school or try to find a job that would be something she'd enjoy.

If she kept it. Right then she wanted to walk up to Lucas and rip it up in front of him.

Pride can cost you everything but leave you with nothing.

The words floated through her mind in her mother's voice.

Pride comes before a fall.

Brooke looked back down at the check. Did it really matter if it came from Lucas? She wanted to say it was a matter of principle, but the reality was...it was a matter of pride. It hurt to think her paintings weren't worth anything except as a way to funnel money to her for Danny's sake.

For Danny's sake.

And that right there was why she'd cash this check. Regardless of the motives Lincoln and Lucas had when they'd bought her paintings—if, in fact, they had—her reasons for painting and selling those paintings had never changed.

For Danny's sake.

Her pride was not as important as being able to care for her son.

She stood up and made her way into her bedroom to change into something a little more presentable before going to the bank to cash the check. After she put gas in her car so she didn't end up stranded somewhere.

CHAPTER SEVEN

AS **HE** pulled up to Brooke's house, Lucas had to admit to being mildly surprised that he hadn't heard from her since he'd left on Sunday. He'd been convinced that she would contact him—through text most likely—to let him know that dinner with his mom was off. Just to be sure—though it wouldn't matter at this point—he took his phone out to check for new messages.

Not finding any, he shut the car off and climbed out into the sweltering afternoon air. He still wore his suit from work and it was just about killing him. The heat had to break at some point...he hoped.

As he went up the steps to the front door of Brooke's house, he noticed the inside door was closed. Frowning, he pressed the doorbell. While he had expected her to cancel, he hadn't thought she might just not be home when he arrived to pick them up.

He was relieved when the inside door opened to reveal Danny.

Danny pushed the screen door open. "Hi. Come on in. Mom said she'd be ready in just a minute."

The minute he stepped inside Lucas realized why the door had been closed. The air conditioning was on. Glad neither she nor Danny had to endure the heat in their home, Lucas smiled at the boy. "You said you liked to swim, right?"

"Yep. I just went swimming yesterday, actually."

"Why don't you bring something to swim in? We've got a pool."

Danny's eyes lit up. "Really? Cool!"

As the boy darted off, Lucas spotted Brooke walking out of what he assumed was her room. She wore a long sundress in several different shades of turquoise with some flowery pattern around the bottom. It had a gathered top and fell in folds to her ankles. The narrow straps showed off her lightly tanned shoulders. He found it a bit surprising that she had any sort of tan given the color of her hair, but it definitely worked for her.

For the first time since he'd met her, she was wearing her hair down. It was a mass of curls that fell to the middle of her back. She carried a pair of white sandals and a purse.

"Will I pass inspection?" Brooke asked as she stopped to slip on one sandal and then the other.

Lucas wasn't sure about his mom and Lindsay, but she looked just fine to him. He'd told his mom that dinner would be casual because Brooke and Danny didn't strike him as the type to "dress for dinner." He wasn't either, but usually did it for his mom's sake. Or rather, he would just stay in his work clothes through dinner and then change.

"You look very nice."

"Thank you." A quick smile curved her lips as she glanced away from him toward Danny's door. "Isn't he ready yet?"

"He was. I told him to bring something to swim in. We have a pool and, with it being so hot, I thought he might like to take a dip."

Before Brooke could say anything, Danny came back out of his room with a bag in hand. He was dressed in long dark denim shorts, a light blue polo shirt and a pair of loafers. The outfit looked similar to the one he'd worn when his grandparents had dropped him off after church.

"Ready to go?" Brooke asked him.

Danny nodded then looked at Lucas. "Do you swim?"

"Yes, I do. I'll probably join you. Anything to get cool in this heat."

Brooke went to the kitchen to pick up a basket that sat on the counter. "Well, let's get this show on the road."

Lucas led the way out to his car, opening the front and back doors on the passenger side for Brooke and Danny.

As he climbed behind the wheel, Lucas heard Danny say, "This is crazy cool."

He glanced back at the boy in time to see him looking wide-eyed at the luxury of the vehicle. Sometimes—often—Lucas took for granted the trappings that his wealth allowed him. It was kind of refreshing to be reminded that not everyone lived as he did. And that people didn't need the wealth he had in order to be happy.

Brooke definitely echoed Danny's sentiment with regards to the car. Compared to her car...well, there really was no comparison. About the only thing they had in common was the use of four tires. There was a subtle scent of cologne that lingered in the car. She watched as Lucas manipulated the wheel with ease as they pulled away from the curb and into the traffic.

Music drifted softly through speakers that made it sound amazing. She recognized the song from her days in church. His music choice brought to mind his comment on Sunday that he'd been on his way home from church when he'd gotten her text. It appeared that perhaps his faith was important to him like it was to her parents. Lincoln certainly hadn't had any sort of faith that she had seen. But then, he probably could have said the same of her even though her family was all Christian. So it was entirely possible that Lincoln had been the black sheep of his family as well.

She clutched the basket of muffins and cookies she and Danny had worked on earlier that day. It had been such a relief to be able to turn the air conditioning back on while they were baking. But now faced with obvious wealth, Brooke felt a flutter of nerves. She was not from a family with money. Eric and Staci were the most financially set, but neither of them really lived any differently. They had nicer cars, but nothing like what Lucas drove.

She listened as Lucas and Danny talked about video games and sports. Thankfully, this visit wasn't about her, so hopefully she wouldn't be required to talk too much. For once, she was feeling a bit out of her depth.

"Oh. Wow." Those were Danny's words as they drove up to a large wrought iron gate. Lucas pressed a button and slowly the gates began to swing inward.

The nerves that had been a flutter earlier grew considerably more active as Lucas drove along a winding treed driveway. When the house came into sight, Brooke realized she'd made a very big mistake agreeing to this meeting. There was no way she and Danny could ever fit in to this world. Nothing intimidated her much, but this did. She wanted this to go well for her son, but right then she was sure that what they wore was totally out of place, and they were going to look like just what they were—the poor relatives.

"That's your house?" Danny asked as Lucas pulled to a stop in front of a huge two story palatial estate home.

"It's my mom's actually, but Lindsay and I live here with her right now."

"It's...big."

"Yeah, too big, really," Lucas said. He shut off the engine and opened his door.

Brooke was a little slower moving which gave Lucas time to get around to open the door for her. When he offered his hand, she paused for a moment before gripping it. Once she had her feet on the ground, she felt him give her hand a quick squeeze before releasing it.

When she glanced at him, he smiled. "They won't bite."

Well, it didn't really matter if they did. She could bite back, if necessary. Danny came to stand next to her and slipped his hand into hers. With the basket of baked goods tucked into the crook of her elbow, she followed Lucas as he walked toward the wide stone steps leading to the front door of the house. Danny stuck tight to her side as they approached the house.

Lucas opened the door and stepped back to allow them to walk in ahead of him. A wash of cool air met them, and Danny's grip on her hand tightened even more. The foyer they stood in was bigger than both her and Danny's bedrooms put together. A sweeping curved staircase on the left side of the room led to the second floor and a balcony.

There was rich, and then there was...this.

"Let's go through to the living room. See if Lindsay and Mom are there."

Walking straight ahead through a short hallway led them into another even bigger—if that was possible—room than the foyer. The way they had come in had them facing a huge bank of windows. There was a fireplace to the right and large pieces of furniture were situated at various angles through the room.

The intimidated feeling from earlier grew even stronger. Keeping Danny pressed to her side, Brooke glanced around looking for some sign of life.

"About time you got here, Luc." The voice came from a room off to the side.

"We left the office at the same time, and I told you I was picking Brooke and Danny up." Lucas responded without any type of defensive tone to his voice.

As he turned to Brooke and Danny, he smiled and motioned toward them. "Brooke. Danny. This is my sister, Lindsay. Linds, this is Brooke and Danny."

Brooke watched as a voluptuous woman about her height stepped into view. Her hair was a few shades darker than Lucas's and looked to have been professionally highlighted. It lay in perfect curls over her shoulders and matched the expertly applied makeup on her face. She wore a gray suit with a hot pink blouse that fit her perfectly.

Given Lucas's laid back attitude and approach, Brooke hadn't really expected his sister to be so...impeccable. Her light gray eyes flitted over Brooke and then focused on Danny. When she took a couple of steps in their direction, Danny pressed more tightly to Brooke's side and his grip on her hand increased almost painfully.

"You're scaring him, Linds," Lucas said with a trace of humor in his voice. "Why don't you go get changed into something a little less intimidating. I told Mom we weren't dressing for dinner even though we were having guests."

Lindsay's gaze met hers for a moment before moving back to Danny and then to Lucas. "I'll be right back."

"That's the professional Lindsay," Lucas said with a grin as he shrugged out of his suit coat and laid it across the back of a nearby chair. "We try not to let her out after business hours."

"Lucas?" This voice was softer, gentler.

Danny's grip on her hand eased a bit as an older woman approached them from the opposite side of the room from where Lindsay had appeared. Lucas went to her and pressed a kiss to her cheek.

"Hi, Mom." He slid an arm around her shoulders as he guided her to where Brooke and Danny stood. "This is Brooke and Danny."

Though this woman wasn't dressed like Lindsay had been, she still exuded an elegance that Brooke knew she'd never in a million years be able to pull off.

"This is my mom, Sylvia."

Though the woman's hair had streaks of silver in it, it looked more like it had been highlighted that way. It was cut into a smooth bob that just brushed the tops of her shoulders. She wore a short sleeve cranberry sweater set over black slacks. Definitely more casual than what her daughter had been wearing, but still elegant. Her eyes were like Lucas's and regarded them warmly.

She smiled and held out her hand. "Brooke? It's nice to meet you."

Thankfully, Danny let go of her hand so she could take the older woman's in a firm grip. "Likewise."

As her hand slid from Brooke's, Sylvia turned her gaze toward her grandson. "And you're Danny."

Brooke was proud of Danny when he nodded and took the hand the older woman held out to him. She gave his shoulder and encouraging squeeze. They'd talked a bit about what the visit with Lucas's mom might entail. So far, so good.

"I'm so glad you could both come for dinner," Sylvia said as she let go of Danny's hand.

As her gaze went to Lucas, Brooke saw pain in her eyes. It hit her then. Until that moment, Lincoln had been the man who'd abandoned her son. But he'd also been a son to this woman. He'd been to Sylvia what Danny was to her. Her heart clenched at the thought of how she'd feel if it were Danny that had passed away.

No wonder Sylvia had wanted to meet Danny. The defensive shield Brooke had put in place before Lucas had come to pick them up slipped a little. A love for their sons leveled the playing field. Wealth or the lack thereof no longer mattered. They were just two mothers who loved their sons.

Lucas reached out and drew his mom to his side. He smiled down at her with affection. "Lincoln would have been so jealous of Danny's hair, wouldn't he?"

Sylvia looked again at Danny and smiled tremulously. "When he was your age he wanted to wear his hair long. Leon—his father—absolutely forbade it. I think that's why he let it grow as soon as he was out of high school."

Danny reached up and touched his curls. "Mom said since it's my hair, I can decide when to cut it."

Sylvia glanced at Brooke and smiled. "Smart mom."

Brooke returned her smile. "Well, I figured there will always bigger battles to fight."

The older woman nodded. "That is so very true."

"Is this better?"

Lucas and his mom turned around as Lindsay walked up behind them.

Gone was the power business suit. In its place was a knee length jean skirt and a gauzy light pink blouse with cap sleeves that flowed out over her hips from the gathering just below her bust line. Her hair was pulled up in a high ponytail and though she still wore some makeup, it wasn't the airbrushed look she'd had on earlier.

"Much," Lucas said with a nod. "What do you think, Danny? Better?"

Danny looked up at Brooke, a panicked expression on his face. She grinned at him. "Your uncle said she wouldn't bite, so I think you can agree with him that this is better."

Brooke looked up to meet Lindsay's gaze head on. The stare-down lasted for about two seconds before a corner of Lindsay's mouth lifted in a half-grin that was so familiar. Brooke felt the defensive shield slip a bit more.

"Yeah, well, it feels better, too," Lindsay said with a grin in Danny's direction. "You hungry? I know I am."

The last of the tension seemed to ease away as Lucas led the way into the kitchen. "Hello, Stella."

A middle age woman turned from the stove to smile at them. "Hi, Lucas. You ready for dinner?"

"The vote has been taken and the results say we're hungry." Lucas gestured to a table that was set for five beside a large bay window in a nearby nook.

Uncertain what to do with the basket still in her hands, Brooke held it out to Lucas as they moved to the table.

He took it from her and lifted the covering to peek inside. When he covered it again, he grinned at Brooke and said, "They look delicious. I can't wait to try them."

"Remember to share," she said as she walked past him to the seat Sylvia indicated.

"Never." Lucas set the basket on the counter and after holding the chair for his mother, went around to take a seat at the other end of the table.

"Stella, this is Brooke and Danny," Lucas said with an affectionate smile at the woman who had joined them from the kitchen. "Stella has been with our family for longer than I can remember. She's the reason my mother and Lindsay have never needed to learn how to cook."

"Or you, either, brother dear," Lindsay said with what looked like more than just a light pat on his arm. "Let's not be sexist here."

"Hey, I can make a mean pot of mac and cheese," Lucas said defensively.

"Will you say grace, Lucas?" Sylvia asked after everyone was seated.

Brooke glanced at Danny, who was already bowing his head. She folded her hands in her lap and followed her son's lead.

Lucas cleared his throat and began to pray. "Father, we thank You once again for Your many blessings. Thank you for health and strength and for the food that has been prepared for us. Bless the conversation around this table and thank you that Brooke and Danny are able to join us. In Jesus's name. Amen."

As the conversation swirled around her, Brooke felt no need to join in. Danny seemed to have settled down and was happily answering questions directed at him by his aunt and grandmother. It was a bit odd to think of these two women in those roles as in the past they had applied only to Victoria and their mom. Her ultimate concern in all of this was for Danny, but she was glad that he seemed to be taking it all in stride.

The meal, not surprisingly, was delicious. Perfectly roasted chicken with perfectly roasted potatoes. Even though she cooked on a regular basis, Brooke knew that Stella even outshone anything she'd be able to cook. Following the main meal came a dessert of chocolate cake that tasted absolutely divine.

Once they were done, Lucas suggested he and Danny go for a swim. Danny enthusiastically agreed, and the two disappeared to get changed.

Brooke felt a little uncomfortable leaving Stella with all the clean-up but when she offered her help to the woman, she refused her offer with a smile.

"We can go sit on the porch to watch them," Lindsay suggested. "Unless you wanted to go for a dip as well."

Brooke shook her head. "I didn't bring a suit."

"I'm sure we could find something for you around here. Right, Mom?" Lindsay said.

"I think Trish left a bunch of suits the last time she was here. Seems she couldn't decide which one to wear and rejected most of them."

"Trish is my cousin's girlfriend. Or she was. I think she was about your size."

"That's okay. Danny is the fish in the family." That wasn't entirely true, but Brooke really wasn't in the mood to get into a swimsuit in front of virtual strangers.

Lindsay led the way out the French doors beside where they'd finished eating. The porch was more like a four season sunroom...nothing like the porches attached to her house.

"It's still very warm out," Sylvia observed as she sat down in one of the chairs facing the large pool beyond the porch. "Can you turn the fan on, darling?"

Lindsay went to the wall and turned the switch that activated the overhead fan.

Keenly missing the presence of Danny and even Lucas, Brooke settled into a chair that also faced the pool. There were plants all over the room. Some with blossoms on them, some with just an abundance of green leaves.

The sound of voices approaching drew Brooke's attention from the scenery. Danny stepped into the room, followed by Lucas. Brooke smiled at the excitement on Danny's face. Then her gaze went past her son and landed on a very masculine chest. Though he wore swim trunks similar to Danny's, there was no doubt that Lucas was all man.

Knowing there was no way she could meet Lucas's gaze without blushing even though his was definitely not the first bare male chest she'd ever seen, Brooke looked back at Danny. "Rules of the pool still apply here."

Danny nodded and then looked up at Lucas. "Can we swim now?"

"Sure thing." Lucas laid his hand on Danny's shoulder as they walked toward the screen door that led out to another porch and then the pool.

"Do you have a boyfriend?"

Brooke jerked her head around at Lindsay's question. "No. Do you?"

CHAPTER EIGHT

LINDSAY lifted a brow at her response then grinned. "No. I don't either. I was just wondering if there was someone else in Danny's life we should be meeting as well. Lucas said he didn't know."

"No. I'm not dating anyone. Danny is my focus right now. And I'm very particular about who I let into my life."

"I hear ya. You just can't be too careful these days. And some guys...well, they're just schmucks."

"Lindsay Marie Hamilton."

"Sorry, Mom, but you know it's true." Lindsay stretched out her legs, crossing her ankles as she propped her heel on the wicker table in front of where she sat. "The last guy I dated managed to hide that he was facing bankruptcy and needed an influx of cash to save his floundering business. As far as I'm concerned, he should have gone into acting because he just about managed to get me down the aisle."

"Really? What happened?"

"Lucas decided to do a background check on him after I forbade him to." Lindsay scowled. "I'm not sure who I hated most in the days that followed that revelation. Me, Lucas or the schmuck."

"I dated a bit after Lincoln, but once I realized I was pregnant, no one was really interested in me. And then I had Danny and knew that he was my priority. I haven't come across a guy yet who has made me regret that decision. I've gone out on a few dates just to pacify my mother, but none of them were guys I wanted anything to do with long term."

"Lucas doesn't have a girlfriend." This time it was Sylvia who spoke. Her gaze was on the pool, but Brooke sensed a loaded message beneath her words.

"Yeah, but he's had some crazy ones in his time, too."

"He told me about the Lincoln test he used to put his girlfriends through."

A sad smile curved Lindsay's lips. "Yeah. I used to feel sorry for the girls, but honestly, if they couldn't resist Lincoln, they didn't deserve Lucas."

"He needs someone who sees him for his worth." Sylvia glanced over at Lindsay. "You both are worth so much more than your bank accounts. I think there's someone out there who will recognize that."

"Maybe for Lucas." Lindsay crossed her arms and sank further down on the seat.

"So do you plan to spend the rest of your life by yourself?" Sylvia asked, her gaze on her daughter.

"We've had this discussion before, Mom. You know my answers. Why don't you ask Brooke?"

When Sylvia's gaze swung her way, Brooke braced herself.

"Do you, like Lindsay, plan to spend the rest of your life alone?"

"I haven't really thought that long term. As I said, Danny is my focus."

"What do you do?" Sylvia asked.

Brooke hesitated then said, "I paint. I have a gallery that sells my paintings."

Interest sparked in Sylvia's gaze. "What kind of painting do you do?"

"Usually I work with oils but I've done some watercolors, too. Mostly nature scenes."

"You'll have to show me some time," Sylvia said with a smile. "Lincoln loved art, too, apparently. He has several paintings up in his room. Maybe you should look at them before you leave."

Brooke happened to glance at Lindsay in time to see her staring at Sylvia and shaking her head. "Sure, I'd like that."

Lindsay's gaze shot her way and in that instant Brooke knew that what she'd suspected earlier was true. Brooke stared at Lindsay as she said, "Does Lucas also enjoy art?"

His sister blinked and looked away.

Brooke turned her attention back to Sylvia when the woman said, "Why yes, now that you mention it, he just brought home three new paintings yesterday."

Gotcha!

"I haven't had a chance to look at them yet because he hasn't had them unpacked. I'm eager to see what they're like." Sylvia beamed. "He assured me that they are quite lovely."

Brooke returned the woman's smile, though she had no doubt it didn't look anywhere as near as beaming as Sylvia's. "I'll have to ask him to show me as well."

Her comment brought a groan from Lindsay, and Brooke looked over at her in time to see her close her eyes and tip her head back against the chair.

"Do you sell many paintings?" Sylvia asked.

"I've sold almost all I've painted. I've been one of the fortunate ones who's had a benefactor for several years. They've purchased every painting I've put up for sale in the gallery."

Interest sparked in Sylvia's gaze. "Do you know who they are? Or are they anonymous?"

"They preferred anonymity, and about six months ago they stopped buying. But, fortunately, another benefactor has apparently picked me up. I just sold three of my paintings yesterday."

"Three? Yesterday?" Sylvia's gaze went to where her daughter sat and then out to the pool. The woman might not have come across as a business woman like her daughter, but she was clearly no dummy.

Lindsay picked up a pillow and covered her face.

"Lindsay?"

The woman pulled the pillow from her face and sat up. She looked straight at Brooke and said, "So what do you do for fun? In your free time?"

Brooke arched a brow in response, but decided to give her a break because as far as she knew, Lindsay wasn't part of the anonymous purchases. "I enjoy baking. That's something Danny and I do together. We usually take some around to our neighbors. We bike a lot in the summer. I enjoy being outdoors so I also do some gardening."

"I saw you brought a basket in with you. Is that some of your baking?" Lindsay asked.

"Yep. At Lucas's request, Danny and I made some muffins and cookies this morning."

"At Lucas's request?" Sylvia asked.

"Yes. The first day he showed up, we'd made some. Apparently he liked them."

"Why don't you go get them, darling?" Sylvia suggested. "And bring back something to drink as well."

Lindsay seemed more than happy to escape the conversation.

"Thank you for bringing Danny over," Sylvia said once Lindsay had left. "I know there's been a lot for the two of you to take in these past few days. And I also know that you haven't been treated well by my son. Thank you for not holding that against us."

"I've had my reservations," Brooke admitted. She figured if the woman was being honest, so would she. "But in the end, it was Danny's call how much he wanted you in his life.

He's known about Lincoln from the time he was old enough to ask why other kids had a daddy and he didn't."

"Lucas mentioned that you had told Danny all about Lincoln."

"Well, what little I knew. To be honest, I really didn't know him that well. We were only together a short time and fun was more the name of the game than getting to know each other. I knew when I first met Lincoln that it wouldn't be anything long term. I just never imagined I'd be left with such a blessing from a casual relationship. I don't regret anything because I have Danny."

"And it seems you've done a wonderful job with him."

"I try."

Lindsay returned with a tray. "Here we go." She set it down on the wicker table. "Drink, Mom?"

Sylvia nodded and took the tall frosted glass Lindsay handed her.

"It's lemonade," Lindsay said as she held out a glass to Brooke.

"Thanks. Perfect for a hot day."

Lindsay picked up the basket and peeled back the cover. "These look wonderful."

"Not quite on par with Stella's chocolate cake," Brooke said. "But we like them."

Lindsay walked over to the screen wall facing the pool. "Hey, Luc! We're eating your cookies."

Brooke watched as Lucas stroked through the water toward them. He placed his hands on the edge of the pool and hefted himself out of the water. As he stood, water sluiced down his body to splatter on the concrete beneath his feet. He grabbed his towel and rubbed it over his head and torso.

"Hey, Danny, let's have a cookie break."

Danny got out of the pool a little more reluctantly. Of course, he ate their cookies all the time. The pool was definitely of more interest to him.

Brooke thought Sylvia might object to them tracking water into where they sat, but she soon realized that the furniture wouldn't likely be harmed by a little water.

"These are delicious," Lindsay said.

"Did you make these, Danny?" Sylvia asked as she held up a cookie.

"Yep. Mom told me that every man should know how to cook and bake because there's no guarantee he'll end up with a woman who can."

Lucas laughed. "Well, that would certainly be the case for any man who ends up with Lindsay."

"Shut up," Lindsay said as she popped the last bite of her cookie into her mouth.

Brooke found the interaction between the siblings interesting. She and Eric had been close as children since they'd been less than two years apart in age, but by the time they hit their teens, they were each reacting to the changes in their lives differently. Eric had tended to withdraw from everything—church, their parents, friends, and family. She, on the other hand, had done her best to make her parents and everyone around her miserable.

Since his return home, they still hadn't reconnected in a way that would allow them to be like Lucas and Lindsay. It had gotten better recently, but they still weren't that close. She struggled with how easily he'd been able to forgive their dad for what he had done to their family. And then there was their mom. Brooke knew that she would have had grounds to divorce their dad without anyone faulting her, but no, she'd stayed with him even after all the pain and humiliation. Who did that?

She couldn't even contemplate taking a guy back after being hurt and betrayed by them on such an intimate and personal level. Lincoln's betrayal had involved Danny and even then she wouldn't have taken him back into her life.

Part of her wondered if her mother had stayed because she just hadn't had any other choice. Two kids. Another on the way. She couldn't exactly do it on her own without a job. Which was why Brooke had never wanted to be dependent on someone who could leave her high and dry without any options.

Only...that's what had happened even without her being aware of it. Six months without a sale and she'd been close to high and dry. Lincoln had made her dependent on him without her knowledge and the same thing could have happened with Lucas, but that wasn't going to be the case if she could help it.

"Mom?"

Danny's voice broke through her thoughts. She glanced around and realized all eyes in the room were on her. "Sorry, sweetie. What's up?"

Before Danny could reply, Lucas said, "I was just asking you if you'd be interested in going out to our cabin for a few days."

"Cabin?"

"Yes. We have a place about four hours north of Minneapolis."

"It's really lovely," Sylvia said. "And lots to do. There's a boat and a couple of Jet Skis."

"Mom!" Danny looked like he was about ready to jump off his seat with excitement. "Can we go?"

Brooke looked at Lucas, hoping that he could see her annoyance at being put on the spot like that. "Let me talk a bit more with Lucas about it before we decide."

"Sounds good," Lucas said as he stood. "Want to go for another swim, buddy?"

"Sure."

Brooke watched her son follow his uncle back out to the pool. She told herself she'd raised Danny to not be swayed by money or things, but for a ten-year-old boy it was a bit unrealistic to think that he wouldn't want to play with the toys that only money could buy.

She was going to have to have a talk with Lucas, just to make sure they were on the same page. His family was not going to be buying Danny's affections. She was going to make good and sure of that.

The rest of the evening passed without further incident. Sylvia actually reminded Brooke a lot of her own mom. Once the guys had finished in the pool, she'd talked to Danny quite a bit about what Lincoln had been like when he'd been Danny's age. Lindsay and Lucas both offered their versions of certain events that their mother recounted.

It alternated between funny and sad, but Brooke could see it was good for the four of them to connect that way. She didn't add much to the conversation and often found her thoughts drifting to the changes that loomed in her and Danny's life. Lucas hadn't broached how much involvement they wanted to have with Danny, but Brooke had a feeling they would want to make up for lost time. She certainly didn't begrudge them that. Lincoln had robbed them of as much as he had Danny by not stepping into the role of father. Still, it was a bit difficult to listen to funny, endearing stories about a man she'd never held in much regard once her letter letting him know of Danny's birth went unanswered.

When it was time to leave, Brooke was more than ready to escape the huge mansion and get back to her little house. It had gone better than she had anticipated it might, but she needed some time with her own thoughts about everything that was going on.

Danny was quiet on the ride home and though Brooke wanted to broach the subject of the paintings with Lucas, she didn't really want to do it around her son. And then there was the subject of the time at the cabin that needed to be discussed as well. She had a feeling they were just two of the many discussions that were to come.

Lucas could sense the tension radiating off Brooke. She did a pretty good job of hiding her agitation with him, particularly around his family and Danny, but he could feel it. Lindsay had given him the heads up that it appeared as if Brooke had put two and two together and come up with four where her paintings were concerned. He didn't know why he hadn't thought to ask his mom not to mention his latest purchases.

When he pulled to a stop in front of Brooke's house, she glanced over at him. "Mind coming in for a few minutes?"

Knowing there was no way he could say no, Lucas nodded as he opened his door and stepped out into the slightly cooler evening air. Danny jumped out of the vehicle and ran to the front door ahead of them, while Brooke followed him more slowly. As he brought up the rear, Lucas figured that nothing good was going to come of whatever it was Brooke had prepared in her mind to say to him on the trip back to her place.

"It's time for bed, sweetie," Brooke said as they stepped into the house. "Why don't you get ready and then come say goodnight to Lucas?"

Danny nodded and trudged into his room.

"Be sure and hang your suit up in the bathroom," Brooke called out after him before turning toward Lucas. She gave him a smile that fooled him not one bit. "Would you like a drink or something to eat?"

Was this her idea of a last meal before handing him his head on a platter? There was a reason he'd chosen to purchase the painting anonymously. He might not know her that well—yet—but he knew she was independent and didn't want to rely on anyone. She wouldn't understand why he'd done what he had.

He sighed. "Any cookies left?"

"Yep."

Lucas followed her to the kitchen and sat down at the counter—it was rapidly becoming his spot in the house—and waited for the other shoe to drop. And waited.

Brooke didn't say anything as she opened a container and placed some cookies from it on a plate. Next she pulled a couple of glasses down from the cupboard and filled them with water. She'd just set them on the counter when Danny reappeared.

"Ready for bed?" She slipped an arm around his shoulders. At his nod, she said, "Say goodnight to Lucas."

Danny came around the counter and held out his arms to Lucas. Fighting back a sudden rush of emotions, Lucas embraced the boy, inhaling the scent of chlorine and toothpaste. "Goodnight, buddy."

"Thanks for swimming with me tonight," Danny said as he stepped back. "Can we do it again?"

"I think so, but that will be up to your mom."

Lucas watched as Brooke and Danny walked to the boy's room. She was with him for a few minutes before reappearing, shutting the door behind her.

"So, your mom tells me you bought some paintings yesterday," Brooke said as she picked up her glass and leaned her hip against the counter.

CHAPTER NINE

Lucas sighed. "Do you want to play the game or just get it all out so you can give me a piece of your mind?"

One of her brows rose at his comment. "Why did you do it?"

"I've always been good at putting pieces of a puzzle together. It didn't take me long to figure out what Lincoln had done." Lucas gestured to the painting on the wall in the living room. "I recognized the style that first day I came to visit you."

Brooke frowned. "Recognized the style?"

"Yes. Lincoln has three paintings hanging in his room at the house that were similar to that one. I took a picture of the signature and compared it to the ones in his room and found them identical. That's when I figured out that the initials were actually yours."

"He has the paintings hanging?" Brooke asked.

"Yes. The one above his bed is the one with the boy and man flying."

Brooke's eyes widened. "I hadn't been sure about selling that one but Dorie phoned asking if I had more to sell and that was the only one I had ready to go."

"I haven't found all the other paintings, but there were some in his closet still in their packaging. And I have a feeling others are in storage somewhere. I'm still in the process of going through all his stuff."

"And all these years I had hoped that people were actually enjoying my work." Brooke looked down at her glass. "I suppose I should be glad he at least hung three of them."

Lucas felt bad as he realized how it must be for an artist to find out that the things they worked so hard on were hidden away.

She tilted her head up to look at him, her hair falling across her shoulder. "What do you plan to do with the three you bought?"

"I planned to hang one at my apartment, one in my bedroom at the house and then give one to my mom."

Brooke nodded and bent her head down again. "Why did you buy them?"

"I think you already know the answer to that."

"It was too much. They're not worth that much. And they weren't worth what Lincoln paid for them either."

"I beg to differ," Lucas said as he picked up a cookie and broke it in half. "You're very talented."

"Then why did the three you just bought not sell until you plunked down way too much money for them?"

"Dorie? Is that her name?" At her nod, Lucas continued, "She told me that Lincoln had told her to not sell the paintings unless someone was willing to match what he paid."

"So even if someone were interested, if they weren't willing to pay what Lincoln would, Dorie wouldn't sell them?"

Lucas nodded. "And there were interested parties but when they wouldn't match Lincoln's price, Dorie wouldn't sell them. Of course, no one could foresee what would happen to Lincoln. Dorie wasn't sure what to do after so many months had passed without him showing up. She'd called his phone but got no answer, of course."

"All this time…" Brooke's words trailed off as she set her glass on the counter and crossed her arms over her waist.

"All this time you were providing for Danny the best way you knew how."

She glanced up at him. "Except if it hadn't been for Lincoln—and now you—I wouldn't have been able to."

"I have no doubt that you would have found a way to take care of Danny. Lincoln provided the only way he thought he could for his son. Emotionally he wasn't prepared to take on that responsibility but you were. He gave you the ability to give Danny what he needed. A mom who was able to do what she enjoyed and still have time to raise her son." Lucas took a sip of his water. "Lincoln wasn't trying to control how you raised your son. He was trying to give you the freedom to do it however you wanted."

A frown pulled her brows together. "I still don't like it."

"I agree that it wasn't the best way to handle things, but honestly, I think we both know from our interactions with Lincoln, that it was the best case scenario."

Brooke seemed to be considering his comments as she didn't say anything in response to that.

"And one more thing. Money will soon be the least of your worries."

Brooke looked at him. "What?"

"You and Danny are Lincoln's only heirs. After my dad's death, the Hamilton fortune was divided into four. You now get Lincoln's quarter. I am named as trustee to help with managing it, but there is enough there that you will never have to worry about money again."

Brooke's mouth dropped open as she stared at him. "When you said that Danny was mentioned in Lincoln's will…"

"I wasn't sure at that point what type of woman you were. I needed to make sure that our company was still protected. I wanted to get a feel for who you and Danny were."

A corner of her mouth lifted. "And now you've decided that we're okay?"

"Better than okay. I know that you'll always put Danny's needs first and part of that is protecting his interests in the company as well."

"I really am not interested in the money. Danny and I have been doing fine."

"I know you have. I can see that Danny is a happy, well-adjusted ten-year-old. The inheritance will just make it easier for you." Lucas looked around the house. "Don't think I didn't realize that the reason you didn't have your air conditioning on when I came that first day was because you couldn't afford to run it. It's things like that you will never have to worry about. You don't need to buy all the latest gadgets, but you will be able to live in whatever state of comfort you deem necessary for you and Danny."

"You live in a mansion," Brooke pointed out.

"Yes, I do at the moment. My own place is not quite as spacious."

"You still have all the trappings of massive wealth. The car. The condo. The clothes."

Lucas couldn't argue with that. "I was raised differently. These things are really just part of the life I've always known."

"Could you live in a place like this?"

If I was living with you and Danny.

The thought was like a lightning bolt out of the sky. What on *earth?* Lucas dropped his gaze to the plate of cookies on the counter. He hadn't even known her for a week. What on *earth* was a thought like that doing in his head?

"Lucas?"

Hoping she wouldn't be able to read anything on his face, Lucas looked up and met her gaze. "What?"

"Could you live in a place like this?" She waved her hand in the air. "This whole house would probably fit in your living room."

"My mom's living room," Lucas corrected. It seemed important that she not associate him with the over-the-top wealthy lifestyle his dad had adopted for him and his mom. There had been no reason for his mom to abandon the home she'd lived in since they'd married. And Lindsay had been quite happy to keep her company at the estate after Leon Hamilton's death. Lincoln hadn't bothered to get a place of his own since he was on the move so much, and Lucas's room had always been waiting for him there as well. "Yes, I could live in a place like this."

Brooke arched a brow, her expression skeptical. "And what about your car?"

"Well, for that, I might need a garage."

As the tension melted into a grin on Brooke's face, Lucas felt something tighten in his chest. He needed to get out of this house. Away from Brooke. This situation was just way too complicated to add in any sort of feelings on his part. He had no doubt anything like that would only ever go one way. She'd already had the Lincoln test.

He swallowed down the water that remained in his glass. "I really should be going."

Brooke looked surprised at the sudden change of subject but slowly nodded. "We still need to talk about the cabin."

"I'll check my schedule and see if we can arrange a time." Lucas stood up. "Thanks for the cookies."

"Why don't you take a couple for the road?"

He gave her a quick smile. "Thanks."

She followed him to the door and out onto the porch. "We had a good time tonight. Thank you for making it so easy for Danny."

"Thank *you* for allowing us to meet and spend time with him. You could have chosen to make it a whole lot more difficult, and I wouldn't have blamed you."

"That wouldn't have been what was best for Danny."

Lucas stood for a moment looking at her, her auburn hair shining in the light spilling from the hallway behind her. "Good night."

He didn't look back as he crossed the lawn to where his vehicle sat and by the time he pulled away, the door to the small house was shut.

Brooke went back to the kitchen and cleaned up the glasses and cookies. Her conversation with Lucas played over and over in her head. The revelation about the inheritance had shocked her. And scared her a bit. No doubt this would give him a fair amount of control over her life even though he hadn't made it sound that way.

Lucas Hamilton was a man used to controlling things. For all that Lincoln had been a carefree gadabout, Lucas was responsible and in control. Even his mother deferred to him. And though Lindsay came across as in charge, she also seemed willing to let Lucas control things.

Oh, he was subtle about it, but there was no doubt that Lucas Hamilton was the man in charge of his empire. He could downplay it all he wanted, but when push came to shove, Brooke had no doubt that he'd do what he had to in order to protect his family and his fortune.

She wondered what he would have done if he'd discovered she was a gold-digger or a druggie and if Danny had been an out of control hooligan. She smiled at the thought. That might have rattled his world a little.

She was a bit mystified by his abrupt departure. In addition to the conversation she'd wanted to have with him about the cabin, she was just going to confirm his presence at the wedding on Saturday. It wasn't a big deal if he changed his mind, though having him there would have made the wedding a fair bit more interesting.

But one thing she was going to have to do between now and then was a little shopping. Now that she had some breathing room in her budget, she was going to get a new outfit for herself and new shoes for Danny. The boy grew out of them so quickly.

Over the course of the next few days, Brooke found thoughts of Lucas popping up at the oddest of times. Like when she was looking for the outfit she wanted to buy for the wedding. It shouldn't have mattered if he liked it or not—particularly when she still wasn't sure he was going with them—yet the thought was in the back of her mind as she looked through dress after dress.

She hadn't heard from him again since he'd left so abruptly. Several times over the days following she'd replayed their conversation trying to figure out if she'd said something that had offended him. She'd started to call or text him a few times but then had stopped. If he wanted to make contact, he knew how to get hold of her.

"Mom, we're going to be late," Danny said as he appeared in the doorway of the bathroom where she was putting the finishing touches on her outfit.

It was to be an outdoor wedding held on the property of Eric's boss, Marcus Black. Thankfully, the stifling heat of earlier in the week had eased off to more moderate temperatures. At least they wouldn't all be melting as the bride and groom said their vows.

Danny wore long pants and a short sleeve shirt with a bow tie and suspenders. Brooke hadn't been too sure about the combination, but with his hair in loose curls and his tanned skin, he pulled it off quite magnificently.

Her own choice for the wedding had ended up being a soft lavender chiffon knee length dress. It had small capped sleeves and ruching that started just beneath her breasts and ended at her hips. From there a filmy chiffon skirt fell in loose gathers to her knees. The square neckline framed the simple silver heart pendant necklace she wore with matching earrings. She'd splurged on a pair of strappy silver heels and hoped she didn't break her neck walking around in them.

"Just let me finish my hair and we can go." She reached for another bobby pin, glad that she'd cranked the air earlier.

The last thing she needed was to sweat her makeup off as quickly as she applied it. She slid one last pin in to secure her curls and then used a liberal amount of hairspray before spritzing on a bit of perfume.

Brooke gazed at her reflection in the mirror. Pleased that her efforts had paid off, she went back into her room and grabbed her purse and shoes. Heading for the door, she slipped one shoe on and then took a couple of steps out the door before pausing to put the other on.

"Ready to go, my handsome date?" Brooke asked as she focused on tightening the strap around her ankle.

"Mom, Lucas is here."

Brooke straightened with a jerk, her gaze meeting Lucas's.

He gave her a lopsided grin. "Hope I'm not late."

"No, you're not. I wasn't sure you were still planning to attend."

"I said I would." He held his hands out to the sides. "Hopefully I'm dressed appropriately."

She took in his light gray suit, white shirt and dark blue tie. Oh yes, he was definitely dressed appropriately. The man could wear a suit, that was for sure.

"You look fine. I just hope you don't sweat to death though. The wedding is outdoors. I suppose I should have mentioned that."

"Wouldn't have mattered. I still would have worn this. I'll be fine. I can always take the jacket off if it gets too hot."

Trying to quell the fluttering in her stomach, Brooke turned her gaze to Danny. "Ready to go, buddy?"

At his nod, they headed out of the house. Brooke paused to lock up and turned to find Lucas standing by the passenger side door of his car waiting for her. More fluttering. This was not good.

As she approached the car, Lucas smiled at her. "By the way, you look very beautiful."

She couldn't believe the heat she felt climbing in her cheeks. She was not a blusher by nature. Yeah, not good. "Thank you."

He waited until she was settled into the seat before closing the door. Danny had already climbed in and buckled himself in the back seat. "I love this car, Mom."

Brooke had to admit that she did as well, but there were other things she was enjoying about the arrangement that she shouldn't have. Like having someone to drive. Someone to open doors for her. To compliment her.

She shouldn't want those things. She didn't need them. And yet there was no denying that she enjoyed them. She just had to remember who Lucas was and all that he represented.

Well, that had been an abysmal failure.

He'd hoped that putting some distance between them would help him get whatever he was feeling under control. Unfortunately, all it had taken was the sight of her hopping on one foot trying to put on a shoe as she'd come out of her bedroom to put him right back where he'd been on Tuesday night.

When she'd glanced up, her eyes wide, to see him standing there, Lucas had struggled to remember how to breathe. He could face down boardrooms of high-powered men and women. He could make difficult decisions without even breaking a sweat. Nothing—absolutely nothing—had reduced him to the quivering mess he became with just one look from Brooke.

Thankfully, she hadn't seemed to notice, but sitting next to her in the car with her light floral scented perfume teasing his senses, Lucas was once again having trouble taking a deep breath.

"So, where are we headed?" he asked as he pulled away from the curb.

Brooke pulled a piece of paper from her purse and gave him the address.

He recognized it as not being too far from his mom's place. "Is that where your brother lives?"

"No. His boss offered him the use of his estate to have an outdoor wedding."

With an idea of where he was headed, Lucas turned toward the closest highway. "That was very nice of him. Who does he work for?"

"He works for BlackThorpe Security."

Lucas laughed. "So are we going to Marcus's or Alex's place?"

"You know them?"

"Yep." He glanced over at Brooke and grinned. "And I think I know your brother as well. I just didn't put two and two together until now."

"You know Eric?"

"Well, if Eric McKinley is your brother, then yes, I do."

"How?"

"Marcus and Alex I know from business dealings we've had. Eric, however, I know from church. He began attending our church around the beginning of the year."

"That was when he met Staci and started going to her church."

Lucas glanced over his shoulder to check for traffic before merging onto the highway. At least he'd know a few people at the wedding in addition to Brooke and Danny. "Your brother shared in our men's group a few months back. I'm not sure why I didn't put it all together. Usually, I'm pretty good at that."

"You had other things on your mind," Brooke pointed out.

Yes, he had...and it hadn't just been Danny. Though meeting up with the BlackThorpe guys at the wedding was fortuitous, he was going to take it as a sign. He'd been praying about it for the past few days with no clear direction or peace about what to do. Maybe he'd be able to move forward now.

"Eric spoke a little bit about his and Staci's journey back to each other."

Brooke shifted in her seat, crossing her legs. It really wasn't good that he noticed the way the silver strap around her ankle contrasted with the tan of her legs.

"Yeah. I had no idea what had gone on for them until after Staci showed back up in his life. Their daughter Sarah is a doll. She loves Danny."

"I love her too, Mom," Danny said from the back seat. "She's going to walk with me down the aisle. "

"Yes, they get along really well even though there's a five year age gap between them."

It had been quite a while since Lucas had last been to a wedding, but this was the first one that had him thinking what it might be like for the groom. To be on the cusp of pledging his life to the woman he loved. To love someone so much that he was willing to commit to her and only her for the rest of their lives.

It wasn't that he didn't want a more serious relationship, but he'd never been able to imagine growing old with any of the women he'd dated. He glanced at Brooke. Something told him that life with her would never be dull.

"Are you planning to catch the bouquet today?" Lucas asked.

Brooke huffed. "Not likely. You won't find me in that batch of women. There will be plenty of single women there who want it way more than me, so I'll leave it to them to battle it out."

Her response didn't surprise Lucas at all. He wondered what kind of man it would take to change her mind. It was fairly apparent she didn't have the highest opinion of the male of their species.

"Do you like Eric's fiancée?" Lucas asked, more curious about the wedding now that he realized who the couple was.

"How exactly am I supposed to answer that?" Brooke said with a laugh. "The short answer is, yes. She's nice and seems to be good for Eric. He's certainly happier with her than he was with any of the other women he's dated since coming back to Minneapolis. And she's a great mom to Sarah. I think she might not be entirely sure how to take me though."

"You can be scary, Mom," Danny piped in.

Brooke turned in her seat. "Really? I don't try to be."

"My guess is that it's your overwhelming confidence," Lucas said.

"Hah. Just because I don't slink around and make like a wall flower doesn't mean I'm scary."

Lucas was curious now to see how Brooke interacted with the members of her family. Danny and Brooke continued to discuss how his friends found her scary too but also cool.

"Are they expecting a big crowd?" Lucas asked as he turned into the driveway which had been marked with an elegant sign reading *Staci & Eric's Wedding*.

"I think around two hundred. Quite a few from Eric's job and also from the church."

There were men dressed in black pants, white shirts and black ties standing along the driveway who pointed to where he should park though there weren't too many cars there yet.

Lucas pulled his car into a spot and turned it off. He opened his door and got out, planning to open the door for Brooke, but she was already standing with Danny by the time he got there.

"The wedding's around the back," she said.

CHAPTER TEN

THOUGH the driveway was smooth blacktop, Lucas offered Brooke his arm. After a slight hesitation—he wasn't sure but maybe he'd imagined it—she slid her hand into the crook of his elbow. Danny trotted ahead of them to the sidewalk that ran along the side of the mansion to the back yard.

When the walkway narrowed, Lucas expected Brooke to move her hand from his arm and walk ahead of him, but instead, she pressed closer to him. He could hear music as they neared the back of the house.

"Sounds like the string quartet is warming up," Brooke said.

The sidewalk ended at a large cobblestone patio, and her hand tightened on his arm. "They certainly didn't think of people in high heels when they designed this thing."

Lucas bent his head as he laid his hand over hers. "I thought you women could walk over anything in heels."

"Not this woman," Brooke said, looking up at him, her eyes sparkling. "I prefer flats to heels."

A gust of wind swept across the expansive back yard, tangling her skirt against his legs. She paused as she gathered the fabric back into place with her free hand.

"Brooke!"

Lucas looked up to see a man in a dark gray suit approaching them from across the grass and recognized him as Eric McKinley.

Brooke slid her hand from his arm. "Hey, Eric. Ready to get hitched?"

The man grinned as he hugged her. "It's about time. I was beginning to wonder if we'd ever get to this point."

"Why? You only proposed to her, what, three times?"

"And almost had to do it a fourth after some of the counseling we went through." Eric's gaze moved from his sister to Lucas. A frown creased his brow. "I know you."

Lucas nodded. "Just realized on the way over here that we go to the same church." He held out his hand. "Lucas Hamilton."

Eric gave it a firm shake. "Mom said something about you being Danny's uncle?"

"Yes. My brother Lincoln was his father."

"Mom mentioned about his passing as well." Eric clapped him on the shoulder. "I'm so sorry to hear about that."

Lucas nodded. "Thanks."

"Lucas? Is that you, man?"

He looked past Eric to see another familiar face. Holding his hand out as he joined them, Lucas said, "Good to see you again, Trent."

Trent frowned. "Sorry to hear about Linc."

Again Lucas nodded his thanks. "I take it you're in the wedding party?"

The man nodded and grinned at Eric. "I don't get into a monkey suit for just anyone."

He'd met Trent Hause a couple of years earlier when he'd come to help set up a virtual security system. Though he had worked mostly with Lincoln since computers weren't really Lucas's thing.

"It's good to see you again." He glanced around at the people busy setting up chairs and decorations. "Are all the BlackThorpe guys going to be here?"

"Last I heard," Eric said. "Of course, Marcus has no choice."

"So how'd you meet up with Brooke?" Trent asked. "Did she run into your car or something?"

Brooke reached out and swatted at Trent, but missed when he took a step back out of her reach. "I am *not* a bad driver."

"So you ran into the car of your last date on purpose?"

Ah, so this was one of the infamous date stories.

"It wasn't on purpose. You could hardly say it was my fault that he parked so close behind my car."

"Or that you put it into reverse instead of drive," Trent remarked with a lift of one eyebrow.

Lucas looked down at Brooke in time to see her put her hands on her hips and glare at Trent. "Oh, shut up."

"So if it wasn't a car accident, how did you two meet?"

"Lincoln is Danny's father," Brooke said before Lucas had a chance.

That rendered Trent speechless for about five seconds. "Wow. Seriously?" His gaze went back and forth between the two of them before settling on Lucas. "So you're Danny's uncle."

Lucas nodded. "Yes, we just found out about Danny last week when we read Lincoln's will."

Eric looked to where Danny was talking with the man Lucas recognized as Brooke's dad. "How's he taking it?"

Lucas deferred to Brooke. She was definitely the better judge of that.

"He's doing pretty good. Seems to be taking it all in stride."

"He's a great kid," Trent said with a smile.

A shout drew their attention. Eric looked over then turned back to them. "Guess I'd better see what's up. Trying to keep any type of stress from getting to Staci today."

"I think I'm going to go find the women," Brooke said. She looked at Lucas. "Will you be okay hanging out for a little while?"

"Don't worry," Trent said. "I'll keep an eye on him."

Brooke's gaze met his. "See you in a bit."

He watched her walk toward the rear doors of the house. When she disappeared inside, he turned back around to find Trent observing him with a grin on his face.

"Is it too late to warn you off Brooke?" Trent asked.

"Warn me off?" Lucas asked.

"Dude, you picked the one sister that really doesn't think too highly of men."

Lucas laughed. "I didn't pick her. We're not dating. I'm only in her life because of Danny."

Trent grinned again and arched a brow. "You just keep telling yourself that." He gave Lucas's shoulder a whack. "Let's go see if the groom needs a hand."

Lucas shot one last glance to the doors leading into the house before following Trent to where Eric had gone.

"You look beautiful, Staci," Brooke said as she spotted the bride seated on a bench in front of a mirror while someone worked on her hair.

Staci smiled at her. "Thank you. Still need to get the dress on though."

"I think Eric would marry you if you walked down the aisle in a bathrobe at this point."

"True," Staci said with a laugh.

"Auntie Brooke, do you like my dress?"

Brooke looked down to see Sarah standing beside her. She wore a light green dress with a satin sash at the waist. The skirt was full and ended just above her ankles. "You look beautiful, too. Just like a princess."

The term brought an immediate smile to the little girl's face. Since having Sarah come into their lives, there had been a few moments when Brooke had wished she had a daughter. Not instead of Danny, but in addition to. It was hard to remember that Sarah was actually five when she looked more like the size of a three-year-old. In some ways, it made her that much more adorable.

"Hey, Brooke."

She glanced up to see Victoria coming towards her with their mom and Alicia in her wake. Victoria wore a dress in the same shade as Sarah's, but it lacked the poofy skirt that the little girl's had.

"Hey, guys."

Her mom wore a dress in a slightly darker shade of green. She was beaming, clearly excited at the prospect of the first wedding for one of her children. "You look beautiful, Brooke. I love that color on you."

"Thanks, Mom."

Alicia hung back. The two of them still hadn't managed to get to a comfortable place the way it appeared she had with Eric and Tori. And even with her mom. Like Brooke, she wasn't in the wedding party so wore a dress in a soft rose. She could pull it off in a way that Brooke couldn't since Alicia's hair was a darker auburn.

"Is there anything I can do to help?" Brooke asked.

"I think everything is pretty much under control. I sent Denise out to check on things outside."

Denise was Staci's maid of honor while her husband was Eric's other groomsmen. Trent was his best man. It was a small wedding party, but that seemed to suit them just fine. Eric had approached her to see if she wanted to be one of Staci's attendants, but Brooke was fairly sure it was out of obligation that he'd asked, not because Staci really wanted her to be a bridesmaid. And she was just as happy to not have that responsibility.

"It looked pretty good when I was out there."

Staci smiled. "I just want to get this show on the road."

Brooke watched as her soon-to-be sister-in-law turned to check her hair and makeup in the mirror. When she'd first heard about Staci and Sarah, she wasn't sure how she'd felt about them. Again, she didn't completely understand how Staci was willing to take Eric back after what they'd gone through, but there was no denying the love they shared.

Eric had been very open about the fact that they'd gone to counseling with their pastor to help them deal with some of the remnants of emotional baggage from their joint past. And it seemed to have helped. Each time she'd seen them together, they'd seemed more and more at ease and in love with each other.

"Well, I'll get out of your way here if you don't need any help," Brooke said. "I'll go and make sure Danny isn't getting messed up."

"Can I go with you, Auntie Brooke? I want to see Danny."

Brooke looked at Staci. "Is that okay?"

"Yep, but Sarah, you stay out of the dirt. Do *not* get your dress dirty, okay?"

Sarah nodded as she slid her hand into Brooke's. "I promise, Mama."

Together they left the room and headed down the stairs. "Are you excited about the wedding, Sarah?"

"Yep. Daddy says it means he doesn't have to go home at night anymore."

"That's true."

"But he doesn't get his own bedroom. He has to share with Mama."

Brooke grinned. Somehow she doubted that would be the hardship Sarah made it out to be.

As they stepped out onto the porch, Sarah added, "And maybe they'll get me a baby brother or sister, too. Mama said that once Daddy didn't have to go home at night, we could maybe get a baby. I don't know where we get one, but Mama said not to worry. She and Daddy would take care of it."

Brooke started laughing at the comment. Ah, out of the mouths of babes.

"Care to share the joke?"

She glanced over to see Lucas walking up the steps of the porch, Danny right behind him. Before she could say anything, Sarah darted over to Danny.

He stooped to give her a hug. "You look beautiful, Sarah."

Sarah held the edges of her skirt and twirled. "I know. Your mommy told me that already."

As Lucas stepped to Brooke's side, Sarah stopped spinning and zeroed in on him. "Are you Auntie Brooke's boyfriend?"

"Sarah!" Brooke said. "Why would you ask that?"

"Grandma said you had a date, and Auntie Tori said it was about time you got a boyfriend."

Brooke fought the urge to roll her eyes. People were going to have to start watching their conversation around this little girl. "No, he's not my boyfriend. He's Danny's uncle."

Sarah tilted her head. "Is he my uncle, too?"

Brooke looked over at Lucas to see him regarding the little girl seriously.

"I'm not, but if you want another uncle, I wouldn't mind."

Sarah beamed. "So I have two uncles now." She lifted her hand and poked one finger up. "Uncle Trent." And another finger. "And you. What's your name?"

Brooke burst out laughing. Danny had been a more reserved child, so this precociousness of Sarah's was new to her. But she liked to see it. This girl wasn't going to let the world overlook her.

"My name is Lucas."

Sarah nodded. "Uncle Lucas."

When Lucas looked at her, Brooke saw humor glinting in his eyes. No doubt he wasn't entirely sure what to make of the little girl.

"Everything okay out here?" she asked him.

"Seems to be. There was some debate on where some flowers were supposed to go, but I think Eric just made an executive decision."

"Lucas Hamilton." The deep voice drew their attention to the door behind them.

Brooke recognized Marcus Black as he joined them. He wore a dark gray pinstripe suit and looked every inch the business owner. Much like Lucas did.

"Marcus. Good to see you again."

The two men shook hands before Marcus looked at her. "Brooke. Right?"

Brooke nodded and held out her hand. He took it and gave her a quick smile. Of all the men Eric worked with, this was the one that came closest to unnerving her. She sensed he was a man who would try—no, not even try—he *would* just control everything. All Brooke knew was that she was very glad she moved in this man's sphere of influence only once in a blue moon.

Leaving the two men to talk, Brooke took Danny and Sarah by the hand and went in search of Eric and Trent. She found them in a group of other men...all of them dressed in suits. It was like a gathering of the Secret Service or something.

"Daddy!"

Eric turned from the group and with a smile, held his arms out to Sarah. He swept her up so she was level with the men he was talking to. She and Danny approached more slowly. Though she didn't know them all by name, Brooke recognized most of the men standing with Eric.

She didn't miss the interest in the eyes of a couple of them. But none of them attracted her in the least.

"Guys, this is my sister, Brooke." Eric gestured to the man on the other side of Trent. "That's Justin. Alex. And you know Than."

Oh yes, she did. After narrowing her eyes in his direction, she turned to the others. "Nice to meet you." She tipped her head back toward the house. "Just met Marcus. He's talking to Lucas now."

"I'd better go have a word with him," Eric said.

Not terribly interested in being left with his work buddies, Brooke fell into step beside him as she retraced the path she'd just taken. "Nice they all showed up for your wedding."

"I think they are happy to come to a wedding, as long as it's not theirs."

"Confirmed bachelors, eh?"

As they walked up on the porch, Brooke noticed Marcus and Lucas had been joined by two women wearing elegant dresses and jewelry that screamed money. One was a little taller than the other, but both were immaculately dressed with perfect makeup. They reminded her a lot of Lindsay. The Lindsay she'd first met.

"Hello, ladies." Eric greeted them as he held out his hand. "So glad you could come today."

"Wouldn't miss it, Eric," the taller one said with a quick smile. "You give me hope for the rest of those bachelors at BlackThorpe."

"Brooke, this is Adrianne and Melanie Thorpe. They are Alex's sisters."

They both smiled at her and shook her hand. The taller one—Adrianne—seemed to be the more outgoing of the two.

"What's your connection here, Lucas?" Adrianne asked.

Brooke wondered if he was tired of the question yet.

"Linc is Brooke's son's father."

Adrianne's eyes widened momentarily as she shot a glance at Melanie. "Well, didn't see that one coming."

"None of us did," Lucas said. "We didn't find out until we read Lincoln's will last week."

A woman with a clipboard approached Eric. "We need to get organized for the start of the ceremony."

Eric set Sarah down. "You go with Danny and Aunt Brooke, okay?"

Sarah nodded and took Danny's hand.

People had begun to arrive and fill the chairs set up in the shade of the towering trees in Marcus's backyard. Brooke turned to say something to Lucas, but he was engaged in a conversation with Adrianne as he walked with her and Melanie to the edge of the porch.

Brooke frowned, not sure why it bothered her that he was enamored with the other woman. It wasn't as if she was interested in him, she reminded herself.

Repeating that a couple of times under her breath, she returned to the coolness of the mansion and found the bridesmaids along with the bride gathered in the large living room. Her parents were there as well.

"I'm just going to go grab a seat," Brooke told them once Danny and Sarah were under Victoria's direction. She gave Staci a smile even as she tried to ignore the yucky feeling in her stomach.

Taking a deep breath, she walked back out on the patio and glanced over the seats. The first row had been reserved for the family, but Lucas was seated further back with Adrianne and Melanie. There was no empty seat beside him.

She tried to find anger to replace the hurt and sick feeling in the pit of her stomach. Rarely did she ever compare herself to another woman, but it was hard to not do that with the two Thorpe sisters. They were definitely more in Lucas's league. But then, she hadn't even been invited to play the game.

And she didn't want to play it anyway, she reminded herself as she walked alongside the white chairs to the row for family. Refusing to look around to see if Lucas saw her, Brooke took a seat on the end of the family row and stared at the string quartet that was playing. She blinked a couple of times, annoyed to find moisture pricking at her eyes.

What was going on? This was ridiculous. If Lucas preferred to sit with them, it wasn't a big deal. It wasn't like she'd be sitting all by herself. Once the processional was over, her parents, Alicia and both kids would be sitting in the row with her.

She saw Eric on the other side of the large floral arch that had been set up for them to stand under while they said their vows. He and Trent were standing together, and Eric was grinning. She didn't miss how his gaze kept going to the house. His anticipation for the wedding to start was clear.

Brooke let out a little sigh. She couldn't remember the last wedding she'd been to. That was probably why she was feeling a little emotional. After all, everyone cried at weddings. Didn't they?

"Brooke?"

CHAPTER ELEVEN

Lucas's voice washed over her. She took a quick breath and looked up to find him bending close to her.

"Am I supposed to sit here with you?"

"If you want, but if you'd prefer to sit elsewhere, that's fine."

His brows drew together, and he stared at her for a moment. "Scoot over. Please."

Telling herself she should not be this happy he'd decided to sit with her, Brooke stood and moved over one chair. As he settled into the seat next to her, he slid his arm along the back of her chair. That would be one way to start a few rumors.

The string quartet changed songs and the pastor led Eric, Trent, and Philip to the arch. She turned so she could see the back doors to the house as they opened. First came her mom and dad, beaming as they slowly walked down the aisle. Once they were halfway down the aisle, the door opened again and this time it was Victoria who came out.

Brooke glanced at the guys, surprised to see a rakish grin on Trent's face as he watched her sister walking down the aisle toward him. She looked back at Victoria, but her sister—though she was smiling—was not looking at Trent. *Interesting.*

Next came Denise and this time when she looked at the guys, Brooke wasn't surprised to see Philip smiling broadly. It was matched by a flirtatious one on Denise's face as she got closer.

Then the door opened again and out came Danny and Sarah. Danny carried a satin pillow, but his attention was on Sarah as she carefully held a basket and dropped red petals on the white carpet as they made their way to the front. They were adorable. And from the murmurs of the crowd around her, Brooke wasn't the only one who felt that way.

Once they were at the front, the quartet changed their music to the bridal march. The crowd stood and turned to face the house. Brooke couldn't see over the people so she kept her gaze on her brother. She knew what Staci looked like already, but she wanted to see her brother when he got his first glimpse of her.

Standing there, she felt the warmth of Lucas as he stood close to her. She glanced up at him and found him watching her. Not wanting him to see the flush that was creeping into her cheeks, Brooke turned back to watch Eric.

The grin from earlier was gone as he stood, feet braced apart, one hand gripping the wrist of the other. Was he having second thoughts? But then she saw it. The rush of emotion on his face that told Brooke he just seen his bride. The woman he loved. Moisture again gathered in her eyes and she blinked to clear it away.

No one had ever looked at her the way Eric was looking at Staci. He loved her. That was why he'd done the difficult things he'd had to in order to make sure this day happened. Brooke glanced over and saw that Staci had reached their row. She paused for a moment and Brooke could see on her face, the same emotion that was on Eric's. Her bouquet shook a little as she took the last few steps to join Eric when he moved away from Trent and Philip.

The couple came to a stop in front of the pastor. He smiled at them then looked out over the gathering of family and friends and invited them to be seated. Once again, Lucas put his arm across the back of her chair. Part of her wanted to give him an irritated look. What was he thinking when he did that? Didn't he know how others would interpret his action? But another part of her wanted to just sink back against him and watch the wedding unfold.

She ignored both parts and sat stiffly, watching as her brother bent and said something to Staci. In the midst of the crowd gathered there, it was a moment of intimacy that just the two of them shared. That was something Brooke had never shared with anyone. Not even Lincoln.

What was it about Eric that made Staci so willing to forget past hurts and promise her forever to him? She glanced down the row and saw her parents sitting close together. Her dad had one arm around her mother while she held his other hand with both of hers. As she watched, her dad looked down at her mom, and on his face was the same expression that had been on Eric's.

Brooke shifted in her seat, inadvertently bumping her arm against Lucas's chest. She shot a quick look at him and found him watching her, his gray gaze serious. When her stomach quivered, she clenched her hands together and looked away.

This had been a mistake...bringing him to this wedding. Of course, when she'd decided impulsively to invite him, she hadn't known how being around him affect her. Hadn't known that he would make her think about things she'd long since dismissed as unnecessary in her life.

When Staci handed her bouquet to Denise, Danny took Sarah's hand and brought her over to where the family sat. There was still an empty chair for Alicia, but she hadn't shown up yet. Brooke glanced around and spotted her on the porch with Marcus. For someone who always appeared so timid, she looked amazingly composed standing next to someone as intimating as Marcus Black.

She turned her attention back to where the pastor was giving Eric and Staci some advice for their marriage. Something told her it wasn't anything they hadn't already heard in their counseling sessions, but maybe one could never hear it too often.

Brooke shifted again. She didn't begrudge Eric and Staci this beautiful wedding, but she really could have done without the sermon.

"Eric and Staci, many here know your story of how—after six years apart—God brought you back together in spite of all odds. Many hearing of your prior relationship might have thought it impossible that you'd be able to make things work now. But when you have God and you have love, nothing is impossible. It has been my joy to work with you over these past few months as you prepared for a God-centered marriage. To see your dedication to each other and your relationship. To witness you forgiving that which you cannot forget and to see the love you have for each other deepen and grow. And now it is my privilege to stand here today to join you two together in holy matrimony."

Brooke watched as her brother and Staci turned to face each other. Again, the look on his face hit Brooke in the heart.

"Staci, when I saw you for the first time after being apart for so long, all I wanted was answers. Instead, you made me question everything I'd ever thought I'd known about you. About us. I have never met a more giving person. A more loving person. I knew pretty quickly that I didn't deserve you at all. But hey, no one's ever accused me of backing off when I want something. Thank you for not making it easy for me. You deserved more than I'd ever given you. Because of you I'm a better man. A better father." Eric lifted their joined hands and brushed his thumb across her cheek. "Today I pledge to continue to seek God with all my heart so that I can love you the way He does. I'm going to make mistakes, but never ever doubt my love for you. I thank God every day for bringing you back into my life. Each night when I go to bed I think that I can't possibly love you more...until I go to bed the night next realizing that, in fact, I can. I can't wait to show you every single day for the rest of our lives. I love you, Anastacia Stapleton, for now and for always."

"I should have gone first," Staci said as she wiped her cheeks. The crowd laughed amid sniffles of their own. Finally, she reached out and gripped Eric's hands in hers. "I was very mad at God about you. I couldn't understand why He'd let you back into my life. I was scared to trust that He would really want us to be together again. I was scared to trust that a relationship now would be better than it had been before. I was scared to trust you with my heart. But that fear could have robbed me of something more amazing than I could have imagined. I had to make the choice—protect my heart or trust that God would take care of me no matter what lay ahead.

"But, as is always the case, God knew what He was doing. He knew that we were better together than apart. It's hard to imagine now that I ever considered life without you. I love you more than I thought would be possible. I look forward to what God has in store for us in the future. I know that there will be ups and downs—there already have been—but I know we're both committed to the long haul with this. The difficult times we've been through have just made the place we're at now that much sweeter. And I can't wait to finally be your wife."

Brooke took a deep breath and let it out. Was it fear that held her back from allowing herself to experience love? She'd always told herself it was because she was strong and independent. She didn't need a man to make her happy. She didn't need love from a man to make her complete. And while those things were true, the underlying reason had been that she was determined to never give a man another chance to hurt her. Like Staci, she was letting fear rob her of the possible happiness that may lie ahead.

She glanced at Lucas, but this time his gaze was on the couple as they exchanged rings. Why was he the one that had her thinking these thoughts? He hadn't even indicated he was interested in any kind of relationship beyond what they had through Danny. Was she brave enough to test the waters knowing that rejection and hurt might lie ahead?

As Eric pulled his bride close for their kiss, a yearning blossomed to life in Brooke that she'd never experienced before. She wanted to love and be loved in the way her brother and Staci did. But was she brave enough to risk the hurt to get it?

Lucas spent the ceremony trying not to think too much about the woman sitting next to him, but it had been an exercise in futility. It hadn't been too difficult to determine that she was not exactly enjoying the wedding. Her back had been ramrod straight and at particularly moving spots in the ceremony, she'd shifted around. Nailing him in the ribs at least once.

It had been a bit funny if he was being honest. Usually, women soaked up the romance that saturated events like this. Married women would recall their own wedding days. Single women would dream of the day that was yet to be theirs. Brooke's body language had screamed her discomfort at being subjected to so many in-your-face declarations of love.

He had to wonder what it was exactly that had made her so jaded when it came to love and romance. Had it been her experience with Lincoln? His brother had been known for his charm and flirtatious nature, but it had never come with promises of a future filled with love.

The crowd around him stood as the pastor presented Eric and Staci as husband and wife. The people clapped and cheered as Eric bent down to kiss his wife one more time before taking her hand and heading back between the rows of chairs.

As the noise settled down around them, Lucas leaned toward Brooke and asked, "So what's next on the agenda?"

Brooke turned to face him but didn't look him in the eye as she said, "I think they're going to take some pictures, but there's a cocktail hour before the reception begins."

"Are you supposed to be there for the pictures?"

Brooke nodded. "Yes. Mom wants some family shots. Since you know people, you could just hang here and visit if you want."

"And if I want to come with you?"

Her gaze shot to his then. "I guess you're welcome to. Don't blame me if you get bored though."

He grinned. "Something tells me it will be anything but boring."

"Brooke?"

At the softly spoken word, Lucas turned to see a young woman with hair a few shades darker than Brooke standing in the row behind them.

"Hi, Alicia," Brooke said, her tone reserved.

"Sorry to interrupt, but your mom wanted to make sure you were coming for the pictures."

"Yep. We're on our way. By the way, Alicia, this is Lucas. He's Danny's uncle." Brooke gestured to him. "Lucas, this is Alicia. She's my dad's daughter."

It didn't escape Lucas that both introductions held no connection to her. *Danny's uncle*. Not *my date*. And *my dad's daughter* instead of *my sister* or *my half-sister*. He was assuming this was the second sister she'd referred to in their previous conversation. Something told him that there were very few relationships she claimed without hesitation. Danny's mom was the one she was probably the most comfortable and eager to claim.

"Nice to meet you." Alicia shook the hand he held out then turned to point to a spot in the far corner of the huge back yard. "They're meeting there for the pictures."

"Okay. We'll be there in just a few minutes."

Alicia left them and headed toward where the wedding party had gathered at the back of the chairs. People were beginning to get up and mill around.

"Guess we'd better go do this," Brooke said with a sigh.

Mindful of the long stretch of grass between where they were and where they needed to be, Lucas once again offered her his arm. She took it after the briefest hesitation, and this time he knew he hadn't imagined it. He wondered if her reactions were because it was him or if she was this way with all men. A part of him really hoped that maybe it was just him. Because then it would mean that she was experiencing some of the same confusions he was where their interactions were concerned.

As the wedding party began to make their way to the spot as well, Lucas guided her toward them. He noticed that Trent was walking alongside Victoria. She held onto his arm as they walked since she was in heels like her sister. Danny ran on ahead with Sarah following him as fast as her legs would allow.

"Don't fall and mess your dress, Sarah!" Staci called out as the little girl dashed after Danny.

"Small world, Lucas," Philip said as they joined the group. "I certainly didn't expect to run into you here."

"Same here. I didn't realize who Brooke was related to when I made contact with her."

"Sorry to hear about Lincoln."

Though Philip hadn't known Lincoln like some of the others had, Lucas appreciated the thought. They had initially met at a Christian businessman's dinner several years earlier and then discovered they attended the same church. They hadn't had any business dealings but had interacted at church events over the years.

Before they could continue the conversation, the photographer, and his assistant began to give instructions for how things would unfold.

"We'll start with the family ones, so if you need to go you can."

"I can take care of that for you," Lucas offered, holding his hand out for Brooke's purse. "You probably don't want that in the pictures."

"True. Thanks." She slid the strap off her shoulder and handed it to him. "Danny! Let me see you."

Danny jogged over to where they stood. Brooke tucked his shirt back in and straightened his suspenders and bowtie. "Now no more running around until the pictures are all done. Okay? You need to pay attention so you don't slow things down."

"'kay, Mom."

"Let's go get this done," Brooke said as she took Danny's hand.

Lucas stood back, watching as the photographer arranged the family members around the bride and groom. Alicia hung back until Brooke's mom motioned for her to join them. It was interesting that the one person who *should* have had a problem with this young woman's presence didn't seem to.

The photographer worked quickly and except for having to get after Sarah once to stand still, things went fairly smoothly. Lucas realized as he watched that Staci had no family present. Everyone there for the family pictures was related to Eric.

"Lucas, why don't you join us?"

It may have been her mom issuing the invitation, but Lucas's gaze went to where Brooke stood, waiting for what she might feel about the suggestion. "These are just for family, Mrs. McKinley."

"And you're family. After all, you're Danny's uncle." She motioned him forward.

Not wanting to delay things, Lucas walked toward the group. He glanced at the photographer for instruction.

"The little guy's yours?" the photographer asked.

Though while not technically true, Lucas nodded.

"Go stand there beside him and his mom."

Hoping Brooke wouldn't hate him—he certainly hadn't planned for this to happen—Lucas positioned himself behind Danny and Brooke. He shifted her purse to his other hand and rested his free hand on Danny's shoulder. The boy looked up at him and grinned.

Suddenly it was Lincoln grinning at him. They were both ten again, and Lincoln was wanting him—daring him—to try the new ramp he'd made. Or the tire swing he'd put up over the lake. Or to race him to the top of the tree.

What are you? A scaredy cat?

"Eyes here!"

The photographer's words pulled Lucas from his drift back in time. Looking over, he tried to pull up what he hoped looked like a decent semblance of a smile. The last thing he wanted to do was spoil the McKinley family photos.

"Okay, Mrs. McKinley, I think we've covered the list you wanted of pictures," the photographer said, addressing Brooke's mom. "Anything more you wanted before we move on to the wedding party?"

When her mom glanced at them and then back to the photographer, Lucas got a funny feeling in his gut.

"Actually, I'd like a picture of my girls and their dates."

"I don't have a date, Mom," Victoria piped up.

"Well, your partner for the wedding then."

"So you want a picture of me and Philip?"

Brooke's mom put her hands on her hips as she frowned at Victoria. "Fine, I want pictures of you with Trent and Brooke and Lucas." She turned her gaze on Brooke. "Probably the only picture I'll ever get of you with a man dressed up so nicely."

"Are you saying I date slobs, Mom?"

Lucas heard a snort of laughter and looked over to see Eric turning away from his mom, a huge grin on his face.

"I'm saying you don't date. Period. So no arguments. I'm going to have proof that you got dressed up and actually let a real live man accompany you to a social event." She turned back to Victoria. "And you, young lady, I want a picture of you with an escort and it's not going to be Philip."

Lucas saw Brooke and Victoria share a frustrated look.

"Okay, if that's settled," the photographer said with a tolerant smile on his face. "Up first. Brooke and her date."

Lucas held Brooke's purse out to Danny. "Hold onto that for your mom, please."

Danny took it, looking as if he were trying to suppress a grin.

The photographer moved them into position. "Lucas, if you could just stand slightly angled and Brooke, you too."

Lucas slipped his arm around Brooke's waist as she rested her hand on his chest. She looked up at him, exasperation clear on her face. "It's like a dumb prom picture. She was going to get it one way or another."

"You want one of you two looking at each other or the camera?"

Brooke turned her head to face the camera so quickly that Lucas almost laughed. He turned his gaze to the photographer and smiled when prompted.

The photographer took a couple of shots but seemed to sense the irritation flowing off Brooke in waves...tsunami-sized waves. They only did the one pose before he let them go.

"Victoria, you're next." Her mom's tone allowed for no argument.

Brooke's sister marched over to where they had been standing. "I'm not doing that pose that Brooke and Lucas just did. For the record."

"How about I get down on one knee..." Trent let the words trail off as Victoria shot a glare at him.

It was so familiar to the one he'd seen on Brooke's face Lucas almost laughed.

"I was just going to suggest doing it that way so the photographer could get all of your lovely dress in the photo and still get my head. Although now that I think about it, you'd probably rather a photo of your dress and me without a head."

"You've got that right," Victoria said, but the grin she gave him took the bite out of the words. "Fine, you can do it this time—this time and only this time for my mother—and I will not be sitting on your knee."

"Ahhh..." Trent lowered himself to one knee and then cocked his head at Victoria.

With a huff, Victoria walked toward him and then swung back around to face the photographer. Lucas waited for the photographer to say something as Victoria had taken up a position right in front of Trent's knee. There was a good six or more inches between the two of them.

"Over to your left just a bit, Victoria, if you would."

With a glance at the group around them, Victoria obviously decided it was better to not stall any longer. She took a step to her left that brought her in line with Trent.

He leaned forward and said something to her which made her smile at him. Lucas wondered if they heard the click of the camera in that instant.

But then the photographer called out, "Eyes here!"

Once those shots were done to Mrs. McKinley's satisfaction, the photographer moved on to the wedding party and bride and groom shots.

Lucas was happy to hang around, but Brooke took her purse from Danny and after telling him to listen to the photographer, suggested they go back to the guests.

He offered his arm once again and together they walked toward the house.

"Thanks for putting up with Mom's requests."

"Wasn't a hardship," Lucas assured her. "I've been asked to do worse things in my life."

He sensed her gaze on him and looked down. She seemed about to say something, but ended up looking away as they approached the large paved patio that was now covered with a variety of tables. People milled around with small plates filled with food.

"Guess cocktail hour is underway," Brooke observed as they joined the crowd.

For the next thirty minutes, they mingled with the guests, but eventually, Lucas found himself standing once again with the BlackThorpe guys, and Brooke had disappeared.

"So, are you dating Eric's sister?" a tall man with dark hair and eyes asked him.

CHAPTER TWELVE

Y EAH, Than needs to know if you're his competition," Trent said with a laugh. "He's got his eye on her."

"He's got his eye on every woman," Justin remarked. He was all muscles. Even the expensive suit he was wearing couldn't hide them.

"You are so right, my friend," Than said with a grin and a lift of one dark brow. "You just never know when the right one will suddenly appear. I rule out no available woman."

"I really don't think Eric would approve of you dating his sister any more than he would have you dating Staci," Trent said.

"You wanted to date Staci?" Lucas asked.

Than shrugged. "Never got that far. First time I met her she was already clearly smitten with Eric. Her loss." He looked back to Lucas. "So? You dating Brooke?"

"The answer to that would be no. I think she's tolerating me in her life at the moment simply because of her son and my connection to him."

"Well, if there's any interest on your part, at least you're in a better position than any man has been in the years I've known her," Trent said with a grin. But then it faded as he sighed. "Of course, I've been having my own battles with a McKinley sister."

"Did none of you guys bring dates?" Lucas asked as he glanced around the group.

"Are you kidding?" Justin asked. "Bringing a date to a wedding is the worst thing to do. They get all kinds of ideas about their own romantic future with you regardless if you've been dating for one week or a year. And man, somehow the groom manages to make all other men look like unromantic schmucks. Yeah, i definitely was going to go solo at this gig even if I did have a girlfriend."

The other men nodded to be in agreement—except for Trent. Lucas thought it rather funny that it was the opposite with him and Brooke. She clearly found the whole wedding thing overrated while it was putting all kind of weird thoughts into his head. He'd barely known this woman a week and already thoughts of her were messing with him.

"You guys socially impaired?"

Lucas turned to see Alex Thorpe had joined them.

"It's like a BlackThorpe cluster with a little Hamilton thrown in." Alex grinned. "You boys need to be mingling. Lots of single ladies here from what I'm hearing."

"Are your sisters among those single ladies you're encouraging us to mingle with?"

"Hands off my sisters, Than."

As he joined the guys in laughing at Alex's response, Lucas's gaze moved across the guests, looking for Brooke. It didn't take long to find her standing with Victoria and her mom. When she suddenly looked in his direction, their gazes meeting across the distance, Lucas got the feeling that she'd been aware of where he was, hadn't needed to look for him.

He smiled at her and after excusing himself from the group of guys, headed in her direction. Though he wouldn't have been surprised if she'd moved on by the time he got to where she'd been standing, she hadn't.

"Having a good time?" Brooke asked him as he came to a stop at her side.

"Sure. Those BlackThorpe guys are something else. Than—I think that's his name—was wondering if you were off the market."

Brooke rolled her eyes. "Than chases anything in a skirt. And when I say anything, I mean anything. I've seen him flirting with sixty-year-old women and then turn around and flirt with a twenty-year-old."

"He's even flirted with me," Victoria commented. "When I called him on it he said that to him every woman is beautiful and deserves to be made to feel special."

"Well, I, for one, would never date a man like that. Who wants a guy who flirts with every woman he meets to make her feel special? How does that make his own girl feel like she's special to him?" Brooke looked at him, an eyebrow arched.

Lucas pressed a hand to his chest. "You're asking me? I'm not like that. And from what I've seen, guys like that tend to fall like a ton of bricks and then have to work twice as hard to convince the woman they love that they're serious."

"I certainly hope I'm around to see it when it happens," Brooke said.

The announcement for dinner came and soon Lucas found himself at a table inside a huge white tent with Brooke, Alicia, Marcus and the rest of the BlackThorpe gang. Somehow Than had managed to get himself seated on the other side of Brooke, and to Lucas's right was Adrianne. Than probably thought he was safer sitting next to Brooke than either Adrianne or Melanie.

The clinking of glasses drew Lucas's attention to the head table. It looked like Eric had no problem indulging the wishes of the crowd as he drew Staci to her feet and dipped her for a lingering kiss.

Lucas had thought he'd just endure the wedding when Brooke had first invited him, that the most fun part would just be hanging out with her and Danny. And while that part was true, having other people he knew at the wedding had made it that much more enjoyable.

The meal drew to a close and speeches began. Settling in, Lucas draped his arm across the back of Brooke's seat. He waited for her to object, but she just gave him a quick glance and turned back to where Trent was sharing some stories about Eric.

When it came time for the tossing of the garter and the bouquet, Lucas had no intention of going but ended up being cajoled into participating. The funny thing about the guys' part of this ritual was that they were more apt to avoid trying to snag the garter than to grab it out of the air.

And this group of men was no different. The garter flew through the air and landed on the ground, smack in the middle of a wide circle of men. Finally, Trent marched bravely into the middle of the group and plucked it from the ground.

"Always gotta be the one picking up after you guys," Trent said with a grin. He twirled the garter on a finger as he meandered back to his seat beside Victoria at the head table.

Lucas was pretty sure that Victoria would be avoiding the bouquet at all costs after Trent had caught the garter.

"You're up next," Lucas said with a grin at Brooke as he settled back down next to her.

Brooke crossed her arms. "I think not."

"At least in your group there will actually be people trying to catch it."

She laughed. "True enough."

"So go support your brother and Staci."

"Okay, fine. But if I end up catching that thing somehow, there's going to be a retoss."

Lucas laughed as she stalked toward the gathering of women. She took up a position at the very back of the group and wasn't participating at all in the friendly jostling going on in front of her. He noticed that she was joined by Victoria and even Alicia was in the rear with them.

Staci stood in front of the head table with the bouquet in hand. She glanced over her shoulder and then turned her

back to the group and whipped the bouquet into the air.
Whipped is the only word Lucas could think to use because
that puppy flew over the hands of all the reaching women to
hit Brooke on the head. From there it fell to the side and,
from what he could see, Victoria instinctively reached out to
catch it.

She held it for about two seconds before dropping it on
the ground.

"Too late," the emcee announced over the speakers. "I
believe the bouquet catcher is none other than the groom's
sister. Victoria."

Brooke stooped to pick up the bouquet and held it out to
her sister. Lucas didn't need to see her face to know that she
was likely taking great joy in her sister's predicament.

"How about we have a picture of the two lucky catchers?"

The crowd cheered the emcee's suggestion even as
Victoria shook her head. Finally, she reached out and
snatched the bouquet from her sister's hands and marched
through the throng of women to where Trent waited.

"That should have been yours," Lucas said as Brooke sat
back down beside him, a smug look on her face.

"Oh no. She deserved that."

"So Trent really does have a thing for her?"

Brooke nodded. "I've kinda sensed something for the past
year or so, but it's become more apparent in the past six or
seven months."

"Why hasn't she agreed to go out with him? Is it because
he's not a little person?"

Brooke crossed her legs and swung her free foot. "I'm not
sure, actually. I don't think it's that. He might be a little too
care-free for her. He doesn't tend to take things too seriously,
and I think that's a drawback for her."

Lucas watched as Victoria and Trent posed for yet
another picture together. These McKinley women were a
prickly bunch, and he felt a new sympathy for Trent.

The wedding festivities gradually wound down though
there were some couples who hung out on the dance floor
after Eric and Staci had had their first dance. Danny had

joined them at their table looking like he was winding down as well.

"Ready to go, sweetie?" Brooke asked him as she reached out to touch his hair. "You did a great job today. Not just as ring bearer but helping Sarah, too."

A quick grin came and went from Danny's face. "They wouldn't let me try to catch that thing Trent caught."

Brooke chuckled. "You're a little too young to be thinking along those lines."

"What does it mean?"

"Tradition says that whoever catches the garter and the brides's bouquet will be the next to get married," Brooke explained.

Danny's eyes widened. "So Trent and Aunt Victoria are going to get married?"

"Eh, I kinda doubt that. It's just a tradition. It doesn't mean it's going to happen. And whoever catches them doesn't have to marry each other. Just marry someone."

"Did Auntie Victoria know that before she caught the bouquet?" Danny asked, his brow furrowed.

"Oh, she most definitely did," Brooke said, humor in her tone. "Maybe don't say anything to her about it though."

Danny nodded and then yawned.

"Why don't we go say our goodnights," Brooke suggested.

Lucas nodded and got to his feet. They made their way through the crowd to where Eric and Staci stood talking with some guests. It took a few minutes, but finally their goodbyes were said and they made their way around the side of the house to where he'd parked earlier.

It was a quiet ride back to Brooke's house. Lucas was mulling over his next step. They needed to meet about the will and all that entailed, but he found himself wanting to ask her out for more than that. Did he dare take a chance? Would it damage their somewhat precarious relationship if she said no?

As he pulled up in front of her place, Lucas said, "Can I come in for a minute? To talk to you after Danny's in bed?"

She'd already opened her door so the interior light allowed him to see the wariness on her face when she glanced back at him, but still she said, "Okay."

Danny was practically falling asleep on his feet so the bedtime ritual went fairly quickly. Lucas waited on the stool at the counter, reading through emails and notifications on his phone.

Brooke reappeared a short time later. She was barefoot since she'd kicked off her shoes almost immediately after walking through the front door. As she joined him at the counter, she started to pull pins from her hair.

"They're driving me nuts."

Lucas could only stare as each pin released a shiny strand. When the last pin hit the counter, she sank her hands into her hair and shook it out. When she was done, her hair was a magnificent halo of silky curls.

Pulling his gaze from the beauty that stood in front of him, Lucas swallowed.

"Did you want something to drink?"

Since his mouth had gone dry, a drink sounded like a very good thing. "Water, please."

After he'd taken a deep swallow of the cold water she poured into a glass for him, he said, "Would you be interested in going out to dinner with me some day this week?"

Brooke's eyes widened briefly. She took a sip of her water and then set the glass on the counter. "Dinner? The three of us?"

"Actually, no. I thought maybe Danny could spend some time with Mom and Lindsay and the two of us could go out." Seeing her reaction, Lucas took it in a safer direction. "I thought it might be good for us to discuss a few things with regards to Lincoln's will and the inheritance."

He wasn't sure what expression it was that crossed her face, but if he had to guess, Lucas would say relief. He was a bit disappointed, but not surprised. She'd made her opinion on men and dating pretty clear. Why he'd thought he'd have a shot, Lucas wasn't entirely sure.

"Okay. I think Danny would enjoy that."

"Yeah, he can go swimming. Lindsay's even wilder in the pool than I am."

Brooke smiled. "What day were you thinking?"

"Whatever works for you."

"And we need to talk about going to the cabin, too," Brooke said. "Danny's been asking me about it."

Lucas nodded. "Yes, we can firm up dates for that as well. If anyone in your family would like to join us, they're welcome. We've got plenty of room."

As the conversation lapsed, Lucas swallowed the last of his water. "I'd better head for home."

When he got up, Brooke came around and walked to the door with him. As they stood on the porch, Lucas turned to look at her. "Thanks for the lovely time."

"Well, now you're just being polite," Brooke said with a laugh.

"Actually, I really did enjoy myself. Our families had more connections than I realized."

Brooke nodded. "I'm glad you knew people there tonight. Thanks for coming along."

Lucas moved toward the stairs then turned back and retraced the steps he'd just taken. He reached out and touched Brooke's cheek. "And in case I didn't say it earlier. You look beautiful."

With one last smile at her, Lucas turned and walked down the steps to his waiting vehicle.

Brooke lifted a hand and touched her cheek. What was this man doing to her? Due to the circumstances that had brought him into her life, she'd had no choice but to let him in. But how close was he wanting to get to her? And how close did she feel comfortable *letting* him get?

He *had* said that the dinner later in the week wasn't a date...hadn't he? But his last comment and gesture had her wondering. She would have brushed aside a gesture like that from someone like Than, but Lucas didn't strike her as the sort of person who said or did things lightly when it came to the opposite sex.

But really, what did she know?

She watched him drive away before going back into the house. After locking up, she went to the bedroom to get ready for bed. As she lay there, her thoughts went back over the day. For the first time in a long time—ever?—Brooke let herself think about loving and being loved. Opening herself up for more hurt than she could possibly imagine. But the flip side, as she'd seen with Eric and Staci earlier that day, was finding joy and happiness in that love.

Not every relationship faced the betrayal and hurt her parents' had. Not every man would abdicate their responsibility the way Lincoln had. And not every guy's head was turned when a prettier girl showed interested in him like her high school boyfriend's had.

What was it about Lucas that made her think maybe he could be that man who was different from the others? Rather ironic considering his own twin brother had been one of the ones who'd contributed to her outlook on men. But it seemed he took the opposite approach to life than his brother did. Not a thrill seeker like Lincoln, he also seemed to take his responsibilities seriously—particularly when it came to his family. Just spending one evening with him and his mom and sister, Brooke had seen that.

And she knew that Lucas would be more of a father figure to Danny than Lincoln had been, even if nothing developed between them. Which just left her with one question.

If Lucas did seem interested in a relationship with her, was she going to take the risk or not?

CHAPTER THIRTEEN

I DIDN'T think I'd be seeing you again quite so soon after the wedding," Alex Thorpe said. He motioned to the chair across his desk. "Have a seat."

Lucas sat down, hoping this conversation would be the first step to putting an end to the niggling in his gut. "Well, seeing you all there kind of cemented something in my mind. Thanks for seeing me so quickly."

"When Lucas Hamilton requests an audience, I'd be foolish to turn it down," Alex said with a grin. "Having a security issue of some sort?"

Lucas shook his head. "I know this might be a little out of the range of what BlackThorpe does, but I figured maybe you could point me in the right direction, if need be."

Alex sat forward, his expression serious. "What's going on?"

"I'm wondering if Lincoln staged his death." *There.* He'd said it aloud for the first time. There was no going back now.

Alex's eyes widened. "That's...an interesting theory. What makes you think that?"

"Well, I was going through his paperwork and files looking for some information and started seeing things—transactions—that didn't make any sense. At least not to me." Lucas rested his elbows on the arms of the chair and intertwined his fingers. "We might not have been very alike personality-wise, but when it comes right down to it, no one else knows Lincoln like I do. There are things that just seem...odd."

"You're right, that's not something we usually take on. However, I'm assuming that you want this handled with a fair amount of discretion."

Lucas nodded. "I really don't want any of this getting out if it's nothing. Obviously, if there is substance to this, we'll have to deal with those ramifications later, but right now, I just want someone to do a little nosing around. See if they can dig anything up."

"That's understandable. " Alex sat back in his chair, a thoughtful look on his face. "We could have Trent look through his computer and online activities. You know he'd be as discreet as they come. And I think Than might be up for a little trip."

"Than?" Lucas didn't bother to hide the skepticism in his voice.

Alex laughed. "Yeah, I wouldn't trust the guy within a hundred miles of one of my sisters, but honestly? He's good at what he does. And because he speaks a couple of different languages, he would fit in good with the tourists and locals down there."

"If you think he's the best one for the job..."

"He is. Believe me, I wouldn't put anyone on a job for you that I wasn't one hundred percent confident in their abilities." Alex leaned forward and snatched the phone from its cradle on his desk. "Beth, can you get hold of Trent and Than and have them come to my office pronto? And Marcus, too, if you can get hold of him."

Alex listened and then shook his head. "Again? That makes how many he's gone through now? I thought that this one might make it." He paused again then said, "Well, get someone to track him down and ask him if he's available for a meeting."

As he hung up, Alex said, "Marcus has trouble keeping assistants. I've had Beth now for three years. I think Marcus has had seven different ones in that same time. He tried to steal Beth from me, but she begged me to hide her."

Lucas smiled. From his own experience with assistants, he knew it could be a demanding job that required someone special. His own assistant, Deb, had been with him for coming up on ten years. Before that, she'd worked with his dad, so in reality, she probably knew more about the business than he did.

They continued to chat for a bit while they waited for the other guys to show up. Trent was the first to arrive, surprise on his face when he saw Lucas sitting with Alex.

"Hey, long time no see!" He held out his hand to Lucas.

"What's up, boss?" Than said as he walked into the room. His expression when he saw who was there was similar to Trent's. "Lucas."

Lucas shook his hand then said, "Oh, just for the record, I'm not dating Brooke...yet. But I have it on good authority that while my chances might not be great, yours with her are nil."

Than grinned. "Ah well. Can't win 'em all."

"Or any, apparently, since you haven't had a long-term girlfriend in what...at least three years?" Trent said.

Before Than could respond, Marcus appeared in the door of the office. Immediately, the joking atmosphere settled into something more serious. As Marcus came to a stop near Alex's desk, he pushed back the edges of his suit coat and put his hands on his hips. "Lucas." He gave him a nod before turning to Alex. "What's going on?"

"Have a seat, guys." Alex walked to the door and shut it. As he moved around the desk to his chair, he said, "I need what we discuss in this room to stay here. Lucas came to me to see if we would do some investigating for him."

"Investigating?" Marcus looked from Alex to Lucas. "About Lincoln?"

Lucas nodded. "I have some concerns that perhaps he staged his death."

Both Trent and Than focused in on his words and all levity was gone.

"Why would you think that, Lucas?" Marcus asked.

Over the next half hour, Lucas laid out the information that had come up as he'd gone through Lincoln's things looking for information on Brooke's paintings. There hadn't been one big thing, but there had been enough little things that seemed odd and out of place. They might be nothing, but in case they weren't....

"Trent, I want you to go to Lucas' s place and have a look at Lincoln's computer and see what he found there." Alex turned to Than. "And you, my friend, are going to head south."

That brought a smile back to Than's face. "Road trip. What exactly do you want me to do down there?"

"I want you to poke around. See if you can talk to people who might have had contact with Lincoln." Alex looked at him. "Lucas, can you give Than an idea of where he'd been in the weeks before the accident?"

"Yes. The authorities down there had pieced some of that together."

"I want you to go beyond what the authorities would have done, Than," Alex said. "Use that insufferable charm of yours and dig up more information than they would have been able to get."

Than grinned. "Will do. You may mock my charm, but it does come in handy."

"I'm counting on that," Alex said with a nod. He looked at Marcus. "Any other thoughts?"

Marcus's intense blue gaze circled the group before he shook his head. Given that the man had hardly said two words during the discussion itself, Lucas wasn't altogether sure why Alex had called him.

When the other men stood, Lucas did as well. As he shook hands with them, he said, "Thanks so much for your help with this, guys. I'm not sure what I hope you find—either outcome will be difficult in its own way."

"Have you planned a service for Lincoln?" Marcus asked.

"We discussed it, but honestly, his friends are spread far and wide...I'm not sure how we'd get people together for it. Plus, he would be appalled—wherever he is—if we tried to do a stuffy memorial service. I had been thinking of doing something just for the family up at our cabin. It was one place that belonged to the family where he was actually happy. But now..."

"Well, I hope the guys can get some answers for you," Marcus said. "I know that unknowns can be difficult. Hard to move forward in those situations."

Lucas wondered if the man had some unknowns in his own life. It sounded like maybe he did.

After making arrangements with Trent, Lucas left the BlackThorpe building and headed back to his own office. Now that he'd started that, he could focus on other things. Namely his upcoming dinner with Brooke.

He was thinking that maybe he should avoid any romantic ties with Brooke for now. If his brother was, in fact, still alive, that might complicate things between them. Waiting for some sort of resolution, in the meantime, would probably be the wisest thing.

Strangely enough, though doing the wisest thing had always been his normal course, when it came to Brooke that wasn't his first consideration. And he had a funny feeling it was going to get him into trouble.

"Ready to go, buddy?" Brooke poked her head into Danny's room. "Don't forget your swimsuit. Lucas said Lindsay would likely go swimming with you."

"Yep, I got it here." Danny picked up the bag from the end of his bed.

"You still okay with hanging out with your grandmother and Lindsay while Lucas and I take care of some business stuff?"

"Sure. It'll be fun."

Brooke was glad Danny seemed fine with hanging out at the house. She, however, was still a little nervous about the dinner with just her and Lucas. When he'd called to check on a time, he'd been all business, leaving Brooke to wonder if she'd imagined those last few moments with him the night following the wedding.

Though she'd offered to drive her and Danny to the mansion—as she liked to call it—Lucas had insisted on picking them up once again. And according to the clock, he would be there any minute.

She picked up her phone, purse and a container of baked goods from the counter then followed Danny out of the house. After pausing to lock the door, Brooke sat down on the top step of the porch beside Danny. She smoothed the skirt of the maxi sundress she'd chosen to wear, hoping it would be appropriate for wherever he planned to take her.

In the four days since he'd asked to have dinner with her to talk, Brooke had tried to think through what they might discuss. The inheritance, obviously, but likely also the time at the cabin and maybe Danny spending more time with Lucas's mom.

"He's here," Danny said, pointing to the street as he stood.

Blowing out a breath to try and calm the nerves that were becoming way too common when dealing with Lucas, Brooke stood up and followed her son.

"Hey, Danny," Lucas said as he came around to open the doors for them.

"Hiya, Uncle Lucas." Danny gave the man a quick hug before climbing into the back seat.

Lucas smiled at Brooke, and her stomach did a flip.

"Hi," she said and returned his smile as she slid into the front seat. As usual, the scent of his cologne greeted her and did nothing to dispel her nerves. Being surrounded by that scent was almost like being hugged by him. That was something she needed to think less about.

"How was your day?" Lucas said after he'd slid behind the wheel.

"Well, we did some baking this morning. Danny insisted that he needed to bring cookies to your mom and Lindsay again."

As they pulled up to a red light, Lucas looked back at Danny. "Your aunt will love you for that, even if she does gripe about needing to lose weight. Put a few aside for me."

"I will," Danny said.

"We went to the community center after lunch. I am teaching a summer art program for nine to twelve-year-olds."

"Really? I didn't realize you taught art."

"I just do local programs at the community center. Nothing too formal but something for kids that are interested in it. I've also done a couple of programs for adults."

"You certainly have the talent," Lucas said as he merged with the traffic on the highway.

"Thank you." Brooke wasn't sure why she felt so ridiculously pleased by his compliment. "I really enjoy teaching others about painting, not just doing it myself."

"Not everyone is willing to share their time and talents," Lucas commented.

"I suppose that's true, but that's not the example I'm trying to set for Danny."

Lucas shot her a quick grin. "You're a good mom."

Again, the warmth that flooded her at his compliment caught Brooke off-guard. He'd better stop with the compliments or she was going to spend the whole evening fanning herself.

Thankfully, Danny piped up and filled Lucas in on his own activities during the afternoon while she'd been teaching. She spent the time giving herself a lecture. This was not her. Men didn't make her nervous or—for lack of a better word—giddy. That Lucas managed to do this to her was alarming. She needed to shore her defenses back up because if this was all one-sided, she was looking at some kind of hurt in the near future.

As soon as Lucas pulled the car to a stop in front of the mansion, Danny opened his door and climbed out.

"Hey, you," Brooke said as she got out as well. "Give me a hug."

Danny ran back to her and wrapped his arms around her. Brooke looked down at his face and felt a rush of love. Now this was one guy she didn't mind loving. She captured his face in her hands and pressed a kiss to his forehead. "Be good for your aunt and grandma, okay?"

"I will, Mom. Promise."

"I know you will, sweetie."

Danny stepped out of her embrace and ran toward the house where Lindsay stood waiting.

"See you guys later," Lindsay called with a wave of her arm as Danny reached her. She slipped an arm around his shoulder, and they disappeared into the house.

Brooke got back into the car, nerves flaring to life anew. *Men will hurt you. They will take what they want and leave you for someone better. Remember how that felt.*

"Here."

Glancing over, she saw Lucas in the open door on the driver's side holding out a bouquet of flowers. Startled, she looked into his gaze then reached for them. Her fingers brushed his as she took the cellophane-wrapped flowers.

The bouquet was large with several different kinds of blossoms in varying shades of purple. It was a truly beautiful arrangement, but it did nothing to quell the nerves now fluttering even more wildly inside her stomach.

"Thank you. They're lovely."

"You're welcome." He pulled around the circular driveway and headed back to the road. "I noticed you had a lot of flowers in the gardens around your house. I thought you might like some inside, too."

"Will they be okay in the car when we go to eat?"

"We'll take them in with us. They'll have a vase we can use."

"You sound pretty certain of that," Brooke observed.

"I am." He looked over at her and smiled. "They know me."

Of course, they would. "Are you a frequent customer?"

"Frequent enough. They're sort of family friends. Plus, the food is terrific."

Brooke hoped she'd be able to eat. Right then her stomach was in knots, and the thought of food—even terrific food—was a bit nauseating.

It wasn't long before Lucas pulled into a small parking lot behind an old brick building. It didn't really look like a place for meetings, and that feeling was reinforced when they walked into the foyer of the building. It had a pub feel with wood floors and large booths along the far wall.

As soon as they neared a small podium just inside the door, a woman approached them, a big smile on her face and arms wide. From the glimpse Brooke got of her before she engulfed Lucas in a hug, she was a stunning woman. Shiny black hair in loose curls. And a figure with curves, that as far as Brooke could see, just didn't quit. She looked like one of those pinup girls from back in the forties and fifties and was even dressed the part. Her dress was a deep cranberry color and was fitted from her shoulders to her waist where it flared out in a full skirt to her knees.

"You still trying to steal my wife, Hamilton?"

Brooke turned to see a tall man striding toward them. He was as fair as the woman was dark.

The woman let go of Lucas and turned to the man with a smile. "No one can steal me from you, babe."

The man slipped his arm around her waist and tucked her into his side. He turned his ice blue gaze on Brooke. "I'm

Thom Declan and this is my wife, Amber. Welcome to our restaurant."

Lucas laid a hand on her back. "This is Brooke McKinley."

Amber held out her hand. "It's nice to meet you. I hope you enjoy your evening."

Clutching her flowers, Brooke said, "I'm sure I will. This place looks great."

"I've got a booth ready for you guys at the back. Follow me." Amber pressed a kiss to her husband's cheek before leading the way through the restaurant.

The booth was large and had a low hanging lamp over it.

"The vase you asked for is there, Luc," Amber said as she pointed to the far edge of the table next to the wall.

"Thanks, Amber."

"Someone will be here in a few minutes to start you off with something to drink."

"Here." Lucas held out his hand. "Let's get those flowers into the water."

Brooke handed them to him and then slid into the booth on the far side. He put the whole bouquet-cellophane and all—into the vase and then pushed it back to its spot near the wall.

As he settled into the booth across from her, he smiled. "You can't really go wrong with anything you order here, but I'm particularly partial to their lasagna. I think Amber said their special today was beef stew when I called earlier. That is also very good."

"Sounds like they specialize in hearty comfort food."

Lucas grinned as he leaned back against the seat. "Yeah, you could say that."

A waitress appeared next to their table. "Hiya, Luc."

Brooke looked up to see a younger version of the woman who'd met them at the door. Her smile was flirtatious as she looked at Lucas.

"Hey, Bernadette." Lucas smiled back at her. "How's it going?"

"Great. How about with you?"

"Doing pretty good. All things considered."

Bernadette laid her hand on his shoulder. "I'm sorry to hear about Lincoln."

"Yeah. Never anything anyone wants to go through."

"So, what can I get you?"

Lucas looked at Brooke. "Brooke? Would you like something to drink?"

Brooke watched as the young woman turned to her. She didn't miss the way smile slipped from her face. "I'll just have water, thanks."

The smile returned when Bernadette looked back at Lucas. "And for you, Luc?"

"Iced tea with lemon, please."

"I'll be right back with your drink."

Brooke watched her walk away then looked back at Lucas only to find that his gaze was on her. "She has a crush on you."

Lucas's eyebrows rose at her statement. "Bernadette?"

Brooke grinned. Guys could be so dense sometimes. "Yes. Bernadette."

"Why would you say that? She's way too young for me."

"Something tells me that is not a problem for her."

Lucas scoffed. "I think you're imagining things."

"You watch her when she comes back. See how she is when she deals with me. She doesn't like me."

Before Lucas could say anything, Bernadette reappeared with a tray.

"Here you go, Luc. Iced tea just the way you like it." Another wide smile that showed every one of her perfectly aligned pearly white teeth. "And water for you." She set the glass down in front of Brooke with a thud, the smile suddenly much dimmer.

"Thank you," Brooke said with a smile at the girl. Unrequited love was not fun. She hated to be the one to put a damper on the girl's feelings even if it was just her imagining that Brooke and Lucas were on a date.

"Are you ready to order?" Again she turned to Lucas first, but he deferred to Brooke.

"I think I'll have the lasagna. Lucas said he recommended it."

Bernadette nodded and then turned back to Lucas. "Same for you?"

"You bet," Lucas said. "Thank you."

"I'll be back with your food shortly. "

As she walked away, Brooke waited for Lucas to look at her. When he did, she saw that he had seen what she had earlier. She arched a brow, waiting for him to say something.

CHAPTER FOURTEEN

OKAY. Fine. Maybe you're right." Brooke watched as Lucas's gaze went in the direction Bernadette had walked. "Why didn't I realize that?"

"Maybe because you're not a guy who wants or needs the attention of every pretty girl that crosses his path. And maybe because you've never viewed her in that light."

"That's for sure." Lucas's brows drew together. "She's Stella's niece. I'd be afraid of poison in my food if I had ever entertained such thoughts about her. Not that I would have even if she wasn't her niece. I mean..."

Brooke grinned. "I know what you mean. Now I just hope she doesn't poison my food."

"Stella?"

"No. Bernadette. She obviously thinks we're on a date."

"Well, sorry, but if it discourages her crush on me, we're on a date."

While she understood Lucas's desire to discourage what Bernadette felt for him, Brooke didn't want to devastate the girl. "Listen, just my being here with you is enough. No need to be overt about anything."

"Ah, shucks," Lucas said with a grin as he reached across the table. "So no holding your hand?"

Unfortunately—or fortunately, depending on person's perspective—Bernadette walked up right then. Lucas pulled his hand back as she plopped a basket of bread sticks on the table.

"Thanks, Bernadette," Lucas said.

The young girl shot a look at Brooke before murmuring, "You're welcome," and walking away.

"Maybe I *will* switch plates with you," Lucas said as he watched Bernadette stomp away.

Brooke laughed. "Such a gentleman."

He winked at her. "My mom taught me well."

Brooke felt a rush of warmth and an overwhelming amount of sympathy for Bernadette. Lucas had a charm that he seemed totally unaware of. It was the total opposite of how Lincoln had been. He'd known how to use his charm and good looks to his advantage. Thankfully, she'd been just jaded enough by men at that point to not take it seriously when he'd turned his attention her way. Otherwise, she'd have been as devastated as Bernadette was when she realized there was no future with him.

"So, what's on the agenda?" Brooke asked Lucas, eager to get this evening back to the main focus.

"Agenda?"

"Yeah. You wanted to have this dinner to discuss some stuff."

"Ah. Yes." Lucas shrugged out of his suit coat and laid it on the seat next to him and then loosened the tie around his neck. "I suppose the biggie is the inheritance."

"And also the time out at the cabin," Brooke added.

Lucas nodded. "Yep. That, too."

"I would imagine there are some legalities involved with the inheritance for Danny?" Brooke asked.

"Yes. There are a few delays at the moment. I've asked the lawyers to hold off for a bit until we get a few things sorted out." He tilted his head. "If that causes you some financial hardship, let me know."

Brooke laughed as she shook her head. "You're kidding, right? Financial hardship? With what you paid for those three paintings, I'm set for at least a year or two."

Lucas's brows rose at her response. "Really?"

"Seriously? You've seen where I live. What kind of car I drive. Do I strike you as the type that needs an excessive amount of money to live?"

"You could move to a nicer neighborhood. Buy a better car."

Brooke narrowed her eyes. "Does it bother you to have your nephew living in the neighborhood we do? Riding in the car we have?"

Lucas regarded her for a moment, and Brooke got the feeling he was trying to figure out what the right answer to that might be. Smart man. "It doesn't bother me. But you can afford to live somewhere safer and drive a more reliable car now."

"We have friends in that neighborhood. And most the places we need to go we just bike to." Brooke sighed. "We will never live in a place like your mom's even if we can afford it. Yeah, it will be nice not to have to worry about how to pay the bills, but that doesn't mean I need to automatically have a more expensive lifestyle. Danny likes his school and being around his friends. I'm not going to move him away from that."

"Do you own your home?" Lucas asked.

"No. I rent. My landlady lives across the street from us. We've rented from her for the past five years."

Before Lucas could respond, Amber appeared at the table with a tray.

"Dinner is served," she said as she set a plate in front of Brooke and then one in front of Lucas. "Do you need anything else?"

"Where's Bernadette?" Lucas asked.

Amber smiled as she shook her head at him. "You've broken my baby sister's heart, Luc."

Lucas sighed. "I'm sorry. I had no idea. Brooke alerted me to the fact that she might have a crush on me."

"It's okay. She'll get over it. I told her that you would never feel the same way for her. She just chose to ignore me."

"The irony is that we're not actually here on a date," Brooke said.

Amber's eyes widened as she looked at Lucas then back to Brooke. "Well, I'm not going to clue Bernadette into that little fact. She can go on assuming you are and will get over this thing she has for Luc all the faster." Amber leaned toward Brooke, a sparkle in her eyes. "Of course, you may have just broken Luc's heart, too."

"I sincerely doubt that," Brooke said with a glance at Luc who had sat back in his seat, a grin on his face.

"You never know." With a wave of her fingers, Amber spun around—her skirt flaring out as she did—and headed toward the front of the restaurant.

"Mind if I say grace?" Lucas asked.

Brook shook her head. "Go ahead."

"Heavenly Father, thank you for this day. Another one in which to see Your blessing and will in our lives. Be with us as we talk things over and strive to do what's best for all involved in this situation. Thank you for the wonderful food and the company. Amen."

Once he'd finished praying, Brooke took her first bite of the lasagna and understood why Lucas had recommended it. A spicy, tomatoey richness exploded in her mouth with the first bite. The noodles were done to perfection and there was plenty of cheese—a definite plus in her book.

While they ate, they made casual conversation, and Brooke watched as the restaurant gradually filled up. Bernadette made a reappearance but avoided their table, resulting in another waitress coming to check if they needed anything.

As they talked, Brooke found herself relaxing with Lucas in a way she hadn't with a man in a long time. He asked a lot of questions about her art and the teaching she did and more about Danny.

"Will you be able to come to the cabin if you have classes to teach?" Lucas asked as he pushed his empty plate toward the center of the table.

Though she knew she probably should have only eaten part of it, Brooke had matched Lucas pretty much bite for bite. It had been so delicious. "I only teach on Wednesdays so if we could plan around that, that would be good. However, I could book one session off if I had to."

"We'll try to work around that for you," Lucas said. He glanced from the table and lifted his hand to the waitress. When she approached them, he said, "I spoke to Amber about the dessert earlier."

She nodded as she picked up their empty plates. "I'll be right back."

"Dessert?" Brooke groaned as she leaned back against the booth. "I don't think I can eat another bite."

"Oh, once you see this, you will. Unless you're one of those rare people who don't like chocolate."

"No such luck there. Chocolate and I get along very well."

"Well, brace yourself."

The grin he gave her set nerves fluttering to life again. She'd appreciated the easy conversation as they'd eaten, but every once in a while it took a turn for feeling like a date and that was one of the moments.

Amber once again showed up at their table with a tray held in the air. "Ready for your dessert?"

"You bet," Lucas said, a look of anticipation on his face.

Amber lowered the tray and set a plate with a beautifully plated chocolate soufflé in the middle of it down in front of Brooke. The aroma of rich chocolate teased her senses, and Brooke knew that even though she had already eaten so much, she was going to eat more.

"Enjoy!" Amber said as she set Lucas's in front of him.

"Oh, we will."

Brooke looked at Lucas and found him watching her. She took a small bite of the soufflé and had to resist the urge to close her eyes and moan. It was *that* good. Rich, warm and everything chocolate should be.

"Good, right?" Lucas said with a knowing smile.

"More than good," Brooke agreed as she took another bite. She ate slowly, as much to savor the taste as to make sure her stomach didn't burst from eating so much.

Plus, she really was in no rush for the evening to end. She loved Danny with all her heart and loved spending time with him, but this evening out had reminded her how much she also liked socializing with adults. Or in this case...one adult, in particular. She just had to make sure she didn't enjoy it too much. The verdict was still out on if something with Lucas would be a good or bad idea at this point.

Lucas watched Brooke scraped the plate to get the last of the chocolate soufflé. As she put the spoon upside down in her mouth, her gaze met his and her eyes sparkled with laughter. Though he'd tried to keep himself from considering this a date, it was moments like that when he wished it were.

Several times over the course of the evening, he'd found himself second-guessing his decision to initiate things with BlackThorpe in looking for Lincoln. If his brother had really wanted to disappear, why should he try to prevent him from doing that? Particularly if his return would cause havoc for several people. How would Danny feel knowing that his father would rather disappear and never actually meet him?

And what about Brooke? How would she feel if Lincoln reappeared?

If he did return, Lincoln wouldn't be able to ignore his role as Danny's father any longer. Their mother would make sure of that. Several times since finding out about Danny's existence, his mother had asked him what she'd done wrong in raising Lincoln that he'd found it so easy to ignore his own son.

Lucas had had no answer for her. She'd raised him the exact same way, and he would never have done what Lincoln had. Of course, their father had had more of an influence on his twin, and no doubt that had played a role in Lincoln's decision where Danny was concerned.

He'd been fifteen when he'd discovered that his father didn't view fidelity in quite the way Lucas had assumed one should when they were married. His father had assured him that he loved his wife but that he needed some variety. Some excitement in that area of his life just like he did in others. The whole conversation had sat badly with Lucas, and he vowed that he would never be like his father. Lincoln, on the other hand, had eagerly adopted Leon Hamilton's philosophy and run with it.

As he looked at Brooke across the table, he realized that they had that much in common. A father who had strayed from their marital vows. He got the feeling, however, that Brooke's dad didn't hold to the same philosophy as his father had.

"I guess we really didn't settle a lot," Brooke said as she sat back, her hand resting on her stomach. "And I ate way too much."

"It's hard not to here."

"It's been lovely. Thank you."

She smiled at him, her eyes shining, and for a moment Lucas was ready to chuck every reservation aside and ask her out for a date. A real one. As if sensing the direction of his thoughts, her smile faded and the sparkling in her eyes was replaced by an emotion that Lucas couldn't name, but it pulled at something deep within him.

"How was everything?"

Lucas closed his eyes for a second before plastering a smile on his face and turning to face Amber. "It was great. Just like I knew it would be."

She turned her smile on Brooke. "I hope you'll be back again."

"Oh, I think you can count on that."

"Glad to hear it. And Thom said to tell you not to be a stranger."

Lucas smiled. "I won't."

Amber stepped to the side when the waitress came to clear the dirty plates. "Tell Aunt Stella I said hi."

"I will. You need to come by some day. Bring your suits and go for a swim."

"Given how hot it's been, I might take you up on that." Amber glanced toward the front of the restaurant. "Well, I need to get back to work. If you need anything more, just let Suze know."

"I think we're going to head out, actually," Lucas said, reaching for his jacket.

Amber pointed to the vase. "Don't forget your flowers."

"Do you happen to have a bag or something?" Brooke asked. "They're going to drip everywhere when we take them out."

"Sure thing."

By the time they got the flowers all bagged up, it was another fifteen minutes later. Lucas didn't bother to settle up the bill as they had his credit card on file and knew what to charge.

Apparently, Brooke noticed the oversight. "You don't pay here?"

Lucas pushed the restaurant door open and held it for Brooke. "They have my information on file."

"I guess you must trust them."

He smiled down at her as she walked past him out into the twilight evening. "I do. I'm a silent partner in the restaurant."

She gave him a startled look. "Really?"

"Yep." He laid his hand on her back to guide her to his car. "It started out as a favor to Stella, but it didn't take long to realize it was a very worthwhile partnership."

Using his free hand, he pushed the button on the fob to unlock the door and reached for the handle as they got close. "Do you want me to put those flowers in the back?"

"Maybe. I don't want to crush them."

Lucas took them from her. "If they get crushed, I'll buy you another."

When she smiled at him, Lucas knew that he'd happily buy her bouquets every single day. After she'd settled in the seat, he closed the door and walked around to the driver's side. He put the flowers on the back seat then grasped the handle of his door. He paused and took a deep breath before opening it.

As he backed out of the parking spot, he said, "Should I call my mom to let her know we're on our way and to have Danny ready?"

"That might be a good idea. I didn't realize how late it was."

He glanced at her. "Time flies."

"It does indeed."

Using his Bluetooth, he placed a call to his mom and she agreed to have Danny ready to go. It wasn't long before they were pulling to a stop in front of the mansion. The door opened, and Danny and his mom appeared.

Brooke got out so he did as well and followed her up the stairs to where his mom and Danny stood. "Thanks so much for entertaining him, Mrs. Hamilton."

"Please, just call me Sylvia. And it was absolutely not a problem to have him here." She looked down at him and smiled. "I think we had fun, didn't we?"

Danny nodded. "We ate and swam and watched some videos."

"I'm glad you had a good time. Ready to go?"

After getting back into the car, Danny held up a one-sided conversation as he expounded more on what he'd done with Lindsay and his grandmother. Lucas was glad to hear that he'd had a good time. He knew spending time with two women might not be every young boy's idea of fun. Thankfully, Brooke had apparently raised Danny to be respectful, and he seemed to easily adapt to the people he was around.

Once they got to the house, he debated leaving right away, but he squelched his common sense and got out with Brooke and Danny. He retrieved the flowers from the back seat and followed them into the house.

"Bedtime, buddy," Brooke said as soon as they were inside. She looked at Lucas. "Bring those to the kitchen, please. I think I've got a vase there."

He laid the bouquet on the counter and watched as she opened a cupboard to reveal a glass vase. She glanced over her shoulder at him and then pointed up to the vase. "Can you get that for me?"

"Sure thing." He walked to where she was and reached up for it. "There you go."

Their fingers brushed as she took it from him. "Thanks."

Standing this close, he could see the dark flecks in her blue-green eyes. And again that emotion from earlier showed in her gaze. Was she feeling the same pull that he was?

"Mom? I'm ready for bed."

"Okay, sweetie. Be right there." She set the vase on the counter without looking at Lucas. "I'll be right back."

While he waited, Lucas decided to make himself useful and began to unwrap the bouquet. The cellophane crackled beneath his fingers as he removed it from around the flowers. He would have just filled the vase with water and stuffed the stems into it, but something told him that Brooke would treat them with a little more care.

He sat down at the counter and stared at the flowers. What was it about this house—this home—that called to him so much? It couldn't have been more different from how he'd grown up. But there was a hominess to it that he hadn't ever thought would attract him.

The appliances were old. The countertops were laminate not granite as was so popular these days. The linoleum looked worn in spots, and the carpet had definitely seen better days. No doubt the windows weren't the latest in energy efficiency either. And yet for all that would make it unappealing to a lot of people—particularly ones in his position—it spoke of family and love and belonging in a way the mansion never had.

He could even understand why Brooke wouldn't want to move. She had made a home for her and Danny that went beyond the building itself. Their life was here—in this house. In this neighborhood. He wasn't sure how he could get her to use the inheritance to better their lives when in reality—in all the ways that mattered—they had it all right there.

"Earth to Lucas."

He blinked. She had returned while he'd been off in his thoughts. "Sorry. I didn't put the flowers in the vase in case there was a special way to do it."

She smiled as she opened a drawer and pulled out a pair of scissors. "Not sure it's special, but I usually trim the stems before I put them in water."

He watched as she added water to the vase then quickly snipped at the stems. She put each flower into the vase arranging them as she went. "This is a truly beautiful bouquet. Thank you."

"You're welcome." Not sure what else to say, Lucas lapsed into silence. He had lots he would have liked to share with her—the stuff Trent had found on Lincoln's computer, for example—but she was too involved to be able to just listen and not allow it to complicate an already complicated situation.

"So time at the cabin? Did you want to set it up for next Thursday?"

Lucas pulled his phone out and quickly brought up his calendar for the month. There was nothing on the schedule that he couldn't take care of before he left or put off until he returned. "That should work for me, and I'm sure it will be fine for Mom. Lindsay...I'll check with her. Is there anyone in your family that might like to come along? We've got plenty of room."

"My family?" Brooke put the last stem of greenery into the vase. She grabbed a cloth from the sink and wiped the stems into her hand. After dropping them in the garbage, she turned back to him. "My folks might enjoy it. Not sure Eric would be able to get off work so soon after taking his honeymoon." She grinned. "And I'm not sure Staci will be keen to leave him this soon after getting married."

"Well, the invitation stands for all of them. Just let me know so we can have the cabins prepared and the boat brought over to the main dock."

"Cabins?" Brooke paused and then said, "So, this probably isn't a cabin-type cabin, is it? Kinda like how your mom's house isn't really a house but a mansion."

"It's not that big," Lucas said with a grin.

"Is the cabin bigger than this house?"

He glanced around. "Yeah."

"Is it rustic?"

"The décor is rustic."

Brooke laughed. "Just tell me all about it."

"It's on an island."

The laughter faded from her face, replaced by incredulity. "You own the whole island?"

"Yes, it's been in the family for several decades."

"Running water? Electricity?"

Lucas nodded. "Cable. Internet."

"Well, I can see why you'd enjoy going to the *cabin*." She made air quotes as she said the word.

"There are also three smaller cabins on the island. The caretaker lives in one, but if Eric and Staci can make it up, they can use one of them and your folks can use the other. Give them a bit of privacy."

Brooke's mouth dropped open. "This is taking some getting used to. All this money."

"Don't ever get used to it," Lucas said.

She tilted her head. "What do you mean by that?"

CHAPTER FIFTEEN

LUCAS waved his hand at the kitchen and surrounding space. "Money can give you the feeling that you're providing for your family in all the ways that matter, but that's not true. My dad gave us a house to live in and my mom tried her best, but what you have given Danny here? Yeah, way more than we ever had—even with all our wealth."

For a second her beautiful eyes seem to liquefy. "Thank you. It hasn't been easy, and I always felt like I had to try to make up for the fact that he didn't have a dad around."

"Sad to say, I think if Lincoln had been active in Danny's life, he would be a much different boy and not necessarily a better one. I hate to speak ill of the...of my brother, but I think you know that it's the truth."

Brooke nodded. "I never would have denied Lincoln the right to be a father to Danny. But I will admit, even though it has had some hard moments as a single mom to a boy, I'm glad for how it turned out."

"Once again, Lincoln solved the problem the way my dad did by throwing money at it. You, on the other hand, took that money and used it to create a stable, loving home environment for Danny. You're a terrific mom."

She beamed at his words, her whole face transformed by her wide smile. "I love being a mom. When I was younger, all I wanted to be when I grew up was a mom. I wanted to have like twelve kids. Then our family went through that huge upset, and it was as if my heart had been ripped out." She traced a pattern on the counter. "We had just taken in a couple of orphaned babies to foster. I fell in love with them instantly and desperately. They were my babies. I helped with them as often as I could when I wasn't in school. And then...everything fell apart. Not only was I forced to leave the only place I'd ever called home, but I had to leave my babies behind, too."

Lucas watched as a tear slipped down her cheek. He reached out and brushed it aside with his thumb, his fingertips touching the side of her face. She pressed her cheek into his palm for a moment, her eyes closed. Tears sparkled on the ends of her eyelashes. Then she lifted her head and opened her eyes. Lucas lowered his hand, his gut wrenching at the pain he saw in her gaze.

"That had been bad enough, but later when I realized exactly *why* we'd had to leave...I hated my dad for that. Who knows what kind of life those baby girls ended up having all because my dad couldn't stay away from that woman. You hear the horror stories of girls like that in places like Africa." Her hands clenched into fists. "I hate him."

It certainly explained a lot about Brooke. The seriousness with which she took her role as mother to Danny. The apathy bordering on disdain she had toward the male gender. And his brother hadn't helped any when he'd chosen his own wants and desires over his son.

Lucas wanted to show her that it could be different—that *he* was different—but until his doubts regarding Lincoln were settled, he couldn't get involved with her. He couldn't tell her about his concerns which was what he'd have to do if they were involved. She would hate *him* if she found out he'd kept this from her. As it stood, she still might.

Brooke's shoulders slumped. "Sorry. Didn't mean to dump all that on you. All that to say, I love being Danny's mother and maybe, in other circumstances, I might have had a lot more children."

"It's not too late for that," Lucas said.

She looked at him, her gaze still damp, a vulnerable look on her face. "Most men out there that I've come in contact with are not interested in me with one child let alone going on to have a bunch more."

"Most men, maybe, but not all. You need just one who is interested." His gaze held hers as the silence that followed his statement grew heavy.

Then Brooke blinked and picked up the cloth from the counter. "That is true. A bit like a needle in a haystack though, and I'd rather spend my time being a good mother to the child I already have rather than trying to find a man to father future ones."

Lucas figured he'd better make himself scarce. He was so close to asking her to give him a shot at being that man. He'd never really thought about having a family. Oh, it had crossed his mind over the years, but there had never been a moment when he'd looked at a woman and thought *I want her to be the mother of my children*. But sitting there across the counter from Brooke, he could honestly say that he had just had that moment.

"Well, I'd better go." He pushed up from the stool. "I'll give you a call to firm up details about the cabin and don't forget to extend the invitation to your family."

She stared at him for a moment then nodded. "Thank you again for a lovely dinner. And the flowers."

"You're very welcome. It was my pleasure." He turned away from her, not certain she would follow him this time. But as he reached the door, he discovered she had, and when he stepped out onto the porch, she did as well.

"Please thank your mom and Lindsay again for spending time with Danny. It sounded like he had a wonderful time."

Lucas turned toward her. "They're trying to make up for lost time, but I told them not to spoil him too much."

"Thank you. For everything."

"You can stop thanking me, Brooke."

"I just feel like you've done nothing but give to us since you arrived on our doorstep."

"Nothing could be further from the truth." He took a step toward her then stopped. "You'll never know all that you and Danny have given me."

Before he could say anything that would increase the tension even more, he said goodnight and left her standing on the porch. It wasn't what he wanted, but it was all he could do right then.

Brooke sank down on the top step, tucking her skirt around her legs. She took a deep breath and let it out slowly, savoring the smell of the freshly cut grass from a nearby yard. It wasn't her favorite scent though. She missed the lilacs that had been present earlier in June. Back then, the cooler night air had carried the light scent from the neighbor's shrubs. She loved the smell. It was a familiar scent that she could count on each spring. It was home. Her neighborhood. The small houses. The postage stamp-sized front yards. The cracked sidewalks. It was where she and Danny belonged.

Her gaze followed the red taillights of Lucas's car until they disappeared around the corner. The man was wreaking havoc on her emotions every time they were together. What on earth had possessed her to share about her desire to have children? That was a dream she'd shelved when she'd realized what her father had done. What if she married and had children with a man like him? She hadn't wanted to inflict on them what she and Eric had endured.

She'd been so shocked—but pleased—when she'd found out she was pregnant with Danny. It had been unexpected and not what she would have planned, but once it was a done deal, she'd been thrilled. And even when Lincoln had bailed on being a dad to her little boy, she'd done her best to be a good mommy for him. And from Lucas had said, it seemed that she'd succeeded.

Would Lucas want children? From what he'd said in their earlier conversation it had seemed as if he might. And when he'd wiped the tears from her face...it was so tempting to believe that he was different. That he wouldn't be like her father and put his needs before others. That he wouldn't be like Lincoln and abandon any children they might have. Nothing he'd done so far supported the assumption that he would be like either man.

But how on earth would she and Danny ever fit into his world? She didn't want to move into a neighborhood like where his mom lived. And she didn't want to send Danny to some elite private school. But Lucas could never live in a place like this. He had an image to maintain being the head of his family's company.

Brooke let out a long breath. At least he knew where she stood with regards to how she wanted Danny raised, and it didn't appear that he felt the need to step in and change things. Yet. They were still really early in this whole situation. Time would tell if he'd be okay with a Hamilton heir attending the local middle school.

With another sigh, Brooke stood up and went back into the house. Daydreaming about Lucas was something she needed to avoid at all costs. In no way did she want to set herself up for any kind of heartache.

Been there. Done that. Had the scars to prove it.

"Are you sure?" Lucas stared at the video chat screen on his laptop, a sick feeling in his stomach.

"One hundred percent certain," Than said. There was a bit of a delay between his image and the sound, but the message he'd had for Lucas had been clear.

Lincoln was still alive.

"Have you spoken with him?"

"A few times, but unless he's an amazing actor, he has no memory of who he is."

"So what's the story then? The authorities said that there was no way anyone could have survived that crash. Is it possible he still intended to stage his death but then something else happened?"

"Anything is possible, man, but from what I'm hearing from people who spoke to the ones who brought him here, he wasn't found with a parachute or anything like that. A fishing boat found him floating on a piece of debris and took him to their home. Because it was a more remote place, they tried to take care of his wounds—to stabilize him—before bringing him to a larger town. Given that he didn't remember anything, they didn't know what else to do apparently. Some of this Lincoln himself told me."

Lucas rubbed his forehead. Of all the outcomes he'd envisioned this search having, this hadn't been one of them. "How badly is he injured?"

"Well, he must have broken his leg because he walks with a limp. It was clearly not set properly and healed wrong. Those who found him tended to him as best they could before they brought him to the closest major city which was here but clearly they didn't have medical training. And because they didn't take him to the area the authorities were searching, no one realized who he was."

"What made you go there?" Lucas asked.

"Well, when you've turned over all the possible rocks, you turn your attention to the impossible ones. Just like others who have survived plane crashes when no one else has, there's always room for the impossible to actually be possible."

"So he remembers nothing?"

"He knows how to speak English and how to take care of himself."

"And you're certain he's not faking?"

"You know, I would never say for certain, but it seems like that. Maybe seeing you might jar something in his head. Any chance you could make your way down here?"

"I'll get the jet ready to go. I really didn't expect you to find anything and definitely not this quickly."

"You and me both. And given what Trent had discovered, I really thought we'd find him holed up somewhere laying low for the time being. But I guess it makes more sense now that none of the money he'd stashed away has been touched. He obviously doesn't remember what he did with it."

"Or he's biding his time." Lucas still wasn't sure he trusted his brother to not try to pull one over on all of them. And what was the likelihood of him ever remembering his past? Of being able to answer the questions that were going to be put to him?

"I'll leave that up to you to determine. I'm going to hang out here and then catch a ride home in luxury."

"I'll email you the details as soon as I've got everything in place." He blew out a breath. "I have no idea what to tell my family. Or Brooke and Danny."

"Yeah, I don't envy you that task, man."

After ending the call with Than, Lucas shoved back from his desk and stalked over to the large glass window. So many emotions coursed through him. Anger. Fear. Confusion. He wanted answers because he knew that others were going to ask him for them. But if what Than had said was true, answers were not going to be forthcoming.

And what of the plans he'd made with Brooke for the cabin. Everything was in place for them to head up there in two days' time with Lindsay and his mom. Her parents, Victoria, and Eric's family were to have joined them on the weekend. Now he had to leave and do it without explanation. He might be able to get away with that with Brooke and Danny, but Lindsay was not going to accept a "business trip" as a reason to miss going to the cabin.

But the sooner he got down there and got Lincoln, the sooner they could move forward and sort out the mess he'd left behind.

He hadn't seen Brooke since the night they'd had dinner. After what had transpired, he'd figured it would be better that way. They had talked a few times on the phone about the plans for the cabin, but now a week later, he really wanted to see her.

Unfortunately, it was going to have to wait.

Within two hours, Lucas was wheels up in the company jet. Once they were in the air, he phoned Lindsay. He'd decided to come clean with her because he needed her help with logistics. But he figured if he'd phoned before getting off the ground, she'd somehow manage to convince him to take her with him.

"Hey, Linds, big favor," Lucas said when she answered. He stared out the window as the plane cut through the billowy white clouds.

"I'm not doing you any more favors," Lindsay said in her blunt way. "You owe me way too many at this point."

"Believe me, I wouldn't ask if it wasn't important."

She must have sensed something in his tone because when she replied her voice was more subdued. "What's wrong?"

Where to start? At that point, Lucas was wondering if anything was actually right. "Well, depending on your perspective—nothing."

"Stop with the cryptic comments, Luc. What's happened?"

He took a deep breath and plunged in, telling her about the suspicions he'd had after finding what he had on Lincoln's computer and then about going to BlackThorpe for help. Finally, he ended with the details of the conversation he'd just had with Than.

"Are you *kidding* me?" In Lindsay's voice, he could hear all the emotions he himself had gone through earlier.

"No. I would never kid about this. I'm in the plane now on my way down to get him and Than."

"This is gonna just shred Mom. Getting him back but with no memory of who he is? Yeah, that's gonna be horrible for her."

"What's the choice here?" Lucas asked. "Leave him down there and let her continue to think he's still dead? You don't think she'd want him back any way she could get him?"

"What if he doesn't believe you?"

"Kind of hard to deny the physical likeness between the two of us. Probably the best way to convince him is going to be just having him look at me."

"I can't believe this. I really..." There was silence on the line for a couple of seconds before she continued. "Do you plan to bring him to the cabin when you get back?"

"I'll see what kind of state he's in. It might be a good place to take him. Out of all the family properties, that was always where he loved being the most."

"True. But what about Brooke and Danny?"

"They have to deal with this news as much as all of us will. We can't just ignore it. At least she'll have her family there with her."

"Are you going to give her a heads up? I'm not sure she'll think too kindly of you springing this on her."

"Yes. I'll give her a call when I have a better idea of how things stand with Lincoln."

"And Mom?"

"Again, once I know a bit more about his condition, I'll talk to her."

Another pause. "Let me know what I can do. You don't need to shoulder this all yourself."

"Just contacting Brooke and letting her know I got called out of town and still getting her and Danny to the cabin is a huge help."

"Sounds like I've got the easiest part of this whole situation."

"Well, brace yourself. Once we're back, nothing is going to be easy."

After he promised to call as soon as he had news, Lucas ended the call. He rested his head back against the seat. The jet had been another foolish purchase of his father's, but he was glad now that he didn't have to rely on commercial airlines to get him where he needed to go. And it would be easier to get Lincoln back to Minnesota this way, too. He had no doubt there were legalities that would need to be dealt with. He'd brought Lincoln's birth certificate as well as copies of other documents, assuming that he no longer had his passport.

He'd made a call to their lawyer as well, who was already working on things on his end. And though he hated to do it, if necessary, he would use whatever he had to to grease a few palms. Most important was getting Lincoln back home.

"Lucas isn't going to drive us?" Brooke frowned as she finished folding the last towel in the basket, her phone trapped between her shoulder and ear.

"No. He had to go away on business, but he'll be back before the weekend and will come join us."

"Should we just wait until he's back?" Brooke wasn't entirely sure she wanted to spend a few hours cooped up in a car with Lindsay.

"No, he wanted us to go ahead up there. And it's still fine for your family to join us there on the weekend. He doesn't want this to change the plans that have been made."

"Why didn't he tell me himself?"

"He will be in contact with you, but since I am going to drive you now, he suggested I go ahead and call to line things up."

Something seemed off, but Brooke wasn't going to call Lindsay on it. She didn't know the woman well enough for that, but there was no reason Lucas couldn't have called her himself with this information. But she wasn't going to cancel things. Danny was beyond excited about this trip to the cabin, and he was bringing his best friend along as well.

"Okay, so when are we leaving?"

After they hammered out the details and it was decided that Brooke and the boys would meet Lindsay at the mansion, she hung up. As she stood there with the phone in her hand, she was tempted to tap the screen on Lucas's name. Surely he could have spared five minutes to tell her himself what was going on. Unless he hadn't wanted to talk to her.

That thought was a bit unsettling, but at the same time, he'd had no trouble calling her over the past week for other things. No, something had happened, she was almost sure of it. For now she'd wait for him to call her, but she'd want some answers when he did.

"How's it going?" Lucas asked when Lindsay answered her phone.

"Pretty good, but why haven't you called Brooke yet? She is going to take your head off when you do. She knows something's up."

Lucas glanced around the cabin of the plane. They had managed to get Lincoln onboard, but he was still more comfortable with Than than he was with his own brother. And from what Lucas had been able to tell, Lincoln wasn't faking the memory loss. Knowing his brother as well as he did, he would have known in a way that Than might not have. They had some issues to deal with once they landed back in the U.S. but for now, Lucas was just glad to have

Lincoln under his care. He looked pretty rough, but a haircut and a shave would help with some of that.

"I'm going to be calling her when I'm done with you." Lucas rubbed his fingers over his forehead. "And go ahead and tell Mom. I'm going to text you a picture of him so she can see for herself. We'll be in Minneapolis later today and hopefully can get him through immigration without too much hassle. I've had Evan working on the legal end of things while I've been down here. If all goes well, we'll come out to the cabin tomorrow. I'm just glad that reports of his death didn't garner much attention, so there should be little to no press about his return to life. Here's hoping, anyway. That's the last thing I want to have to deal with."

"I know this has been hard on you," Lindsay said, her voice soft. "Don't think I don't know that Brooke has stirred things in you that have never been stirred before. Having Lincoln back in the picture, especially like this, has got to be the best and the worst case scenario for you."

Had he been that obvious? "Well, it is one reason why I haven't tried to push to spend more time with her. When it comes to girls, Lincoln has always come out ahead. And they have that link now with Danny."

"You deserve a shot at happiness, Luc. Don't step aside for Lincoln in this situation. Be there for her. From what she's said over the past few days, men have let her down like they have me. The most attractive quality in a man now would be to have one stand beside me while I'm going through a difficult time. Not trying to fix everything, just being there to offer support and understanding."

"Well, let's just see if she's still talking to me after I make this phone call to her."

"Do you want me to tell her? Would that be easier?"

"Easier, definitely. The right thing? No." Lucas sighed. "I'll call her. Is she able to talk now?"

"Yep. She's sitting out on the dock with her phone while the boys are swimming."

"Okay. Thanks. Give me a call when you're done talking with Mom."

After disconnecting with Lindsay, Lucas clutched the phone in his hand and bent his head. He wasn't sure he'd done the right thing in not telling Brooke about this sooner, but it had seemed best at the time. He had wanted to have more information before letting her know what was going on.

After breathing a prayer that God would give him the right words to say to Brooke, Lucas let out a deep breath and tapped the screen to bring up her information.

"About time you called," was Brooke's greeting when she answered.

"Yes, I'm sorry about that. I've had a lot of stuff going on that I needed to take care of." Lucas stretched out his legs and leaned back in his seat. "How are things going at the cabin?"

"Well, I was right about one thing. This place is not a cabin. At least not by most normal people's standards. It has marble countertops and jetted tubs. Those don't belong in any cabin I know of."

Lucas found himself smiling. It was truly refreshing to view his wealth through the eyes of someone who hadn't lived that lifestyle. He realized how much he'd been taking it all for granted for most of his life. "I hope you're still able to enjoy it despite having to suffer the presence of marble countertops and jetted tubs."

"Shut up," Brooke said, a humorous lilt to her voice. "You know it's absolutely beautiful here. I don't know how you ever leave."

"You're welcome to stay as long as you like." Forever, if she wanted.

"If Danny didn't have to go to school... This place is winterized, isn't it?"

Lucas did laugh at that. "Yes, it is. And you can just ice skate across the lake to it in the dead of winter."

"Are you kidding? I expect to be ferried across on a sleigh with bells and lap blankets pulled by two glorious white horses."

"I'm sure I could make that happen for you," Lucas told her. And he would. If she was still talking to him after all this was sorted out, he'd do whatever he could to give her the desires of her heart.

There was a beat of silence then Brooke said, "I was just joking."

"I wasn't."

CHAPTER SIXTEEN

Mᴏʀᴇ silence, but this time Lucas knew he had to break it before it got any more intense. "Look, Brooke, there's more to my trip away than I've told you."

"Well, considering you haven't told me anything about it, that's pretty much a given."

He looked toward where Than and Lincoln sat. His brother was slumped sideways in his seat, clearly asleep. His gaze met Than's for a moment before looking away.

"I just need you to listen to everything I have to tell you before you say anything, okay?"

Silence then, "Okaaaaay?"

"Back when I realized that Lincoln had been buying your paintings, I had to go through his computer and financials to find out the gallery he'd purchased them from and what he'd paid for them. During that time, I came across some things that raised some questions in my mind about Lincoln's death." He paused but in line with his request, Brooke didn't say anything. "Some of what I saw had me wondering if maybe Lincoln had...faked his death."

He heard a sharp intake of breath, but still she said nothing. He told her about talking with Alex and the BlackThorpe guys. About the information Trent had found on Lincoln's computer. And finally, about Than heading to the Caribbean to follow up on his suspicions.

This time she didn't stay silent. "What are you saying, Lucas?"

"Than found Lincoln. He's alive but has no memory of who he is or what happened."

"Well, isn't that just convenient." There was no disguising the undercurrent of anger in her voice. "Do you believe him?"

Even though it would paint Lincoln in a worse light if he said no, Lucas knew it wouldn't be right. "Yes. I believe him. There is no recognition in his eyes when he looks at me. Mannerisms that he used to have are gone, too. It's just not...him."

"What am I supposed to tell Danny?" Her voice was low and tight. "The father he thought was dead is alive, and oh yeah, he doesn't remember he has a son?"

"Brooke, listen, I know this will be confusing for him."

"You think?"

"While I'm not convinced Lincoln *was* planning to fake his death, I do think he had plans underway to move down there permanently."

"And that's supposed to make Danny feel better? If he hadn't been declared dead, we would still be living our normal lives. Now Danny gets to meet the man who denied his existence for ten years and can't even get any answers from him. Lincoln owes him answers, Lucas."

"Yes, I know he does, but, unfortunately, unless things change, he doesn't have them to give."

When Brooke lapsed into silence, Lucas could hear yells and shrieks in the background. It sounded like Danny and his friend were having fun. He hated to think how the next few days might change that for him.

"And why didn't you tell me about this sooner?" More anger in her voice now. "I had a right to know. This affects *my* son. I get to tell him this news. I get to deal with the ramifications of it all. You should have told me as soon as you had suspicions."

"I did what I thought was right, Brooke. There was every possibility that my suspicions were wrong. I didn't want to get anyone's hopes up or create stress about something that may not be—"

"Your mom. You didn't want to get your mom's hopes up."

"No, I didn't. Since we'd never found his body, she already harbored hopes. I didn't want to feed those hopes without more concrete proof." Lucas drew his legs in and leaned forward, bracing his elbows on his knees.

"I know you're used to calling all the shots for your family, but you don't have that right with me and Danny. If this didn't involve Danny, I wouldn't care that you kept it from me, but it *does* involve him." She paused. "You know he's become attached to you, Lucas. You may not have been his dad, but he connected with you in a way he never has with my dad or Eric. Now how is he supposed to have that relationship with you when his father is still alive?"

Lucas swallowed hard and pressed a hand to his chest. How did he put into words what Danny meant to him? How many times over the weeks since he'd first met them had he wished Danny *had* been his son? It had started the first time the boy had wrapped his arms around him in a hug. But he wasn't his son. He was Lincoln's.

"Brooke, I'm sorry. Was I supposed to just leave him down there? Not tell my mom the truth about her son? If you were in her shoes and it had been Danny, wouldn't you want him back in whatever shape you could get him?"

"Low blow, Lucas."

His heart hurt at the tone of her voice. "I need you to understand why I did what I did."

"And what if I said that I didn't want Danny to know. That I don't want him to meet Lincoln?"

Lucas paused. That was something he hadn't considered. For some reason, he'd just assumed that the next logical step was having the two of them meet. "I don't know how we can keep that from happening."

"It can happen if you step back out of our lives as easily as you stepped into them."

"No." The word came out harshly, but Lucas just couldn't allow that to happen. "You wouldn't do that to Danny." *And please don't do that to me.*

He heard Brooke sigh and the band that had been tightening around his chest eased slightly.

"No, I wouldn't. You've made good and sure he would object to us not having anything more to do with you."

At that point, it sounded like she didn't care one way or the other for herself, and that pained Lucas more than he cared to admit. "That wasn't my intention. I didn't know how this was going to play out. He's my brother, Brooke. I love him. I love my mom. And, believe it or not, I love Danny, too. I'm not doing this to hurt him."

"I know." These words were whispered and heavy with emotion. Another deep breath. "I'm just worried about my son."

"You've raised a fine boy, Brooke. I think he'll be able to take this in stride. We'll all still be there for him."

"I suppose you're going to want this to happen sooner rather than later?"

"Time isn't going to change anything at this point. I'd like to bring Lincoln up there tomorrow. I'm taking him to see our doctor in the morning, and then we'll come afterward."

"So soon?"

"My mom needs to see him. Lindsay is telling her right now."

"What does Lincoln think of all this?"

"He was confused when he first saw me, even though Than had talked to him a bit about it."

"What was he doing down there?"

"Working in a bar. Hanging out at the beach."

"And no one realized who he was?"

"He was in a different part of the area than where they'd been focused on searching. That's how Than found him. Looking in the impossible places."

"Lucas, I am glad for your sake and your mom and Lindsay's, too, that he's okay. It's just a...surprise. I had never imagined having to deal with him again when he didn't respond to my letter. Then you showed up and said he was dead. This is a bit of a shock for me, and I'm not entirely sure how I feel about it."

That wasn't really what Lucas wanted to hear. He wanted her to say she didn't care one way or the other about Lincoln. It had been the main reason he had held back from pursuing anything with her and though it wasn't easy, he was glad now he had. One less complication for them to have to deal with.

"Will you talk to Danny before we come or would you rather wait until I get there?"

Brooke sighed. "I'll tell him tonight. I think he'll need a little time to adjust, but I don't want to interrupt his fun right now."

"Just tell Lindsay and Mom that you're going to wait."

"My family was going to come out tomorrow, too. Should I ask them to not come now?"

"I think they should still come. Be a support for you and Danny. There is plenty of room out there—as you've seen. If your mom wants to bring some groceries so they don't have to go to the main house to eat for each meal, that would be fine. Both the cabin for them and the one for Eric and Staci have a complete kitchen."

"Of course they do. Along with their marble countertops."

Lucas was glad to hear the trace of humor in Brooke's voice. "Yes, but a cheaper kind."

She chuckled and then sighed. "So you're going to be out here tomorrow afternoon, huh?"

"Probably around supper time, depending how things go with our appointments in the morning."

"Okay. I'm sure Stella will have a big spread for everyone. My family is supposed to arrive mid-afternoon."

"If you need anything, just give me a call. I might not be able to answer if I'm in an appointment, but I'll call you as soon as I can."

"Still taking care of everything for everybody?"

Lucas paused then said, "That's my job."

"Well, some of us would rather not be viewed as a job." She said the words softly, and left Lucas wondering exactly what she meant. "Anyway, drive safely. We look forward to seeing you tomorrow."

Before Lucas could respond, the line went dead. He lowered the phone from his ear and stared at it. What a mess.

"Woman troubles?"

Lucas looked up as Than settled into the leather seat across from him. "Women. Family. Business. It's always something."

"But the women ones are always the most challenging."

"They really haven't been up until now."

Than lifted a dark brow. "Miss Brooke got to ya, huh?"

"Yeah, I guess you could say that, but he got to her first." Lucas looked to where his brother sat still slumped to the side in sleep. "And now I'm bringing him back to her."

"Won't matter. He is her past, and it's a past they don't even share anymore since he can't remember it. Brooke needs someone like you."

"I think she'd probably sock you for saying that."

"Wouldn't be the first time."

Lucas stared at Than. "She's punched you?"

The other man shrugged, an amused look on his face. "Let's just say she didn't appreciate my flirting. We came to an understanding after that."

"Well, all I know is that if she liked a guy like Lincoln, she'll find me incredibly boring."

"Hey, at least you know she likes your looks."

Maybe he'd give Than a punch to go with the one Brooke had apparently given him once upon a time.

Correctly interpreting his expression, Than jerked his chin up and grinned. "Go for it."

Lucas chuckled and settled back into his seat. He let out a long sigh. "No. I owe you one for finding Linc." He gave Than a serious look. "And I mean that. I don't think I'll ever be able to repay you for your help."

Than lifted one shoulder in a half-shrug. "Just doing my job."

The look they shared told Lucas that it had been more than that to the man, but he didn't press the issue.

"Will you need me once we land?" Than asked.

"I don't think so. We've just got to get through customs and then back to the house. I'm hoping that it's not too soon to take him up to the cabin, but it was his favorite of all the properties we own. I'm hoping—perhaps in vain—that something there might jog his memory."

"I hope it works out for you guys."

He heard the skepticism in Than's voice and felt it himself, but he had to hold onto something at this point. Anything.

But by the next afternoon, Lucas didn't have as much hope as he'd had the day before. In times like this, he was doubly glad for his wealth. It had meant being able to afford the immediate attention of their doctor and the tests that Lincoln had needed. The initial results of the scans and x-rays had supported what they already knew.

Although the good news was that Lincoln's brain scans hadn't shown any permanent damage, there was no explanation for his continued memory loss. The doctor thought it was likely a combination of the initial physical impact on the brain in the accident and also the shock of everything.

X-rays had revealed his leg had been broken in two places and had healed badly. The only possible solution was to re-break the bones and set them properly. For now they were going to leave that.

One unexpected wrinkle in everything had been Lincoln's insistence that Than stay close by. In some ways, it reminded Lucas of imprinting. Than had been the first person to connect him with his missing past, so Lincoln had somehow formed a bond with him. Than had stayed at the mansion the night before and had accompanied them on their morning round of appointments.

And now Lincoln was riding in Than's car as he followed Lucas to the cabin. He'd been grateful that the other man had been willing to come along with them. It was a weird position to be in given that he didn't really know Than all that well. But Eric would be out at the island, too, so at least Than wasn't going to be surrounded by strangers. Not that that would have bothered the man. Lucas was pretty sure Than had never met a stranger.

Once everything had settled down the night before, he'd been able to call his mom. It had been an emotional conversation, as he'd known it would be. But at least with her there had been no complexities. She was glad her son was back and that he was safe. End of story.

Halfway through the four hour trip to the cabin, Lucas hit the button on the Bluetooth to call Brooke. After such a draining day, he'd decided not to call her again the night before, but he knew he needed to touch base before he got there to find out how things had gone with Danny. Lindsay had said she thought it had gone fine, but he wanted Brooke's opinion—as Danny's mother.

"Hey," she said when she answered.

"How's it going?"

"As well as could be expected. Lots of questions."

"I can imagine. I think we all have lots of questions." Lucas looked in his rear view mirror at Than's car. "What's his biggest concern?"

Brooke didn't answer right away but then said, "He's worried that he might not like Lincoln as much as he likes you."

The breath squeezed from Lucas's lungs, and he found himself fighting moisture in his eyes. The tightness in his throat kept him from being able to answer right away.

"Lucas?"

"Yeah." His response was gruff with emotion. He hadn't expected her to say that. For Danny to feel that way about him.

"I told him that you can't always control how you feel about a person." She paused. "And that none of us expect him to force feelings for Lincoln. I told him that all I expect from him is that he be respectful and spend some time with him. If that's what Lincoln wants."

Still trying to get his emotions back under control, Lucas cleared his throat. "I agree. I don't want to force Danny to spend time with him if he's not ready for it. I talked to Lincoln about him last night. Showed him pictures of the two of you."

"What was his reaction?"

"Nothing, really. I'm having a hard time getting a read on him. Lincoln used to just put it all out there."

"Yeah, I remember that about him."

Not wanting to dwell on Brooke's memories of Lincoln, Lucas said, "He is just not showing any emotion at all. I talked to him about Mom and Lindsay, too. The only thing he's had any sort of strong feeling about is Than."

"Than? What in the world does he have to do with this?"

"I think Lincoln kinda sees him as his best friend. They spent a few days together before I got down there. I think he has some kind of bond with him now. So, just a heads up that Than's coming up to the cabin, too."

"Oh, man." Brooke groaned but then said, "Hey, has he met Lindsay before?"

Lucas laughed at the question. "No. He hasn't."

"Ah. Fresh meat. At least I won't have to worry about him."

"You wouldn't have had to worry about him anyway."

Silence. "I wouldn't have? Why is that?"

"I just told him you weren't interested in him."

"He already knew that and it's never stopped him before."

Realizing that he was quickly moving into a position where he'd have to reveal more than he could right then about how he felt, Lucas tried to redirect things. "Yeah, he mentioned that you punched him."

"He deserved it." The line went quiet for a moment and then Lucas heard muffled conversation. "I gotta go. The boat just got here with my folks and the rest. How long until you arrive?"

Lucas let out a sigh of relief. He had to be more careful about his conversation for now. "Probably another hour or so."

"Okay. We'll see you when you get here."

Feeling a little more relaxed after his talk with Brooke, Lucas turned on some of his favorite worship music and tried to just zone out for the remainder of the trip. There were plenty of stress and emotional moments to come so he was going to try to chill while he could.

Brooke listened as the boat's engine faded into the distance. From what she remembered of the length of the trip from the mainland to the island when they'd arrived, the guys should be there in about half an hour. Nerves were alive and well in her stomach as she stood on the front porch of the cabin where she was staying with her parents, Tori, and Alicia.

She settled down on the top step of the porch and watched Danny and his friend down at water's edge not too far from the cabin. They had spent hardly any time in the cabins since arriving. She was so pleased that he was enjoying himself and knew it had been a good idea to bring his buddy along, too.

He'd taken the news about Lincoln relatively well. However, Brooke didn't have a lot of experience in how boys were supposed to act when the father they'd been told was dead was actually alive. No doubt coming face to face with him would be the true test of how well he was doing.

After talking a bit with Lindsay, they'd decided that it would be best if Brooke and her family stayed at their cabins while Lincoln met with his mom. Depending on how that went, next would be Brooke and Danny, and then they'd all gather at the main cabin for the supper Stella had prepared for them.

"You doing okay, darlin'?"

Looking up, she saw her mom standing next to her. She turned her gaze back to Danny and Jeff as her mom sat down beside her.

"Yes. I'll just be glad to get this part over with. Then we can move on from it."

"We're praying for all of you. I'm sure it's not easy for anyone involved."

"Thanks." For once, Brooke found herself willing to accept their prayers. "I get the feeling that if Danny and I weren't involved, this would be a more positive event. But because of our previous relationship—or lack thereof—with Lincoln, it's made it all a little more confusing."

"And there are other emotions involved, too." Her mom gave her a knowing look.

Rather than trying to deny it, Brook just said, "Yeah."

She felt an arm go around her shoulders. After a moment's hesitation, Brooke laid her head against her mom.

"Trust God that if the two of you are to be together, it will work out. I'm not saying it will be easy, but it will be worth it."

"And was Dad worth it?" It was a question she'd pondered a lot over the years. Truly, the man he was now—if she hadn't experienced what she had as a result of his behavior—was a man to be liked, if not admired. She didn't really like to admit it, but he had become a good husband and was a good father to his kids—when they'd let him be.

"Yes. He is. Your father has changed a lot since we were in Africa. You kids really only saw one side of him."

Brooke glanced over to see her mom gazing out toward the water. "And we didn't see that much of that one side either. He was always pretty busy."

"That's true. He was a very proud man when we went to Africa. He took great pride in the fact that we were going to do the Lord's work and were willing to make the sacrifices involved." Her mom sighed. "He came back from Africa a broken man. That's what happens when you think you're immune to the weaknesses other people have. He didn't guard himself against his own desires. Didn't think he had to."

The man her mom was describing didn't sound much like the man she knew now.

"Did I love your father through all of that? I can't say that I did. In fact, I came close to hating him for what he did to me. To you children. To the babies. It took time to build up that trust and love again. I can't say we rebuilt our marriage because after everything was torn down in Africa, there was nothing left. The foundation we'd built on up to that moment had been made of pride. So we had to build it up from nothing. But that second time around we made sure God was a part of the foundation we were building in a way we hadn't the first time. Your dad understood that even though he'd said he was sorry and I'd forgiven him it was still going to take time to heal those wounds."

"And you had to deal with being pregnant on top of it all."

"Yes. Sometimes I look back and marvel that I made it through, but when you're in the midst of the fight, you're just looking to make it from one day to the next. If I'd known then how long and hard the battle would be, I probably would have walked away. But thankfully, God kept that knowledge from me and instead gave me the strength to get through one day at a time."

Though on a lesser emotional level than her mother's experience, Brooke knew what it was like to just try to make it one day at a time. Being a single mother, she had struggled to provide the best she could for Danny. Sometimes that had been incredibly hard. When she'd wanted to be a mother to her many children, she had imagined she'd be staying home with them, baking cookies and having only to focus her love and attention on them without worrying about money. Her husband would have taken care of all that. She'd been so naïve.

She felt her mom stroke her hair. "There's only one thing keeping him from finally closing the door on all that happened back then."

Brooke glanced at her mom, aware that that one thing was her inability to forgive her father. "But didn't Alicia's appearance open it all up again?"

"No, sweetie. Alicia is an innocent in all of this. Though we didn't seek out information on Sherry and what happened with her after we left Africa, we always knew it was a possibility. Slight, but it was there."

"Have you guys ever thought of buying a lottery ticket?" Brooke asked as she pulled her legs up and wrapped her arms around them.

"What?"

"I mean, the chances of two people in one family being born with dwarfism were slim to none and yet we have Victoria and Sarah. And then the slim possibility that Sherry would get pregnant and yet there's Alicia. Our family seems to defy the odds. We might win a few million if we bought a ticket."

Her mom chuckled. "Well, as far as I'm concerned, I've already won the lottery with all you kids and your dad."

When the sound of a distant motor reached Brooke, she straightened and looked toward the far side of the island though she couldn't see anything through the trees. She felt a touch on her arm and turned toward her mom.

CHAPTER SEVENTEEN

ONE more thing, sweetheart." Her mom laid a hand on the side of her face and gave her a gentle smile, her blue eyes soft with love. "You will never have room in your heart to fully experience love as long as there are things you haven't forgiven. Those things will always have a corner of your heart that you could be giving to those in your life who love you."

Could she forgive her dad? Could she forgive Lincoln? More importantly, could she let go of the anger she felt toward God?

"I think for the first time in a long time—maybe ever—a man has touched your heart. I would hate to think that because of the unforgiveness you hold there that you're not able to fully love or be loved." She smiled again. "Just think about it."

Brooke was sure she'd be thinking of nothing else over the next little while as the two men who'd hurt her most were now on the same island. In thinking of Lincoln, she realized that he wouldn't understand how she felt because he didn't remember what he'd done to her and Danny. Truly, forgiving him would only be for her sake not his.

The boat motor suddenly shut off, and silence flooded the island. Brooke saw Danny look toward where she sat. He was aware of what the boat's arrival signaled. His father was there.

"Can I pray for you, sweetheart?"

Brooke knew that her mom's question wasn't asking if she could pray for her later in the privacy of her room. She wanted to pray for her right there, right then. Brooke nodded.

Gathering her close once more, her mom rested her cheek on Brooke's head. "Father, we come to you right now asking for peace and wisdom for the situation that's unfolding around us. Two people that I love dearly..." Her mom paused and Brooke heard her swallow before continuing. "Two people that I love dearly are being affected. Protect them from hurt, I pray. Give Danny peace as he meets his father for the first time and help him to be able to accept and deal with all the emotions that will come with that meeting. And for Brookie, I pray that you give her strength to do what she needs to do with regards to Lincoln. And finally, I pray for Lucas. So much responsibility is falling on his shoulders. Give him strength to handle it all and to trust You with what he may also be feeling in his heart. We know that You are in control of all this and believe You will work out if we will only trust You. In Jesus's name. Amen."

Brooke wasn't sure what was contributing to the softening of her heart. In the past, she'd rejected any attempts by her parents to draw her into spiritual things. Maybe it was watching Danny embrace it so readily. Maybe it was meeting Lucas and seeing how his faith fit into his life. Or maybe it was just looking at the incredible complexity of their current situation and knowing that they weren't going to be able to get through it all on their own. Whatever it was, for the first time in her adult life, Brooke was searching for the peace that had eluded her for so long.

Her mom had a peace that surpassed any situation they faced. Brooke, on the other hand, only knew peace when things were going exactly as she wanted. She needed that to change.

"Brooke?"

Brooke straightened from her mother's embrace, and they both turned to see Lucas standing at the corner of the porch. She drank in the sight of him. Dressed in jeans and a T-shirt, the most casual she'd seen him yet aside from the swimsuit he'd worn to swim with Danny, she could see the signs of strain on his face.

"I'll just go back inside," her mom said as she patted her on the knee and then stood.

Once her mom had gone into the cabin, Lucas walked to where Brooke sat and then turned toward Danny and Jeff. Brooke wanted so badly to go to him, wrap her arms around his waist and lean on his strength and offer him her own. But she didn't have that right. It wasn't her place to draw on that strength, particularly when so many others needed it more than she did.

"How's he doing?" Lucas asked as he settled on the porch step beside her. Leaning forward, he rested his elbows on his knees, interlacing his fingers.

"He's nervous. But I've tried to keep him and Jeff busy with stuff so he didn't think too much about it." She looked at Lucas's profile, again pulled to him in a way she'd never been to a man in the past. Right then, with everything going on, it was the scariest thing ever. "How are you doing?"

He glanced over at her, and their gazes held for a few seconds before he looked back out to the water. "I'm tired. It's been a long few days."

"I meant about Lincoln."

Lucas bent his head. "Yeah, I know what you meant. It was just easier to answer the other way."

"How was your mom doing when she saw him?"

"Over the moon. It doesn't matter to her that he doesn't remember her. She'll take him any way she can get him. Impaired memory is better than dead in her mind."

Brooke found her gaze going to Danny. "Yeah. I understand that."

"And I'm not sure how Lindsay's doing. I think she's wavering between being happy to see him and wanting to vent the anger she's held toward him since hearing about the plane crash."

"She was angry with him?"

"That's Lindsay's go-to emotion when the alternative is a weaker one. And yes, she was angry that his thrill-seeking had led to his death."

Brooke understood the anger Lindsay must be feeling. It was an emotion that had filled her life on more than one occasion. But right then, the anger she'd been harboring for so very long was slowly dissolving away. It was like a castle on the beach that was eroded by the relentless waves that kept dragging more and more of it out to the ocean to disappear.

"Did you want to talk to Danny before he meets Lincoln?"

"Yeah." He stood up and turned to face her. "Do you mind if I talk to him alone first?"

"Sure. Just send Jeff up to me."

Brooke watched Lucas make his way down to where Danny and Jeff played. The boys had stopped to watch as he approached. Lucas held out his hand to Jeff and after shaking it, the boy darted up the path toward Brooke.

"Do you want to play on your tablet for a bit?" Brooke asked him when he reached her.

"Sure." He climbed up the steps and disappeared into the cabin. Brooke knew that her mom would take care of him until all of this was done for Danny.

Her breath caught in her throat as she watched Danny and Lucas stand side by side at the water's edge. Then Lucas lowered himself on a large boulder and put a hand on Danny's shoulder. Eye to eye now, they continued to talk.

Then Danny threw himself at Lucas and without a moment's hesitation, the man embraced him and held him close.

Brooke didn't bother to try to stop the tears that flooded her eyes and overflowed onto her cheeks. She'd told herself that for so long it had just been her and Danny and they were fine, but here was a man that was everything they both needed. However, Brooke wasn't sure they could ever fit into his life—even if he wanted them to. As nephew and mother of nephew sure, but as anything more? Brooke wasn't sure that would work, especially now with Lincoln back.

When Danny finally stepped back from Lucas, they talked for another minute or so before heading in her direction. Brooke quickly swiped her fingers over her cheeks to make sure any tears were gone. She stood as they got close, brushing off the back of the jean capris she wore.

"Ready to go?" Lucas asked as they came to the bottom of the stairs.

No! was what Brooke wanted to say, but instead she nodded. Putting it off wouldn't change the outcome. When she stepped off the bottom step, she reached for Danny's hand. Together they followed Lucas along the path that led from the guest cabin to the main one.

Danny's grip on her hand tightened as they climbed the large stone steps to the huge porch and approached the front door.

Lucas reached out to the door handle then looked over at them. "Let's do this?"

Brooke glanced down at Danny and their gazes met. "Ready?"

Danny looked back to Lucas. "Let's do this."

Lucas had tried not to have any preconceived ideas about how this meeting between Brooke, Danny and Lincoln would go, but he was taken totally off-guard when Lincoln looked right at Brooke and said her name.

Of all the people his brother had to remember, it had to be her?

Brooke shot Lucas a startled look but all he could do was shrug. Lincoln got up and made his way toward them, the limp in his right leg very pronounced. Lucas turned his gaze to Danny. The boy almost looked like he wanted to hide behind Brooke but was doing everything in his ten-year-old power to stand his ground.

"Brooke?" This time her name came out as a question.

"Yes."

"You're as pretty as Than said."

Relief flooded Lucas. He hadn't remembered her. He shot Than a look. The guy needed to keep his yap shut. Than just gave him a grin that told him he didn't really care what Lucas thought.

"And you must be Danny."

Lucas pulled his attention back to the matter at hand. He saw Danny nod and look quickly in his direction, but he didn't say anything. Though he had positioned himself a distance from Danny and Brooke, he saw his brother's gaze go from Danny to Brooke and then to him. He may not have his memory, but clearly Lincoln could still read body language fairly well.

It was all Lucas could do to not go stand with the two of them and wrap his arms around them. But right then the situation needed fewer complexities, not more.

"So, Lucas tells me you like to ride bikes and swim."

Lucas looked over to where his mother sat. She was absolutely beaming as she watched the interaction between her son and grandson. But when he glanced at Lindsay, she wore a far more reserved expression. She had her arms crossed as she sat on the arm of the chair beside their mom.

"Yes. I do." Danny answered him this time, drawing Lucas's gaze back to him.

"They say I liked to do that, too." Lincoln smiled at Danny as he thumped his leg. "But something tells me that the bike riding, at least, will be more difficult than it used to be."

Danny shuffled his feet, not staying completely plastered to Brooke's side. Clearly, he was relaxing a little. Though

Lincoln had had no interest in being a father before, losing his memory of what had prompted that decision had apparently meant he was willing to give it a whirl now.

Lucas just hoped that Danny didn't happen to pay the price for that in the future. Especially if Lincoln's memory did come back. However remote that possibility might be, Lucas didn't completely dismiss it. After all, Lincoln had been dead and yet here he was.

The bigger question in Lucas's mind at that point was if Lincoln would feel that he should also try to build a relationship with Brooke again. And as difficult as it was to watch him with Danny, the thought of him turning his attention to Brooke made Lucas sick. Because in spite of everything he'd told himself ever since the doubts had been raised about Lincoln's death, Lucas couldn't deny that he'd fallen hard for the mother of his brother's child.

"Why don't we go ahead and eat," Lindsay suggested as she stood.

Lucas glanced at Brooke and could see an uncertainty in her gaze. For the first time since he'd met her, she looked lost. Maybe having her family around would help with that. He was finding it incredibly frustrating to not be able to offer her support the way he wanted to.

"Brooke." When Brooke looked at Lindsay, she said, "Do you want to let your family know that we're going to eat?"

Brooke nodded as she pulled her phone from her pocket. She let go of Danny's hand but didn't move away from him as she tapped out a quick message. Her phone chirped a reply right away. "They'll be here in a few minutes."

An awkward silence fell over the room, but then Than said, "Hey, Lindsay, are you busy next Friday night?"

Lucas almost laughed at the annoyed look that momentarily passed across his sister's face, but it did help to break the tension in the room. He even caught a glimpse of a smile on Brooke's face.

Too bad that Than had *no* idea of who he was messing with.

Lindsay looked his way before tilting her head and turning her gaze back to Than. Lucas tried to feel sorry for the guy, but just couldn't dredge it up.

"Why yes, Than—what kind of name is that, by the way?"

Than had leaned forward in his seat. "It's short for Nathaniel."

Lindsay moved in his direction. "I actually prefer Nathaniel. Is it okay if I call you that?"

Than actually shot him a somewhat concerned look at that point. Now it was Lucas's turn to just shrug and grin.

"Uh, sure. Though usually the only one who calls me Nathaniel is my mom when I'm in trouble."

"Oh, well something tells me you are trouble with a capital T." Lindsay settled on the couch next to him. "So I'm assuming that since you're wondering if I'm busy, you'd like to make some plans with me."

"I was, uh, thinking about it."

"Time for thinking ended when you asked me if I was busy." Lindsay reached out and tapped the tip of his nose while she batted her eyelashes. "Pick me up at six and take me someplace nice. And by nice, I mean someplace you need to be wearing a tie to get through the door."

Lucas managed to turn his laugh into a cough, but he knew that Than could see the humor in his eyes when he looked at him. In all the stress of the return trip with Lincoln and the appointments that morning, he hadn't had a chance to warn Than about Lindsay. But then again, maybe it would be a good experience for the guy. Get a little bit of what he gave out.

Voices drifted through the open window, drawing the attention from Lindsay and Than. Lucas went and opened the door for Brooke's family. Immediately, he could see the concern on her parents' faces. He wished he could ease it, but only Brooke would be able to do that for them.

After quick introductions had been made, Lucas led them in prayer before they filed into the large dining room where food had been laid out for their evening meal. Stella had outdone herself once again in pulling together a spread like this for so many people. Once people had their plates filled, they began to find seats.

As Lucas watched, Lincoln followed Brooke, Danny and Jeff outside. Lindsay also went out onto the deck with Than right behind her.

"How're you doing, Lucas?"

He glanced over to see Eric standing beside him with a plate full of food. "I'm fine. How are you? Enjoying married life?"

Eric grinned. "That goes without saying. It was a long time coming, but worth every second of waiting."

Lucas was genuinely happy for Eric and Staci. From what he'd heard, their road to marriage had been rocky and uncertain.

"Why don't you grab a plate of food and join us?" Eric suggested.

With a nod, Lucas went into the nearly empty dining room and picked up a plate. His mom and Brooke's parents had settled at the table in the nook on the other side of the kitchen. Brooke's two sisters and her niece also joined them. In the end, he, Eric and Staci found space at the table in the dining room to sit and eat.

"I know you said you're fine," Eric began, "But seriously, how are you doing with this whole turn of events? I couldn't believe it when Alex told me what was going on."

"It's been a bit crazy, that's for sure," Lucas said. "To be honest, I'm just trying to make sure everyone gets through this with the least amount of emotional upheaval." He gave Eric an apologetic look. "I'm afraid your sister is bearing the brunt of this because of Danny."

Eric nodded. "But Brooke's strong. And Danny's got a good head on his shoulders. I think they'll be fine."

"I'm praying they will be. The last thing I wanted to do was to disrupt their lives so much." Lucas pushed the potato salad around on his plate. "If I'd had any inkling..."

"It's hard not to wish you had done things differently," Staci said. "I know all about that. After meeting Eric at that singles retreat all I could think about was how I wished I'd made a different decision. Once he'd found out about Sarah and things were really rocky there for a while, I spent a lot of time wishing that I hadn't gone to that retreat. But you know, God obviously had a plan for us. It took us a little while to get with the program, but in the end, it was worth it."

"I hope that will be the case for Brooke and Danny. Too bad it took Lincoln losing his memory before he'd agree to meet Danny. He should have stepped up long ago."

"Speaking from experience, I can say that Sarah was better off without me in her life for those early years," Eric said, sadness on his face. "I wasn't in any position to be a good father to her and might, in fact, have done more damage than good. Staci did better on her own than we would likely have done together."

"It's possible that Lincoln wouldn't have been a good father to Danny back then either. Maybe this memory loss is a blessing in disguise."

For Danny maybe, but it was breaking Lucas's heart. His gaze went to the large windows that looked out over the deck and the group gathered at the table there. He had wanted to be a part of Brooke's life in a more intimate and permanent way, but now that seemed a remote possibility. This was not a girl he had wanted to put to the "Lincoln" test.

Sadness filled him and robbed him of his appetite, but he forced himself to smile. "I think it might take a little while, but in the end I do think this will be good for Danny and Lincoln. My brother wasn't a bad guy even before his memory loss, he was just more focused on the next adventure than on anything that might tie him down."

He saw Eric and Staci exchange glances then Eric said, his voice low, "Don't give up on Brooke. You're the first man I've seen get this close to her."

"I only want what's best for her," Lucas said.

Before Eric could say anything more, Than came in with Danny and Jeff. As soon as he spotted them at the table, he settled in a chair beside Eric while the boys went back for seconds.

He pinned Lucas with a look. "Seriously? You couldn't have warned me about Lindsay?"

Lucas gave a shake of his head. "You asked for it, buddy. If you weren't so keen on wooing everything in a skirt, you wouldn't be in this predicament."

Than leaned forward, bracing his arms on the table and said, "Do I need to be wearing any sort of protective armor when I take her out? I mean, is she likely to try and emasculate me?"

"Only if you get out of line," Lucas said with a grin, glad to be able to focus on something else again.

"Well, that's certainly not going to happen. Not that it would have even without the threat." Than leaned toward Eric. "And I thought *your* sister was tough."

As people filtered back into the cabin, Lucas spotted Brooke with a stack of plates headed to the kitchen. She didn't even look in his direction.

"So, we have a couple hours of daylight left," Lindsay said as she came out of the kitchen. "What do you say we fire up the Jet Skis?"

Lucas sat listening as pretty much everyone got on board with the plan. Again, though he hadn't really had a picture of how things would unfold, for some reason he hadn't seen this. Danny seemed anxious to move past the emotions involved with meeting his father. Lucas couldn't really blame him, but it was as if Lincoln had never been gone. Never been declared dead. Was he the only one struggling with it all?

"Are you sure you're up to it?" his mom asked as she touched Lincoln's arm. At one time she would have slid her arm around his waist, so maybe things weren't completely back to normal.

"I think it will be good. Get back to the things I'm told I used to do."

As soon as it was agreed on, everyone planning to participate scattered to get ready. Though Lucas wasn't really in the mood, he knew he needed to be there since he and Lindsay were the only ones with experience to run the machines.

Once everyone got down to the boathouse and dock, Lucas quickly realized that Brooke wasn't among those prepared to participate.

"Where's your mom?" he asked when he spotted Danny.

"She said she might come down later."

Not what Lucas wanted to hear, but it was probably for the best. With Lindsay's help, he pulled out the life jackets and found enough for everyone to wear. Their Jet Skis were top of the line three seaters so that they could pull waters skiers or tubes behind them.

"You boys both know how to swim, right?" Lucas asked as they prepared to take them out on the first run.

Danny and Jeff nodded enthusiastically, big grins on their faces.

"Okay, Linds and I each need a spotter on the back as well."

In the end, Than went with Lindsay while Lincoln went with Lucas. Alicia and Victoria settled into the chairs on the dock with Staci and Sarah to wait their turns.

"You head to the north, Linds," Lucas called out as he began to bring the Jet Ski up to speed. Danny and Jeff were on the tube behind him while Eric was on the one behind Lindsay and Than. Mindful that it was the first time for both boys, he took it easy. They spent about fifteen minutes out in the open water beyond the island before heading back to allow the others to have a turn.

Over the next hour or so, they continued to switch off people on the tubes while Lucas and Lindsay did most of the driving. Eric tried his hand at it and once he'd driven a couple of times, he managed to get Staci on the Jet Ski with him and put Sarah in the front. Lucas sank down on the end of the dock to watch.

"You guys look like you're having fun."

His heart jumped at the sound of Brooke's voice. He glanced over his shoulder to see her standing next to where Alicia and Tori were sitting. She still wore what she'd had on at supper so clearly had no plan to join in on the Jet Ski fun. Once again, it didn't escape Lucas's notice that she didn't look in his direction.

It was for the best.

Unfortunately, no matter how many times he told himself that, it didn't make him feel any better.

CHAPTER EIGHTEEN

BROOKE wasn't sure it had been the best idea to come down to the dock. The past few hours had left her feeling like she'd been through an emotional wringer. All she'd really wanted to do was crawl into bed and go to sleep. Maybe in the morning things would have been better. But she knew that wouldn't have been the case.

Seeing Lincoln had been difficult. Not because it had brought up old feelings—there were none of those left—but seeing the physically broken man he'd become was hard. It was probably a blessing that he had no memory of the man he'd once been. That Lincoln would have not been able to accept the limitations an injury like he had would have put on him. Thankfully, this Lincoln without any memories seemed interested in building some sort of relationship with his son.

Brooke knew it was probably wrong of her, but she really did hope that his memory never returned. Who knew what would happen if he remembered all the reasons he'd decided not to be part of Danny's life and then walked out once again.

That would be devastating for Danny and not something she could protect him from.

Worst of all though, had been the way Lucas had pulled back from her and Danny. After promising to be there for them, he'd stepped away and left them alone to deal with Lincoln. As soon as they'd walked into the house, as soon as they'd come into Lincoln's presence, he'd left them. Just like every other man, he'd abandoned her when she had needed—wanted—his support.

"You don't want to go for a ride?" Victoria asked. Her damp hair and suit made it clear she'd been at least once. "It's more fun than I thought it might be."

"Not tonight," Brooke said, grateful to have her thoughts pulled from the direction they'd been going in. "I'm sure there will be other opportunities while we're out here."

She glanced to where Lucas sat on the end of the dock. His hair was dark with moisture and stood in spikes on his head. He had his hands braced on either side of him as he stared out to where the Jet Skis were on the lake. Before today, she might have gone and sat beside him. Flirted with him a little. But now... He'd distanced himself from both her and Danny when they'd gone in to meet Lincoln and had remained that way through dinner. If that was how he wanted to play it, she could do that. She could take a hint.

When the ache in her heart threatened to overwhelm her, she looked away from him to the sparkling blue of the water. She lifted a hand to shade her eyes as she looked for Danny and Jeff. Given all he'd had to deal with too, she was glad to see him having fun.

"Here, Brooke, have a seat," Than said, getting up from where he'd been sitting next to Alicia.

"Very gentlemanly of you, Than, but I think I'm going to head back up to the cabin. I just wanted to see how Danny was getting along."

"The boys are doing great," Than said. "I think they're going to be asking to go out at every opportunity."

"Tori, can you send them to me when it's finished up here?"

"Sure thing," her sister said, a concerned look on her face. But thankfully, she didn't say anything further.

With one last look at the back of Lucas, Brooke turned and headed up the steps and the path that led to the cabin. Though she knew she shouldn't feel hurt, she did. He'd told her if she ever needed anything, to let him know. Well, right then she needed his strength. His support. His...*love*. But it was clear that first and foremost, his loyalties lay with his family.

As she reached the top of the path where it split off to the different cabins, she looked back at the dock. Lucas was standing now, hands on his hips. He was facing her direction, but was he looking at her?

It doesn't matter.

That's what Brooke told herself as she turned back to the path. Clearly now that Lincoln had returned, the whole dynamic had changed. Lucas's role in Danny's life had shifted. And apparently it had shifted in hers, too.

Did he think that Lincoln's return had brought back old feelings she'd had for him? Because if that was the case, nothing could be further from the truth. Lincoln had never made her feel anything close to what she was feeling for Lucas. But maybe it was just too weird. If something serious had developed between them, he could have ended up being Danny's stepfather and uncle. It would be a clear reminder to people that she'd been with his brother first. And maybe that was just too weird for Lucas.

As she stepped into the cabin, her parents and Lucas's mom looked toward her from where they sat.

"How are they doing down there?" Sylvia asked.

Brooke tried her best to pull up a smile. "It looks like they're all having a lot of fun. Eric even had Staci and Sarah out on one of the Jet Skis."

"You didn't want to give it a go?"

She shook her head. "I think they're going to be calling it a day soon. I'll give it a try next time." Looking at her parents, she said, "I've got a bit of a headache. I'm going to go lie down. I asked Tori to send the boys to me when they're cleaned up."

With the extra visitors, they had shuffled around who was sleeping where and Brooke had ended up in the three bedroom cabin with her folks and Victoria and Alicia. The boys were up at the main cabin with Lucas's family, and Eric and Staci had the smaller two bedroom cabin with Sarah.

"There's some medicine in my bag at the cabin if you need it, sweetie," her mom said, concern clear on her face.

"Thanks, Mom."

As she left the main cabin, she could hear the roars of the Jet Skis along with the yells and shrieks. Any other time she would have joined in, but her heart just wasn't in it right then. Frankly, if she could have, she would have gotten in her car and left. She wasn't one to run from problems, but this one just promised to involve too much heartache if she stuck around.

But she'd stay. For Danny's sake. After all, his needs had always and would always come first.

Realizing that the excuse she'd given her mom had turned into a reality, Brooke went looking for the medicine before lying down in the room she'd claimed after giving her parents the larger master bedroom. Alicia and Tori would be sharing the other one.

Curled on her side, Brooke finally allowed the tears she'd been holding back to fall. They were tears of anger, frustration and hurt. Was this God's way of making sure that as long as she was at odds with Him she'd never find happiness? He'd let her have just the tiniest sample of what having a good, stable man in her life could be like and then had tossed his unpredictable, mess of a brother back into the mix.

Thanks a lot, God.

Lucas and Lindsay were the last ones to leave the boathouse and the dock. Once the sun had begun to sink, they'd put an end to the fun for the evening. The others had trudged back up to the main cabin while the two of them had put away the Jet Skis and all the life jackets.

"Well, that was fun," Lindsay said as they walked along the dock.

The solar lights on the edges of the dock and lining the path leading to the cabin were beginning to shine in the waning twilight.

"Yep, it seems like everyone enjoyed themselves."

"Except you," Lindsay pointed out. She laid a hand on his arm as they reached the spot where the dock ended and the path began. "I'm sorry."

"For what?" Lucas asked. "You haven't done anything."

"I know, but I'm sorry that things have gotten all messed up for you because of Lincoln's return."

"We need to focus on what's best for Lincoln and Danny right now," Lucas said, staring out across the lake behind Lindsay.

"For too long you've put aside what you want. And don't think for a minute that I didn't see how you were with Danny. And with Brooke."

"I was just doing what I could to make up for how Lincoln abandoned them. I needed to show her that our family wasn't all like that."

"You were already looking at Danny like he was your son." Lindsay's words were spoken softly, but they hit him in the gut like a punch.

"He's Lincoln's son, not mine."

"Lincoln will never be half the father to Danny that you would be. Danny needs you in his life." Lindsay sighed. "Lincoln might not have his memories but Danny does. He will always know that you stepped up when his own dad didn't. And I think he will always look to you for the stability he needs. I can see you backing out of his life. And Brooke's, too. Don't do it. They both need you."

"It's not that simple, Linds. I wish it was, but it's not."

"Actually, I think it is, but you're letting other things cloud your judgment. And I'm pretty sure you're not communicating with Brooke to find out how she's feeling in all of this."

"She's got her family here, she doesn't need me."

Lindsay gave a huff in clear frustration before turning toward the path. "Sometimes, you men are so stupid."

Her irritated words didn't make Lucas smile like they might have another time. He had been stupid. He'd allowed himself to fall too hard and too fast for a woman he had no right loving. The fact that she'd been Lincoln's girlfriend at one time should have been enough to warn him off. But no, he'd let himself feel things that he shouldn't have.

With a sigh, he followed Lindsay as she stomped up the path toward the cabin. It was relatively quiet when they walked in the door.

"Did you have fun?" his mom asked when she saw them.

Lindsay tossed him a look and kept on walking to the stairway. He saw his mom's gaze follow her daughter then she looked back at him, her brows drawn together. "You two fighting?"

"Just a difference of opinion. Nothing new. She'll get over it." He smiled at Brooke's parents. "I think everyone had fun. I'm sure we'll be out there a few more times before the weekend. You should join us."

"I just might," Brooke's dad said, but his wife was shaking her head. As was his mom.

"I've gotta go get changed," Lucas said. "See you in a bit."

He climbed the stairs to the second floor where all the bedrooms but the master were located. He met Danny and Jeff in the hallway. They'd already changed out of their swimsuits.

"Where you boys off to?" Lucas asked as they came to a stop in front of him.

"We're supposed to go say goodnight to Mom. She's at the other cabin lying down. Grandma said she had a headache."

Lucas frowned. "Is someone walking down there with you?"

"I think Grandma and Grandpa are going with us."

"Okay. But you're staying up here, right?"

"Yep. In that room," Danny said, pointing to the smallest of the rooms.

Of the four rooms on the second floor, only one had a larger bed and Lindsay had claimed that one. The other three rooms had single or bunk beds. The boys had one, he had another, and, thankfully, Than and Lincoln would share the fourth.

"Okay. I'll see you when you get back from your mom's."

Danny nodded and then the boys raced down the stairs as only ten-year-old boys could. As he watched them, Lucas felt incredibly old. And yet it brought back memories of when he and Lincoln had been that age. They, too, had raced down the stairs like Danny and his friend. And they'd spent hours exploring and playing on the island. He was the only one with those memories now.

Once inside his room, Lucas quickly changed out of his wet clothes into a pair of shorts and a T-shirt. He tried to keep his thoughts from going to Brooke and wondering if she really did have a headache or was just trying to avoid him.

Lucas sank down on the edge of the bed. Part of him wanted to plead a headache, too. He was so frustrated and angry with everything that had transpired over the past few days. And then he felt guilty for feeling that way. He should be glad his brother was back—even without his memory. But all he could think was that things had been going just fine until he'd showed back up. And the only person he had to blame for that was himself.

But then he would think about the look on his mom's face when she saw her son alive and well, and Lucas knew he'd done the right thing. Danny would adapt and Brooke would continue to be the great mom she'd been all along. And he would try to put aside the feelings that had developed and pray that at some point God would bring him the right woman.

After all, he had prayed about all of this, especially about finding Lincoln. He had to trust that God had a plan in place for each of them. The hardest part for him would be continuing to have Brooke in his life, but not in the role he'd begun to imagine for her.

He'd always laughed when people had talked about love at first sight or falling in love so quickly, but now he knew that it was possible. And he really wished he didn't.

"Did you guys have fun?" Relieved that the medication had taken the edge off her headache, Brooke listened as both boys began to excitedly recount their time on the water. She was glad to hear they'd had fun.

Danny hadn't said much about Lincoln, but it was a bit difficult with Jeff there. She hoped that sometime the next day she'd have time to talk with him. She did notice that most of the comments about their time with the Jet Skis included references to Lucas and not Lincoln.

When she saw Jeff try to stifle a yawn, Brooke said, "C'mon. Let me walk you back to the cabin. I think you guys need to go to bed. Tomorrow will be another day to do stuff."

They left Brooke's room and found the rest of her family gathered in the living room.

"I'm just going to run the boys back and get them into bed," Brooke said.

After Danny said goodnight to his grandparents, she followed the boys out to the path that led up to the main cabin. It seemed almost like being at a resort with the cabins and lighted paths. Too bad there was too much turmoil for her to truly enjoy it. If she'd known what was to come, she would have declined Lucas's invitation to the cabin.

Right then she really wanted to be in her own home. She wanted the privacy of her own room. The comfort of her own bed. But that wouldn't be for another few days. Although it had been the original plan to stay through to the following Tuesday, Brooke was already contemplating asking for a ride back with Eric and Staci when they went home on Sunday.

The boys took the steps up to the porch two at a time, but Brooke followed more slowly. By the time she walked into the cabin, they were already talking with Lucas's mom.

"You boys going to bed?" she asked them.

"Yep. Mom says we need our rest to do more stuff tomorrow."

Sylvia looked at her and smiled. "Like I said before, your mom is smart."

Brooke tried to return her smile but doubted it looked all that sincere. "Okay, guys. Say your goodnights."

It didn't take long for Danny to say goodnight to Lindsay and his grandmother. None of the others were in the room so they headed for the stairs.

"Can I say goodnight to Lucas, Mom?"

"Lucas?"

"Yep. And to thank him for today. I forgot to do that before."

"Okay. I'll just make sure your beds are ready for you."

She went into the room where they'd stayed since arriving two days earlier. As she waited for them to join her, Brooke picked up the clothes that lay in heaps on the floor. Then she straightened up their beds so that they could be tucked in properly.

Muffled voices got closer as she worked and she looked up in time to see the boys appear in the doorway with Lucas behind them.

She plastered a smile on her face. "Ready for bed?"

The boys nodded and went to their respective beds. Once they were lying down, Brooke went to each of them and tucked them in and kissed them. "If you need me for anything, just use Jeff's phone to call me."

"Or come get me," Lucas said from where he stood. "I'll make sure your mom knows you need her."

Brooke ran her hand over Danny's hair and bent to whisper, "Love you, sweetie."

"Love you, too, Mom." And then he looked toward the doorway. "Love you, too, Uncle Luc."

There was a pause then Brooke heard Lucas say, "I love you, too, buddy. Sleep well."

She closed her eyes briefly, fighting off a wave of emotion. "See you in the morning."

With one final kiss on his soft curls, Brooke stood and walked toward the doorway. She turned off the light as she left the room and pulled the door closed. There was a nightlight in the room she'd brought with her that gave them light if they needed to get up in the night.

She didn't want to look at Lucas. Didn't want to talk to him, but he grasped her arm as she walked past him.

"Can we talk?" His voice was low and rough.

She looked toward the large glass windows along the front wall of the cabin that ran from the main floor to the second floor ceiling. Darkness was rapidly settling over the island and while she'd enjoyed that the first couple of nights, tonight it didn't move her at all.

"What about?"

"Everything."

She couldn't keep from glancing at him. Her breath caught in her lungs at the emotion in his dark gray eyes. "I'm not sure we should."

"Please. Just for a few minutes. There are things we need to discuss."

Before he could respond, a door opened across the landing, and Than and Lincoln came out. Both men paused at the sight of them standing there, Lucas's hand still holding her arm.

"Everything okay?" Lincoln asked.

"Everything's fine," Lucas said, his words clipped.

"Why don't we go downstairs?" Than suggested.

Lincoln looked at Than then back at them before nodding. Brooke didn't realize she'd been holding her breath until they moved towards the stairs.

"Let's go to the dock," Lucas suggested. "Hopefully, we won't get interrupted there."

Brooke had imagined spending time on the dock in the moonlight with Lucas, but it hadn't been under these circumstances. "Okay."

He released her arm as she headed for the stairs that Than and Lincoln had just taken. As they passed through the living room, Lucas paused beside Lindsay and bent to say something to her. When she nodded, he followed Brooke out onto the porch.

"Watch your step," was all he said as they made their way along the path to the dock.

The nearly full moon glinted off the dark water, and Brooke wrapped her arms across her middle when a breeze from the lake swept over them. Unlike the heat of the city, it was relatively cool on the island at night. It truly was an idyllic life, and she could imagine spending time out there to paint, but she was feeling like maybe this would be her last trip to the Hamilton "resort."

"Danny said you had a headache earlier. Are you feeling better?" Lucas asked as they approached the end of the dock.

Brooke settled into one of the chairs that were still sitting out from earlier. "Yeah, I took some medication that helped."

"That's good." Lucas stood staring out at the lake, his hands shoved into the pockets of his shorts.

Brooke pulled her legs up and wrapped her arms around them. As she rested her chin on her knees, she let out a soft sigh. She would be enjoying this immensely if the events of the past few days had never occurred.

Lucas turned from the lake and sat down in the chair across from her. "I'm sorry for how all this has turned out."

"You're hardly to blame for what' s happened with Lincoln." Although she did blame him for pulling back when she and Danny had needed him. She knew he was in a difficult position, but it still hurt that he'd acted that way. For some reason, she hadn't expected that he would.

"No, but perhaps I could have handled it all differently. Although Danny seems to be taking it all in stride. Or am I imagining that?"

Brooke shrugged. "I'm not sure. I do know that he's not connecting to Lincoln the way he did with you. When we came upstairs tonight, it was you he wanted to say goodnight to, not Lincoln."

She heard Lucas's quick intake of breath.

"I thought maybe he'd already said goodnight to him."

"Nope. The problem is that no matter how this new Lincoln tries to work things with Danny, in the back of his mind is the knowledge that his dad chose to not be part of his life before. You, on the other hand, came to him as soon as you realized who he was. I'm not sure that Lincoln can do anything to make Danny forget that."

"So you don't think there's any hope for a relationship between them?"

"I think there will be something there, but I think it's too late for the father-son relationship that your mom might want them to have." Brooke sat back, resting her hands on the arms of the chair. "Does Lincoln even want a relationship with Danny? Or is he just trying because it seems that's what everyone around him wants?"

"Good question. I guess I never really asked him. When I told him about the life he'd forgotten, I just included you and Danny. Didn't really give him a choice."

"Well, maybe it's time you did. Have a heart to heart with him and find out what he really wants. Like I said though, I'm not sure he'll ever be able to have that close father-son relationship with Danny if that's what he's hoping for."

"I'm worried that he might make the effort now but if his memory comes back, he'd head out and leave Danny again. And maybe not even his memory but if parts of his old personality are still there, he might not want to hang around."

Brooke didn't know what to say to that. It had crossed her mind, but it was too late now. "Perhaps if you'd told me what was going on before it got to this point, we could have looked at some other options."

"What do you mean?"

"If you'd talked to me about this as soon as you heard that Lincoln was alive, I could have looked into getting some advice from a counselor on how to handle it with Danny. Maybe we could have used some professionals to help with the transitioning."

"You're saying I screwed up," Lucas said bluntly.

"I'm saying that you were so busy trying to handle this all on your own, you weren't able to look at it from all angles. You were so intent on taking responsibility for everything that you didn't think to ask those of us who are also involved what we might think about how it should be handled."

"I didn't want to say anything until I was sure."

"I get that," Brooke said. "I'm saying that once that call came that they'd found Lincoln, you needed to let me know. Instead, you took off determined to take care of it all by yourself. This involved my son and, for the record, *I'm* not your responsibility. And I'm the one who makes decisions for Danny. You trampled all over that."

When Lucas didn't answer right away, Brooke was afraid that maybe she'd pushed it too far. But there were so many emotions inside her right then that it was hard to keep them all tightly reined in.

Lucas leaned forward, bracing his elbows on his knees. "So what do we do now?"

"You have that talk with Lincoln about Danny, and I'll have a conversation with Danny about Lincoln. Then we compare notes and go from there."

"Okay. I guess that's the best plan of action."

"I'm not going to force Danny into anything with Lincoln that he's not comfortable with, so even if Lincoln *does* want that sort of relationship with him, it's going to have to be on Danny's terms."

"I understand," Lucas said as he ran a hand through his hair.

Brooke was a bit surprised that he was agreeing so easily. The slump of his shoulders as his head bent forward suddenly brought into focus for her exactly how much the weight of the responsibility he bore must press down on him. If she knew anything about him now, it was that he just wanted the best for all those he felt responsible for. But when push came to shove, whose needs would he put first? His family's? Or Danny's?

"Is that all you wanted to discuss?"

His head lifted at her question, and he turned toward her. The solar lights that gave some illumination along the dock weren't strong enough to cast light on his face, so Brooke had no idea what he was thinking.

"No." He looked away from her. "We need to talk money."

"I don't think so," Brooke said.

"Yes, we do. Since Lincoln is alive, the terms of his will are no longer valid."

"So? Danny and I are doing fine."

"I just wanted you to know that I will be making financial arrangements to make sure that you and Danny are taken care of."

Anger surged through Brooke. "I am quite able to take care of myself *and* Danny."

As soon as she said the words, Brooke realized that wasn't quite true.

And apparently Lucas did too because he said, "Really?"

"I don't need or want your handouts anymore. I'm going to tell Dorie that she's supposed to sell my paintings to whoever wants them from now on."

"You think she's going to give up the hefty commission she gets from holding on to the paintings to sell to me?"

Brooke's fists clenched. "Why would you do that?"

"Because it's the only way I'm going to be able to take care of the two of you, apparently."

"I'll take my paintings somewhere else."

Lucas sighed and ran his hand through his hair again. "Why does this have to be such a battle, Brooke? There are countless women who'd be taking what I'm offering without argument."

"Maybe it's because I don't want what you're offering." Brooke lowered her feet to the deck and stood up.

Lucas also pushed up out of his chair which gave him a distinct height advantage over her. "You don't want financial security for yourself and Danny?"

Of course, she did. And in reality, it wasn't that she didn't want what he was offering, she just wanted *more* than that from him.

"You just don't get it, Lucas," Brooke said.

"Then explain it to me." Frustration was very clear in his words. "I need to understand."

Before she could stop herself, Brooke reached out and grabbed the front of Lucas's shirt in her hands. In one step, she was close enough to pull him down and press her lips to his. Though she might have taken him off-guard at first, it didn't take him long to react.

CHAPTER NINETEEN

LUCAS'S arms folded around her, trapping her hands between them where she still clutched the fabric of his shirt in her fists. As his hands splayed across her back, Brooke felt like she'd just found her home. The sensation of being in his arms—of finally feeling his strength surrounding her—rushed through her. Everything she'd been feeling in her heart over the past couple of weeks meshed with the sensations swirling in her as they kissed. Emotions collided with physical sensations in a way she'd never experienced before.

She wanted her arms free to wrap them around him, but Lucas held her so tightly she couldn't move. It was as if he didn't want to let her go. As if he was afraid to loosen his grip in case she escaped. But she wasn't going anywhere.

In his arms, she felt as if they could handle anything because they'd be doing it together. Leaning on his strength didn't mean she was weak like she'd always thought it would when it came to depending on a man. In return, she could offer him the strength she had, too. Together. That's how she wanted them to be.

Her heart belonged to this man, and as she felt his lips move over hers, Brooke allowed herself to hope for the first time that his belonged to her.

The kiss seemed to go on forever, and yet when Lucas lifted his head, it was over too soon. Far too soon.

He pressed his forehead to hers. "This is just so complicated."

Complicated? For Brooke, everything had come into shocking clarity as they'd kissed. She wanted to spend the rest of her life with this man. They'd known each other less than a month, but after waiting so long, she knew this was what she wanted.

She felt Lucas take a deep breath and step back from her. Brooke's fingers numbly loosened their grip on his shirt as he took another step away. The fabric slipped out of her grasp as she realized that he moving away from her. Just like he had earlier, he was putting distance between them.

Stupid. Stupid. When would she ever learn?

"Brooke..."

"Never mind, Lucas. Set up whatever you have to to make you feel like you're still in control of your world. Just stay out of mine."

"Brooke. Wait."

She would not give him the satisfaction of seeing her run, but Brooke spun on her heel and moved as quickly as she could for the path leading away from him. She'd kissed him and all he'd said was that it was complicated.

Why had she thought Lucas would be different? He wanted to control her life just like every other one of his responsibilities. She had clearly misread every interaction they'd had.

Stupid.

As soon as she reached the end of the dock, Brooke took the path that led to the cabin where her family was. She broke into a jog and then a flat out run. She had to get away. This would be the last time—ever—she would make herself that vulnerable to someone. She had been stupid to think that Lucas would look past all that lay in their way to see how they could be together. Instead...all he'd said was how complicated it was. Well, she hoped his complications kept him warm at night.

Brooke slowed as she neared the cabin then pulled up short when she spotted her dad sitting on the top step. His head was bent over his folded hands. She considered retracing her steps but then thought back over the conversation she'd had earlier with her mom. It came as a surprise that right then she wasn't viewing him through the anger and resentment she had for so many years.

"Dad?"

His head jerked up as she walked up the stairs. "Hey, Brooke."

She settled down on the step beside him, pulling her knees close as she stared out at the dark water of the lake. It had been years since she'd sought out her dad's company. But she'd realized over the past few days—as she'd struggled to make difficult decisions for Danny—that it would just kill her if her son looked at one of the decisions she'd made as bad and decided not to talk to her for years. Granted what her father had done had been more than just a bad decision, but everything lately was making her rethink the way she'd dealt with her relationships as an adult.

"Everything okay?" Her dad spoke the words softly, tentatively, as if he wasn't sure how she'd receive them.

"Not really. Everything has kind of gotten all messed up, and I think I'm just making everything messier."

"It's a difficult situation," her dad agreed. "A strange twist of events, that's for sure."

"What would you do?"

"Me?" He paused then let out a long breath. "If I were in your position, I'd do what you're already doing. You're doing your best to protect Danny while at the same time letting him make some of the decisions in this situation for himself."

"I feel like I'm forcing him to view Lincoln as his father. I feel like Lincoln is also forcing himself into the role when he has no memory of Danny's existence."

"Ideally, what would you like to see?"

"Ideally? I guess I'd like Danny to be able to choose who he wants to view as a father in his life. Choose a man by their contribution to his life rather than because they donated half his gene pool."

"And for yourself?"

"I'd like to be seen as more than a responsibility. Someone that needs to be taken care of."

Her dad chuckled. "Unfortunately, some men are born with a strong drive to take care of those they care for."

"Well, Lucas must have gotten Lincoln's dose along with his own."

"Sometimes it's the only way a man knows how to express his love." He paused then said, "And sometimes it's the only way a man *can* show his love."

Brooke thought of the bags of groceries he and her mom had brought her. As she sat there, she realized just how selfish she'd been. Her dad had made a mistake—a big one—but by all accounts he'd done what he could to rectify things. She had just been unwilling to forgive him. And what right did she have, really, to continue to hold it against him when the person he'd wronged the most had been willing to forgive him?

"Why did you do it?"

The silence that followed her question was long, and Brooke wondered if her dad was even going to answer her question.

Finally, he cleared his throat. "Is that what it will take for you to forgive me, Brooke? Me answering that question?"

Brooke couldn't honestly say. "I just need to understand. What was it about Sherry that made her more important to you than your family? Mom. Me and Eric. The babies."

"Any reasons I try to give will only sound like excuses and what I did was inexcusable."

Brooke turned to look at him, but he was staring out at the lake. "Was it something Mom did?"

His head whipped around to her. "No. Don't for a minute think that your mom played a role in what happened. She didn't. The blame for that rests squarely on my and Sherry's shoulders. We made the decisions that led to what happened. My failings as a husband actually started long before that incident in Africa. I didn't take the spiritual lead the way I should have. I was determined to live my life the way I thought it should be led according to the knowledge I had in my head, and God let me do it. He let me tear it all down with my own prideful choices so I'd have no one else to blame. It's a real wake-up call to be sitting in the midst of the rubble of your life and realize that the only person there for you is God."

"I thought Mom stuck by you."

"Oh, physically she was there, but in every other way, she was gone from me. And for weeks she wouldn't even look at me. That more than anything else up to that point, broke me down. She had once looked at me with love and admiration— not that I deserved either—but then it was anger and hate. I knew it would take time and hard work, but it was important to me to make amends as best I could for what had happened in Africa."

Brooke pondered what he'd said. She wasn't sure what had started it, but the hardness she'd harbored for so long against her dad was slowly eroding. "I think what made me the most angry at you back then had more to do with the babies than Mom. I didn't understand the affair part at the time the way I did later. It just added to what I was already feeling toward you."

"The babies are fine, sweetheart."

Brooke straightened. "What?"

"The babies—well, they're not babies anymore—are doing just fine."

"How do you know?"

"Your mom kept in contact with the orphanage they'd been in and another missionary family took them in. We've been helping to support them financially over the years."

"Really?" Brooke felt a rush of emotion. Until then she hadn't realized just how much it had weighed on her, not knowing what had happened and imagining the worst. "Why didn't you tell me?"

"I'm not sure. I thought we had, but with everything going on back then, I guess we didn't. And it never came up in later years."

"Do you believe in love at first...or second sight?" Brooke knew she was jumping all over the place, but it was a reflection of her emotions because they were all over the map, too.

"Sure." It appeared her dad didn't have a problem keeping up with her changes in topics.

"Why? Lots of people don't."

"Well, your mother and I have been praying for a long time that God would bring someone into your life."

There was a hitch in her heart at her dad's comment. "But that doesn't explain why you believe in love at first sight."

Again he chuckled. "Well, we might have also prayed that love would come quickly so you wouldn't have too much time to think or over-analyze it."

"Seriously?" Brooke found herself smiling for the first time that evening.

"Seriously. We knew that it would take a very special man to make you reconsider your opinion of the male gender. And it was pretty clear it would have to be something that happened quickly or you'd be able to talk yourself out of it."

"And you think Lucas is that man?"

"Don't you?"

"I did, but it seems he's more interested in seeing the complications in the situation than the possibilities."

"This is all a very complex situation, sweetheart. You need to cut him just a little slack. The very things that draw you to him are the things that make him feel the way he does about what's going on."

Brooke sighed. "So what am I supposed to do?"

"I would actually suggest you pray about it. Trust God to work this out."

She wasn't surprised at his suggestion. What did surprise her was that her usually knee-jerk response to the suggestion of praying didn't kick in. Maybe it was time for a change in that relationship, too.

Brooke pushed up off the step and then, for the first time in longer than she could remember, she bent over and pressed a kiss to her dad's cheek. "Thank you, Daddy."

Before he could respond, she walked down the steps and headed for the water's edge. It was time to really think about everything. So far, her emotions had been ruling her reactions more than anything else. She needed to take a step back and gain some perspective on it all.

Lucas could hear the footsteps as soon as the person stepped onto the dock. He had a few guesses who it might be, but none of them were people he wanted to talk to right then.

"Guess things didn't go well, huh?"

Lucas looked over as Lindsay settled into the chair Brooke had been sitting in earlier. "Not so much."

"So now you're sitting out here trying to sort out all the world's problems by yourself?"

"At least the ones in the Hamilton world."

Lindsay let out a snort. "When are you going to learn?"

"Learn what, exactly?"

"That it's not your responsibility to make everything right for all of the rest of us."

"I have to at least try. Once Dad died, that became my responsibility."

"Really?"

He could hear the disdain dripping from that one word.

"Dad didn't take responsibility like you do. In fact, the only place he truly cared about his responsibility was to the company. It certainly wasn't to us kids or Mom. As long as he provided money for the lifestyle he wanted us to have, he figured he'd done his part. That has *never* been how you've approached things."

Lucas couldn't argue that. But it was partly because of his dad's lack of responsibility that he'd picked up the slack. Particularly where Lindsay and his mom were concerned. "There are so many lives tangled up in this mess right now. I'm just trying to figure out a way to sort it out with the least collateral damage."

"Honestly, Luc, the only people who are messed up in it are you, Brooke and Danny. Mom's happy to have her son back and to have her grandson. I'm pretty sure any decision you make with regards to Brooke and Danny, as long as it doesn't take them out of her life, she'll support. Me, well, I'm dealing with my own stuff and it has nothing to do with you. So you don't need to fix things for me. I'm a big girl and can deal with it on my own."

"And Lincoln? What do I do about him?"

"You accept that he had his chance to be a father to Danny, and he abandoned him. You accept that anything he and Brooke had in the past is just that...in the past. Lincoln remembers none of that. I think right now he's just trying to fill the roles people are telling him he needs to." Lindsay stretched out her legs. "Danny needs a good, stable man in his life and you're that man. And while I don't quite understand it myself, Brooke seems to have taken a fancy to you. If you're feeling anything similar for her, well, I think you should give it a whirl."

"Give it a whirl?" Lucas laughed. "I'm afraid this is way past the *give it a whirl* stage. And when Danny's involved, I'm not going to do anything lightly with Brooke."

"So you're worried about how Danny would react if you and Brooke did get together?"

"No, I'm more worried about what would happen if it didn't work out. It's not like we can both just move on without having to deal with each other ever again."

Lindsay fell quiet for a bit then said, "I guess this is where you have to decide if it's worth the risk. I know you're not the risk-taker in the family, but maybe—just maybe—this is one case where you should be."

"Maybe."

"You overthink things, Lucas. You throw up obstacles that don't need to be there." She paused. "Have you prayed about this?"

Lucas shot Lindsay a glance. Though his sister did attend church regularly with him and their mom, he was more involved in the church than she was. It was rare that they had any sort of spiritual discussions. "Yes. I've been praying daily about all of this since the day we opened that will and found out about Brooke and Danny. Of course, the prayers have changed as circumstances have shifted."

"I think it's maybe time that you and Brooke sat down and had a real heart to heart. Although I kinda thought that was going to happen earlier."

"Things kinda got a little...intense."

Lindsay kicked at his foot. "Do tell."

"I don't think so," Lucas said with a laugh.

"You're a tease."

"You could say I learned from the best."

"Ah, fine." Lindsay sprang up from her chair. "I'll just leave you to your thoughts. But as you're figuring out all the problems to fix, remember to leave my life out of it."

Lucas sighed as he watched her march away. For the second time that night, he was basically being told to butt out.

Then she turned and called back to him, "And maybe you should find Brooke and have another intense moment."

He doubted Brooke would be interested in a repeat of earlier. Something told him that he was now top on her list of men who'd messed with her life.

He stared at the water, reliving those moments when he'd held her in his arms, his lips pressed to hers. It had felt so right. And she had been the one to initiate it, which told him that he hadn't been alone in what he'd been feeling. Surely if she felt for him what he felt for her, it wasn't so easily dismissed. Ever since she'd walked away earlier, he'd been fighting an emptiness edged with desperation. He couldn't let this evening end without at least trying to talk to her again.

Resolutely, he pushed up out of the chair and followed the path both Brooke and Lindsay had taken. As he neared the cabin she was staying at with her family, he saw her father sitting on the porch.

The man turned toward him as he approached the steps. Lucas figured he'd have to ask to see her, but instead, Doug McKinley gestured toward the lake. "She's down by the water."

"Thank you."

"You're welcome." Brooke's father stood up. "I'll leave the two of you to some privacy."

Not sure if Brooke had heard him talking with her dad, Lucas approached slowly. She sat on the small dock that served this area of the island. It wasn't as big as the one by the boathouse, but it still had small lights along its edges. There were no chairs on this dock so Brooke was seated at the end of it with her feet dangling over the edge. She had her hands braced on the wood, her head bent.

"Brooke?"

She didn't turn to look at him or in any way indicate she'd heard him. He couldn't blame her for that. It was what he deserved.

With a sigh, he slipped his shoes off and sat down beside her, his feet dipping into the cool lake water. Still she just sat there, not acknowledging him at all.

Lucas turned to look at her and that's when he saw them. The trails of tears down her cheeks turned silvery by the moonlight. His heart clenched, and he found it difficult to breathe. He had done this to her. From what he knew of her,

Brooke McKinley was not a woman given to tears, and yet here she sat...crying. Because of what he'd done.

"Baby, I'm sorry." With little effort, he turned and slid one arm behind her back, one under her legs and lifted her onto his lap.

Without hesitation, she wrapped her arms around his neck and buried her face in his shirt. And then it was more than just tears. The sobs were harsh, pulled from somewhere deep within her.

This depth of emotion scared Lucas. Was he responsible for this? Had he really hurt her this badly? He wrapped his arms more tightly around her and just held on.

"It's going to be okay," he murmured against her hair. "Just hang in there."

The ache in Lucas's heart grew with each shuddering sob that shook Brooke's body. When he'd walked into their lives, he had wanted to make things better for them, but right then it felt like all he'd done was make things worse. So much worse.

Dear God, please give me the words to make this right. Give me the words to let her know how sorry I am for everything that's happened. Help her to find peace in the midst of all this. I just want it to all work out and everyone to be happy. I need...wisdom and strength. Please, God.

Gradually, her sobs lessened in intensity though her breaths still came in shuddering gasps.

"It's going to be okay, baby. It's going to be okay."

CHAPTER TWENTY

As THE intense emotions finally receded, Brooke continued to rest against Lucas, drawing on his strength the way she'd longed to almost from the day they'd met.

"It's going to be okay, baby."

His repeated words soothed her, whether they were true or not. He probably thought she'd lost her mind. With everything else that was happening, she hadn't been able to share all that was going on in her heart. Yes, part of the emotional response was because of him, but after the conversations she'd had with her parents it had gone much deeper.

They had been tears of hurt, anger and regret...but now she was at peace. Nothing had changed in her circumstances, but talking with her parents had showed her that facing difficulties didn't mean one had been abandoned by God. That was how she'd felt from the time they'd been ripped away from Africa. She hadn't understood as a child how God could have let that happen. The faith she'd been taught from so young, the commitment she'd made to Him at the tender age of five, hadn't been able to withstand the onslaught of fear, confusion and anger that had come from those events that had taken place on the other side of the world. And that had set the stage for everything that followed in her life.

Brooke took a deep breath and blew it out, relaxing her grip on Lucas's neck.

Lucas shifted her slightly but kept his arms around her. "Hey, sweetheart? You okay?"

Another deep breath. "Getting there."

"I'm sorry for what happened earlier."

"It's okay. I know you only spoke what was on your mind. And you're right, it is complicated."

"I may have spoken what was on my mind but not what was in my heart."

Brooke pulled back a bit so she could look into his face. In the light of the full moon, she was able to see his familiar features but not the emotion in his eyes. "What do you mean?"

"I wanted everything sorted out with Lincoln. I wanted to know what role everyone was going to play in this tangled mess before I said anything. *If* I said anything, depending on how things played out."

"And now?"

"Now..." Lucas looked down at her. Keeping one arm around her waist, he lifted his hand to touch her cheek. "Now I want to stand beside you as we sort this out. I want you to stand beside me. I want the two of us to decide what's best for Danny." He paused, and Brooke felt him take a deep breath. "The thing is, I don't just love Danny. I know it's too soon. I mean, we've...uh...not known each other very long, but I..uh...kinda feel that way about you, too."

Brooke smiled as he stumbled over the sentence. Clearly, this wasn't the type of sentiment he was used to expressing. Which was fine by her. She just needed to hear him say the actual words once.

She looped her arms loosely around his shoulders again. "Are you saying you love me, Lucas Hamilton?"

A slow smile chased away the seriousness of his expression. "I just might be."

"Well, I might just be kinda feeling the same way."

She felt as much as heard his chuckle. "You're gonna make me say it, right?"

"But, of course." She fished her phone out of her pocket and held it up to him. "Although if this is gonna be a rare occurrence, I'd better record it."

Lucas snatched the phone from her hand and set it down on the dock. "No. Just for you, I will learn to say it more often."

Brooke moved closer so their faces were just inches apart. "Well, we can just start with one time here."

He leaned his forehead against hers much like he had earlier, but this time around he had a different message for her. "Don't ask me how, because I sure don't know, but you make me feel things no one else ever has. Suddenly I'm thinking about a home—not just a condo or a mansion—but a home like you have with Danny. And I'm thinking kids. Lots of them. Maybe even adopting a couple from someplace like say...Africa. But most of all I'm thinking about love, and how very much I love you, Brooke. And I don't want that home with anyone but you. And those children? I want them to have the best mom in the world and that's you."

"Oh, Lucas." Tears flooded Brooke's eyes once again, but for a very different reason this time. "I love you, too. I never thought I'd find a man who I felt safe with. Who I could trust with not just myself, but with Danny, too. And then there was you. Trying to control everything but only with the best of intentions. And the first time I saw you hug Danny...you breached the walls I'd kept in place for so long. Then somewhere along the line, my heart began to soften toward others, too, not just you."

Lucas drew in a quick breath. "Your dad, sweetheart?"

"Yes. My dad. Lincoln. And God. My mom told me I needed to forgive in order to free up my heart to love as fully as I could. And she was right. Ever since meeting you, that anger has begun to ebb away. And now...well, I think it's pretty much gone." Brooke took a deep breath and let it out. "I want to love you and Danny with my whole heart. Not just the parts that weren't full of anger and resentment."

"I am so happy to hear that. I understood why you felt how you did, but I'm glad you've found freedom from that anger." He paused. "You still realize it's not necessarily going to be smooth sailing from here on out, right?"

"I know, but as long as we're in the same boat, I'll be able to deal with it. I want to face the challenges head on and move forward with our lives."

She rested her head on his shoulder, and they sat in silence for a few minutes. The only sound was the lapping of the water against the shoreline.

Then Lucas touched her chin, lifting her face up to his. "And let's do this properly this time."

Brooke smiled as their lips met. It was gentle and tender, filling her heart to its very edges. She laced her fingers behind his head as he deepened the kiss, drawing her closer into his embrace.

Warmth spread through her body as their love washed over her. When they parted, Brooke tried to catch her breath. She felt Lucas reach into his pocket for something then heard a thud on the dock, but before she could ask what he was doing, they were falling.

She was still in his arms when they hit the water. Thankfully, it wasn't super cold but it still took her breath away as they sank into it. She didn't know how deep it was, but apparently Lucas did because his feet touched bottom and they didn't completely submerge.

"Thought we could maybe use a cool down." Humor laced Lucas's words.

"No doubt about that," Brooke agreed just before she pressed her lips to his again. She felt his smile against her lips which made her smile, too. Love grew and expanded in ways she'd never imagined possible.

Under the moonlight of that warm summer night, she whispered, "I love you, Lucas."

"I love you, too, baby. Forever."

Lucas carried her to the water's edge and helped her over the rocks to the dock. When he bent to pick up her phone, she realized the thud she'd heard earlier was him making sure his own phone didn't get ruined in the water.

She took her phone from him but couldn't slide it into the pocket of her soaking wet jean capris. "My parents are going to think I'm crazy when I walk in the door soaking wet."

"I think they're just going to be happy for you." Lucas slid his arm around her waist and pulled her close as they walked toward the cabin. "I want to stay longer, but I still need to deal with a few things before I call it a day." As they reached the foot of the stairs, he turned her toward him. "You understand, right? I don't want you to feel I'm abandoning you."

Brooke reached up to cup his cheek, enjoying the feeling of his stubble under her palm. "I understand. More than you know, I understand. I'll see you in the morning."

He bent his head, and they kissed again. A soft, lingering goodnight kiss.

As he walked away from her, Brooke stood watching until he disappeared from sight. She wanted to run after him for just one more hug. Just one more kiss. But there was always tomorrow.

Shivering in the cool night air, she climbed the steps to the cabin, prepared to share all that had transpired with her parents.

"Why would you do that?" Though his mother's words were softly spoken, Lucas heard the accusation in them. Of all people, he hadn't expected this reaction from her, especially after what Lindsay had said earlier.

"Yeah. Why? You brought me back here to connect with my son and his mother." Lincoln stood beside their mother's chair, his hands clenched into fists. "Now you're telling me that you've got something going on with Brooke, which could end up being serious enough that you'll be taking the role of father in my son's life."

Lucas hated confrontations with those he loved, but this time around it was different. "You had your chance with her, Lincoln. And I have a letter that proves that you had a chance to be a father to Danny. You walked away from both responsibilities ten years ago. You don't get to object to what's going on between Brooke and me."

"And if I want to be a father to Danny now? To make amends for the past? You're not even giving me a chance. As soon as he finds out how you feel about his mother, he's never gonna give up the bond he feels with you."

"Please give him a chance, Lucas," his mother said, a pleading look on her face.

"A chance for what, Mom? To win Brooke's heart? To convince Danny he's the father he's always wanted?"

"Yes. Give them a chance to see if they can be a family."

Pain pierced Lucas's heart. How could she ask him to step aside and let Lincoln try to woo the woman *he* loved? How could she? His own mother? Hurt clouded his mind and he had no words to express what he felt at that moment.

"This. Is. Bull." For the first time, Lindsay spoke up. "Mom, I love you, but you are *so* very wrong. How could you ask Lucas to give up the woman he loves for Lincoln? Lucas has done so much for all of us. He stepped up when Dad was a philandering schmuck to protect you. He's worked hard to keep the company going while Lincoln was off living his carefree lifestyle. So no. I won't let this happen." Lindsay turned to Lucas. "You are going to stay with Brooke and love her like you do and let her love you back. And Danny is going to see who the real man is here." Spinning around, she pinned Lincoln with an angry glare. "Because it certainly isn't you. Ten years ago and every year since you've had the opportunity to step up and be the father Danny needed, but not only did you not do that, you kept him from us. We had the right to know we had a nephew. A grandson. You've robbed us of ten years with that precious boy all because you didn't want to give up your lifestyle. So no. You don't get a chance with Brooke. And no, you don't get to try and replace Lucas in Danny's life. All our actions have consequences and these are yours, whether you remember them or not."

"Lindsay, please." His mom held out her hand to her daughter, tears on her cheeks.

Lindsay's hands were fists at her side. Lucas had seen his sister angry on many occasions, but he had to say he'd never seen her quite *this* angry.

"No, Mom. If you can't see how wrong what you're asking Lucas to do is, then I'm done with this." Lindsay's hand slashed through the air. "And I will make my displeasure abundantly clear to everyone here if Lucas gives in to your wishes."

Lucas felt compelled to try and rein her in. "Lindsay."

She spun to face him. "Do *not* give in to this. Do *not*. If you do, I will never respect you again." Tears sparkled in her eyes now, too.

Lucas went to her and gathered her rigid body into his arms. "I'm not going to, Linds. I'm not going to."

She looked up at him. "You're not?"

He shook his head and shrugged. Giving her a half smile, he said, "I can't. The woman's got my heart and she's not going to give it back. And that's exactly how I want it."

A smile eased the anger from Lindsay's face. She wrapped her arms around his neck. "I'm so proud of you."

When she stepped back, Lucas turned to face his mother and brother. "The thing is, even if I *was* willing to step aside—and I'm most definitely not—Brooke wouldn't allow it." He looked at Lincoln, the brother he no longer knew and said, "I'm not going to stand in the way of a relationship between you and Danny—if that's what *he* wants. You made your choice regarding a relationship with him ten years ago. He gets to make his now. Yes, I do hope to call him son someday, but he will always know that you are his father."

Even though she'd hurt him more than she ever had before, Lucas went and knelt in front of his mom. He took her hands in his. "I know you love us both, Mom, and that you want to make things right for Lincoln, but right now my heart is telling me to do what is right for Danny and Brooke. I love them. I'm not going to deny it anymore. There's lots of stuff that still needs to be worked through, but my relationship with Brooke and with Danny is no longer part of that. It's been settled. I hope in time you can understand and accept why that is."

Tears continued to spill from her eyes as she cupped his face in her hands. "I'm sorry, Lucas. I should never have asked that of you. Forgive me."

Lucas smiled and leaned forward to press a kiss to her forehead. "All is forgiven, Mama."

The next morning, Lucas was downstairs bright and early with Stella in the kitchen. He couldn't sleep anyway, so he'd decided to see if he could give her a hand.

"You know you don't need to help me," Stella said as she handed him a carton of eggs.

"Well, I have it on good authority that women like a man who can cook. So I figured I'd better learn."

Stella laughed. "I'm more than happy to help you. And in future years I expect to hear from Brooke that you've cooked her dinner or served her breakfast in bed."

Lucas grinned at the thought. "I could probably do the breakfast in bed. Not sure about the dinner though."

"Aim high, dearie. Aim high."

Danny and Jeff walked into the kitchen then, and Danny's eyebrows rose when he saw Lucas attempting to crack eggs.

"You need some help?" he asked as he came to stand next to him. "I know how to do that. Mom taught me."

"Yes, I think I do need some help. I need to crack them all and I'm pretty sure I'm supposed to avoid getting eggshells in the mix."

Danny laughed. "Yeah. Here, let me show how I do it."

Lucas watched as the boy expertly cracked an egg into the bowl. He had a feeling that egg cracking was going to be the first of many things this young man taught him. Already Danny was teaching him how it was to love a child of his heart if not his blood.

Danny was surprisingly at ease in the kitchen while his buddy Jeff hung out on a stool at the counter. Stella gave Danny instructions and the boy jumped right to it.

People began to straggle in slowly. First were Eric, Staci, and Sarah. Then Than and Lincoln and his mom made an appearance. Brooke's folks showed up with Alicia and Victoria.

"Brooke just got up," her mom told him. "She'll be along shortly. She said to go ahead if breakfast was ready before she got here."

Brooke couldn't believe she'd slept in, but honestly, it had been the best sleep she'd had in ages. She hurried along the path toward the main cabin, hoping she wasn't too late for breakfast.

When she walked in, she could hear voices coming from the dining room and headed in that direction. People were standing in a circle around the table but the food on it was still untouched. As she stepped into the room, Lucas looked toward her and when their gazes met, she couldn't help but smile. She just couldn't contain the love she felt him any longer.

He held out his arm and without hesitation, Brooke moved to stand beside him. As he slid his arm around her, she put hers around his waist. He bent and pressed a quick kiss to her lips. "Good morning, babe."

She hadn't expected him to put their relationship out there quite like that, but she was glad. "Good morning, sweetheart."

Eric cleared his throat. "Well, I've clearly missed out on a few things. Why don't you say grace, Lucas, so I can get caught up?"

As Brooke looked around the room, she saw mainly smiles as people looked at her and Lucas, and the biggest one belonged to Danny. When her gaze met his, she couldn't contain her own smile as the love she felt for her son joined the love she felt for Lucas. They filled her heart so completely.

There might still be rough patches ahead, things that had to be worked out, but Brooke had no doubt they would be able to weather them. This was the beginning of their forever, and she couldn't wait for what was to come.

The End

Available Now!

When There Is Love

The McKinleys

Book 3

Chapter One

VICTORIA McKinley slumped back against her chair and scowled at the error screen on her monitor. "No. Please..."

She squeezed her eyes shut and said a quick prayer before opening them again, hoping against hope that the error message would have magically disappeared. But no such luck. It had been happening more and more frequently, and once again, all the data she'd entered—and not saved—was gone.

Her gaze went to where her cell phone sat beside the keyboard. She had been putting it off for weeks, but in the past few days, on top of the error messages and system shutdowns she'd been getting, the tower had begun to make a horrible sound. She simply couldn't afford to lose everything that was on the computer.

The only choice left to her was to call the person who'd set it up in the first place. The one who had threatened her with all sorts of dire consequences if she ever dared take it to anyone but him for servicing.

Trent Hause.

If she hadn't been so worried about losing all her data, she would have happily defied him and gone to some random computer place. But in addition to that, carting the tower anyplace was pretty much impossible for her. She'd have had to call her dad or Eric and then they'd want to know why she didn't ask Trent to help. After all, he took care of all the computer issues in their family.

With a sigh, Victoria reached out and picked up her phone. After the briefest of hesitations, she tapped on Trent's contact information then put it on speakerphone. It rang three times, and she was just about ready to hang up when the call went through.

"Hang on. I need to look out the window."

Frowning, Victoria looked down at the phone. Had she called the wrong person? It sure *sounded* like Trent's voice. "What?"

"To see if pigs are flying. Fortunately, I cannot confirm that hell has frozen over, but I figure pigs flying would be easy enough to see."

Victoria couldn't keep the corners of her mouth from turning up in a smile. "Pigs are not flying."

"Then why are you calling? I'm pretty sure that was the requirement that had to be met before you'd call me."

"Yes. I know." Victoria sighed. "Unfortunately, I'm in dire straits here, and you're the only one that can help me."

"Really now?" Trent dragged the words out. "Those are words I never thought I'd hear from Miss Victoria McKinley."

"I suppose I could take my problem to Drake's Fast Computer Repair Shop down the street."

"Oh no, you don't."

Victoria could almost picture him sitting straight up in his chair. "So you'll help me?"

"Of course, I'll help you, babe. I have a meeting this afternoon but should be done by five. I can stop by your place afterward. Would that be okay?"

"Yes, that would be fine." She paused. "Thank you, Trent."

"You're very welcome."

Silence stretched between them before Victoria said, "Well, I'll let you get back to work."

"Yep. See you in a few hours."

After she hung up, Victoria gave one last withering glare at her computer before sliding off the chair and heading for the kitchen. She mentally flipped through the contents of her fridge and cupboards to see what she could pull together for a meal. It might not be the wisest decision, but if the man was going to come fix her computer, the least she could do was provide him with dinner.

Thankfully, she'd gone shopping with her mom earlier in the week. It was a chore she disliked, but her mom always turned it into a girls' day out with lunch included so it was a little more tolerable. Victoria hated that she had to rely on her mom to help her, but there was just no way to reach a lot of the stuff on the grocery shelves by herself. That left her with two alternatives: ask someone for help or let her mom come along. Since she hated the thought of asking random strangers for help, the choice really was a no-brainer.

Victoria slipped her arms into the cuffs of her crutches and gripped the handles. She tried not to think about how often she needed to use the walking aides lately. Though she still didn't need them all the time, she knew that point was coming sooner rather than later. Once that happened, her family would know just how much pain her hip caused her. Hoping to keep that knowledge from them as long as she could, she used the crutches whenever she was alone. Too bad it wasn't a permanent solution.

She walked into the kitchen and climbed up on the stool she kept there to see what was in her freezer. Though fridges with freezers on the bottom had gained popularity in recent years, hers was still the older style since she needed access to the freezer portion less frequently.

With a package of frozen chicken breasts in her hand, she climbed down to put it on the counter. It would be nice to cook a meal for more than just one. Even though she lived on her own, Victoria still took the time to cook for herself since cooking was something she enjoyed doing. Her mother had made certain that both she and her older sister Brooke had learned to bake and cook at a young age.

Now that her plan for the afternoon had been squashed, she had time to prepare a meal. It wasn't a big sacrifice to put off doing the paperwork for her business—The Accessibility Solutions Company—since it was her least favorite part of the job, but because of the computer issues, she'd been putting it off a bit too frequently of late. Hopefully, Trent would be able to fix it quickly so she could keep from getting too much further behind.

It was just after five thirty when Trent pulled his Jeep to a stop behind Victoria's car in her driveway. He still couldn't believe she'd actually called him, even if it was for a computer issue. No doubt she'd debated going against what he'd asked of her when he'd set up her system—that she wouldn't go anywhere but him for repairs.

He grabbed the plastic bag from the seat next to him and then got his laptop bag from the backseat. As he walked along the sidewalk that led to the covered porch, Trent noticed the bright flowers planted in the beds in front of the house. The small front yard was immaculately landscaped, and he would bet dollars to donuts that Victoria took care of it all.

That woman didn't let anything stop her from doing what needed to be done. It was one of the many things he admired about her.

He pushed the doorbell and looked around as he waited for her to answer the door. She'd chosen a quaint little neighborhood to live in. It was definitely a world away from the somewhat sterile apartment he called home these days. Truth was, he hesitated to buy a house for himself just yet because he hoped to share a home with a wife one day and wanted it to be something she would like, too. Or, alternatively, if she already owned her own place, he could just move in with her. After getting married, of course.

When he heard the door open, Trent swung back around, a ready smile on his face.

"Hey, Victoria."

"Hi, Trent. C'mon in." She moved back and once he'd stepped into the house, she closed the door behind him.

His stomach rumbled at the wonderful smells permeating the air. A clear reminder that the sandwich he'd had for lunch had been hours ago.

"Here. I got this for you." Trent reached into the plastic bag and pulled out an ice cold bottle of the specialized water he'd seen Victoria drink on more than one occasion. He'd stopped at the convenience store just down the block from her house and bought cold drinks for both of them.

"Thanks." She smiled as she took it from him. "How did you know I like to drink this stuff?"

Trent shrugged. "I've seen you with it a few times."

"You're one of those observant kind of guys, huh?"

"About some things," Trent replied, although in truth—given his job with BlackThorpe—he was pretty observant about everything. It was something Marcus Black and Alex Thorpe drilled into them on a regular basis.

Be alert. Be aware.

"Well, come observe what my computer's doing and tell me it's not at death's door."

As he followed her into the living room where her computer was set up, Trent noticed that she wore a white denim skirt and turquoise T-shirt. Her hair was gathered into a ponytail that swept back and forth across her shoulders as she walked. She seemed to be favoring her left leg, but he couldn't be completely sure. He wasn't often in the position of watching her walk like this, so perhaps that was her normal gait.

"That's what popped up," Victoria said as they reached the computer desk.

The message on the monitor drew his attention from Victoria. He frowned as he read it, settling into the chair she'd turned toward him. "Is this the first time you've seen it?"

"No. It's shown up a few times."

A sudden rattling sound came from the tower at his feet. "And how long has it been doing that?"

"About a week?"

He glanced over and saw she was standing at the corner of the desk, a sheepish look on her face. With him seated, they were almost at eye level with each other. Her chocolate brown gaze met his. He lifted his eyebrows at her response.

"Okay. It's been about two weeks since it first started making that sound."

"And the messages?" he asked with a jerk of his head in the direction of the monitor.

She bit her lip for a second and then said, "I've been getting them off and on for about a month or so."

"A *month or so*, Victoria?" Trent sighed, looking down at the tower as it gave a particularly loud rattle. "Why didn't you call me sooner?" When she didn't answer right away, he lifted his gaze to find her watching him, one eyebrow quirked. "Yeah. Never mind."

He turned his attention back to the computer. So he'd maybe been coming on a little strong with his flirting lately. It was a bit disheartening to realize that she'd only contacted him out of sheer desperation. She'd put off calling him for over a month at the risk of losing her business and personal records.

Well, he'd do what he could to get her back on track computer-wise and then he'd need to rethink his approach to things. Though they'd only met because of Eric, he'd liked her almost from the start. At first, she'd been a curiosity for him. He'd never been around someone with dwarfism before, so their initial interactions had more to do with him wanting to learn more about her as a little person. Slowly, they'd become friends of a sort, and he'd enjoyed spending time with her and the rest of the McKinleys when he could.

It wasn't until earlier that year that things had kind of changed for him. Quite out of the blue he'd realized he was accepting Eric's invitations in hopes of being able to spend time with Victoria. And the disappointment he'd experienced if it turned out that she wasn't there was far more than it should be for just a friend. A few months ago, he'd begun to test the waters to see if she might be interested in him as well. He'd been wary of facing it head on since he realized it might take Victoria a little bit longer to get used to the idea, not just because he was her brother's best friend, but also because he was of average-size.

Unfortunately, his lighthearted attempts at flirting hadn't had their intended effect. It seemed she'd never viewed him as more than a friend and now even their friendship—such as it was—had been strained because of how he felt about her. He hoped it wasn't too late to get back to that friendship, because this whole computer situation brought home to him how truly uncomfortable she was with his attempts to take things to the next level.

"This is going to take me a little while. If you have plans, I can work on it at my place," Trent said as he tapped some keys to get rid of the error screen.

"I have no plans, but if you do, feel free to take it with you and work on it when you have the time."

"Since my best friend up and got married, my Friday night and weekend social life has dropped drastically. I had no plans that my DVR can't take care of."

"Well, in that case, I made some supper if you're hungry."

Surprised, Trent glanced at her. "Uh, sure. It smells delicious."

"It's nothing too fancy."

"And what about me makes you think I only eat fancy food?" Trent asked as he turned his attention back to the computer. "Let me just get this set to back up the hard drive and then we can eat while it does that."

"Sounds good. I'll just go finish it up."

Trent resisted the urge to turn and watch her walk to the kitchen. Instead, he groaned when he saw how long it had been since a backup had been run on the system. He was going to have to teach her a few more things this time around.

He used his own credit card to purchase a backup program for her. It took a few minutes to get it all set up, but soon the program was backing up her system online. At least this way, if the machine took a dump, her work files were protected.

Knowing the backup would take a while, Trent pushed back from the desk and went to the kitchen. As he took in the round table that was set for them, his gut clenched. His resolve to keep things friendly threatened to crumble around him. This setting came way too close to resembling the intimate dinners for two he'd pictured over the past few months.

"What would you like to drink?"

He looked to where Victoria stood behind the counter, obviously on a stool of some sort. She dropped the cucumbers she'd just finished slicing into the bowl of salad in front of her. With quick movements, she mixed it all together.

"Water is fine."

"Can you just grab the glasses from the table and fill them there, please?" She tilted her head toward the fridge.

With a nod, Trent grabbed the two glasses and went to the water dispenser on the front of the fridge to fill them. Pushing one glass against the dispenser, he watched over his shoulder as Victoria climbed down the stool and reached for the salad bowl. She put it on the table then returned to the kitchen. She grabbed the stool by its upright handle and moved it to the stove.

He returned both glasses to the table. "Is there anything else you need me to do?"

Victoria glanced at him then back to the stove as if debating. "Actually, if you'd drain the vegetables for me, that would be great."

Happy that she'd accepted his offer of help, Trent joined her at the stove. She still stood on her stool which brought the top of her head to his shoulder. When she glanced up at him, it seemed that she realized how close they were, too, as her brown eyes widened briefly.

OTHER TITLES BY

Kimberly Rae Jordan

Marrying Kate

Faith, Hope & Love

Waiting for Rachel (*Those Karlsson Boys: 1*)
Worth the Wait (*Those Karlsson Boys: 2*)
The Waiting Heart (*Those Karlsson Boys: 3*)

Home Is Where the Heart Is (*Home to Collingsworth: 1*)
Home Away From Home (*Home to Collingsworth: 2*)
Love Makes a House a Home (*Home to Collingsworth: 3*)
The Long Road Home (*Home to Collingsworth: 4*)
Her Heart, His Home (*Home to Collingsworth: 5*)
Coming Home (*Home to Collingsworth: 6*)

This Time With Love (*The McKinleys: 1*)
Forever My Love (*The McKinleys: 2*)
When There is Love (*The McKinleys: 3*)

A Little Bit of Love:
A Collection of Christian Romance Short Stories

**For news on new releases and sales
ign up for Kimberly's newsletter**

http://eepurl.com/WFhYr

Please visit Kimberly Rae Jordan on the web!
Website: www.kimberlyraejordan.com
Facebook: www.facebook.com/AuthorKimberlyRaeJordan
Twitter: twitter.com/KimberlyR Jordan

Made in the USA
Middletown, DE
27 July 2015